When the Roll Is Called Up Yonder

Anne Arrandale

DEDICATION

To all the men in my family who served, and the women who made their service possible. Thank you.

Disclaimer

This is a work of fiction. Names, character, places and incidents either are the product of the writer's imagination or are used fictitiously, and any resemblance to actual persons, living or dead, business establishment or locales are purely coincidental. Besides, if you want to sue me, I don't have much of anything, unless you want custody of the cat.

Chapter One

October 3, 1915

Tadhg Nagel rode his big dapple gray horse along the side of the airfield. The noise was deafening. Air machine engines being started, fire trucks idling in case they had to be rushed into service, automobiles still driving into the area trying to find a place to park in the adjacent field. Then there were the people in the stands. No wonder the Prince Georges County Sheriff called for extra help.

Nagel and Sergeant Johnny Allen, with Allen's horse Major and Tadhg's Brian Boru, usually called "The King", had been sent down last night by train to College Park's Aerodrome, the first airfield in the state. Allen was currently patrolling the parking area, riding his black horse around looking for all the world like a cowboy calming a milling herd.

The men had been chosen for two reasons. First, because their mounts were the largest and calmest on the force, but at the same time were capable of riding down miscreants and fighting their way through an unruly crowd with hooves and teeth. The other reason for their selection was because the Captain deemed them the best looking men in the unit.

Johnny Allen had indeed been a cowboy in his

youth. He had worked on a cousin's ranch in Texas for a couple of years and had finally been considered old enough to make a cattle drive north. Riding drag behind two thousand smelly bovine, sleeping on rock hard ground, and a steady diet of beans was enough to make Allen take his pay from the three month long trip to get on the next train east.

Allen had arrived in Baltimore City shortly after the Great Fire in 1904. Because it was what he knew, he got a job working in the City's stables, caring for the horses of the first mounted unit in the country. Four years later, on his twenty-first birthday, Johnny Allen joined the Police Department.

For four years Allen walked a beat downtown. He was a popular cop with his boyish good looks and gentle southern drawl. He hated every minute of it.

One of the mounted officers who frequented the area to which Allen was assigned rode the big horse called "Major". Major was a gentle giant who loved to have the kids pet his nose and give him apples or carrots. Major had been instrumental in running down a purse snatcher on Howard Street at Christmas time. The big black beast had caught up with the miscreant, trapped him against the wall of a building, squeezing him in place while his rider dismounted and calmly walked to a corner call box to summon the wagon.

Major's assigned officer was injured on the job during a non-mounted assignment and was forced to take retirement. He knew he couldn't keep the horse without his position on the force, and he looked for another officer to take over. Johnny Allen had been the first to speak up. Allen loved that horse. More importantly, the horse loved him and would do anything   he   asked.   With   the   personal recommendation of Major's retired owner Allen got the posting.

Nagel liked Sergeant Allen. Although Allen was his superior, they were frequently assigned to the same patrol and worked well together. Best of all their horses got on well. Too often one animal would take a dislike to another and the horses would spend more time trying to bite each other than controlling crime.

The two men rode in the box car with their horses from Baltimore to College Park, and had spent the night with them in the barn. This morning the animals were well rested but the officers were achy, tired and testy from trying to sleep in an empty stall rather than in their feather beds at home.

Sunday, October 3, 1915. It was cold that morning when they had to get out in the saddle. Tadhg had hoped the cold would keep the crowd down. No such luck. People were pouring into the bleachers like somebody was giving out free cotton candy at the circus.

Tadhg had been watching a group of young women sitting in the front row. The girls seemed determined to draw the attention of three of the fliers who were standing beside one of the brand new French Nieuport 11 Bebes. The men were all young, around Tadhg's age, and rather dashing in their uniforms with the polished leather and brass.

The show was supposed to start in the next half hour. Tadhg felt something touch his right boot and he looked down. "Rose!

Rose O'Donovan, Tadgh's steady girl, was looking up adoringly. He really wanted to pull her up into the saddle and ride off to find a quiet corner. It took him a moment to realize their friends, Rose's employers, Millie and Dylan Shay, were standing behind her.

Tadhg hooked his left leg over the small pommel

and took a moment to relax. He had to be careful of the saddle holster where his service revolver hung. "You have any trouble getting here?"

Dylan laid his hand on the big horse's rump. "Not getting here. But I thought I was going to have to pull a gun to get a taxi to bring out here."

"Yeah," Tadhg chuckled. "It's awful crowded today. We could have used two more mounties today but Cap said he couldn't spare them. I don't know why. The horses are off on the weekends."

"Maybe because you won't be back until Monday, then these big boys will get Tuesday off too."

"Yeah maybe. Don't be reasonable, Dylan."

Dylan, still laughing, took Millie by the elbow and led her to an empty spot in the bleachers.

"Tadhg, when will you get a break?"

He pulled out his watch to check the time. "In about forty-five minutes. The King here gets a bag of oats and I get a sandwich. You see that tent down there?" He pointed to a red and white candy-striped pavilion set up in the field beside the aerodrome. She nodded. "Meet me there in around an hour. I'll buy you a hotdog."

Tadhg swung his left leg back over the saddle and slipped his toe into the stirrup. He leaned low in the saddle so none of the passersby could hear him. "See if you can leave Millie and Dylan when you come to meet me."

She squeezed his ankle through his boot, giggled and ran to where their friends were sitting.

The University of Maryland Marching Band marched out onto the field. With much fanfare they began to play the *Star Spangled Banner*. The crowd stood, the men removed their hats, and the uniformed officers, including those on horseback, were at attention holding a salute. After the final drum roll they played *la Marseaillaise* in deference to the French officers present today.

Tadhg's attention had been on the field during the performance. As soon as he broke his salute he spotted movement out of the corner of his eye. Three girls on the front row who had been trying to draw the attention of the French flyers had ducked under the barricade and were running toward the planes.

The three officers were oblivious as they were helped into their flight suits and helmets by their mechanics. There was nothing else he could do. Tadhg wheeled his horse, rode past where the aeroplanes sat, then turned in, jumping the big draft horse over the wooden and steel barricade onto the airfield. Nagel pushed the animal to greater speed in order to cut the girls off. He could see one of them was running directly into the propeller.

He didn't hear the crowd cheering nor did he hear Johnny Allen riding behind him. All Tadhg Nagel knew was he had to stop these stupid girls before they were shredded.

The King seemed to know what to do before he was told. He ran close enough to the now spinning propellers that Nagel's cap was blown off. Tadhg rode directly into the group of teenagers, making them scatter. Johnny Allen and Major came in behind him, riding around the girls, heading them back to the barricades where two Prince Georges County deputies were waiting to take them into custody.

The crowd went wild! The two mounted officers got a standing ovation. Allen nudged Tadhg's boot with his foot. Both men stood in their stirrups and took a bow to the crowd. Nagel looked up and found Rose staring at him as if she had never seen him before. Well, maybe she hadn't. Not like this, anyway.

Nagel felt the King blowing. The big horse was

getting tired. Riding in an impromptu rodeo was a lot different than meandering the City streets telling people not to jay-walk or keeping children from getting run over after school.

He raised his arm to get Rose's attention, gestured to the pavilion and told Allen, "I need to take the King for a break."

"Go on. I'll watch for any more wayward women trying to rush the field."

"Thanks, Sarge. We'll be back in an hour."

"Tell your girl I said hello."

"Oh hell no. You get your own girl."

"At least ask her if she has a sister."

Tadhg shook his head. "She doesn't. But there's a sweet little nursemaid where she lives who might give you the time of day."

He rode back to retrieve his hat from one of the French mechanics and rode down the line to the refreshment pavilions. Even though the horse was tired he still managed a rather showy trot, allowing Nagel to show off even more as he posted in time to the gait. They both knew they looked good and played it for all it was worth.

They rode up behind the food tent. Tadhg had already scouted out the public tap. He kicked his right leg over the cantle and slid down from the modified cavalry saddle. From the bag behind the cantle he pulled The King's nose bag and a bag of grain and led him to a horse trough at the tap. He turned on the water to give the animal a drink.

After allowing him some time at water Tadhg slung the nose bag over The King's head to let him have a bite. Rose came behind him and put her hand on his shoulder while Nagel was loosening the saddle girth. He recognized her touch. They both would have liked a few minutes alone, but that wasn't going to happen. Nagel couldn't leave his horse, and he didn't dare do anything that might dishonor his uniform. A policeman wasn't allowed to light a cigarette while he was on duty. Tadhg could only imagine what would be said if someone reported he was found in a passionate embrace in a public place with a young woman.

"Oh Tadhg, that was so exciting!"

He grinned as he sat on the edge of the horse trough. "It was, wasn't it?"

"I was so worried about you watching The King running toward those planes." She handed him a box Millie had sent from the bakery. "I brought you some fried chicken.

He took her hand and pulled her down beside him. "Careful. If you lean back you're apt to get a wet bum."

She scooted closer to him so they were touching from hip to knees. "What will happen to those girls?"

He answered between bites of chicken. "The deputies will take them to jail. After a few hours they will call their parents to come get them. If they're lucky their daddies will cut a willow switch and wear them out."

"And if they're not lucky?"

"He'll do nothing. They'll wind up taking up with some cadet for a few minutes of fun, and we'll read a report about another murdered girl pulled out of the harbor, or one who drinks laudanum to escape her lot."

She sighed and squeezed his hand. "Why does it always seem to come down to that Tadhg? Why is it always some stupid girl who allows some man to take advantage?"

"That's just it Rosie. They're not stupid. They're trusting. If you weren't working for Millie and Katy you'd never know about half of this stuff. You're a good girl, Rosie. But the girls you work with, some of them would be considered 'bad'. Do you think Siofre or Frances or Annie are bad?"

She shook her head. "Of course not. Oh they talk sort of coarse sometimes. But not in front of men."

"That's right. But you know what they were." All the women he had named had been members of the Oldest Profession. "And every one of them was tricked into the life in one way or another. Some of them were snatched off the street. Annie left home when she was fifteen thinking she was going to marry her boyfriend. Instead, he beat her and passed her around to his friends until she was willing to work for him."

"I never knew that about Annie."

"She doesn't like to talk about it because she thinks it's makes her seem stupid. She told me one night when we all went to a dance at the church hall."

"I remember that. I think I went with Thomas Mulalley."

"You did. I hated it."

She smiled and leaned closer. "So did I."

"Then why did you go?"

"So I could be with you."

This time he squeezed her hand. "Have you heard from Thomas or Alex?"

"Not since they left for Boston." Tadhg had met both young men on an undercover assignment. The two had been living and working at the bakery since they were released from what amounted to indentured servitude in a railroad camp. Of the original nineteen young men those two had stayed the longest. They had finally gone north to work in the shipyards from where America was keeping Great Britain and France supplied with equipment and food. With the war in Europe ramping up the two Irishmen had gone to join their friends in Boston where they could make more money than they had waiting tables and killing rats in Baltimore. "Frances really misses Alex, too."

"He's too old for her. She's only fifteen." They sat together, barely touching other than where they held hands. "Let's take a walk." He stood and tended to his horse first. He removed his feed bag, dumped out the crumbs and returned it to the cantle bag. He waited while The King got another drink, then Tadhg took Rose's hand and the three of them walked further away from the pavilion.

Tadhg noticed Rose was pulling her light jacket more tightly around her. "Are you cold?"

"Millie has a blanket. I'll be fine once I get back to the bleachers." She wrapped her arms around herself a little more. He looked over his shoulder to make sure no one was around and wrapped his arms around her, pulling her close.

Rose O'Donovan didn't care if she was warm or not. She was where she wanted to be. "Tadhg?"

"What sweetie?" His voice vibrated in his chest against her cheek.

"Will you be home tonight?"

"I don't know yet sweetie. It depends on how late we have to stay tonight."

"Will you be working tomorrow?"

"Nope. The King gets off Monday and Tuesday. So I'm off too."

"Good.

"Go with me tomorrow night. We'll go to Keith's." He named the movie theater with the ballroom above.

"Just us?"

"Unless you think you want a chaperone." He felt her shake her head.

"If I go with you, just you and me, will I be one of those stupid, trusting girls?"

"Never with me, sweetie." He heard The King

whicker a greeting. Tadhg released his hold on Rose and stepped back just a little when heard the sound of hoofbeats. A sergeant on a large black horse rode up beside them. Tadhg knew what was expected.

"Rose O'Donovan, I'd like you to meet Sergeant Johnny Allen. He's outranked by his horse Major. Sarge, this is my girl, Miss O'Donovan."

Allen kicked one leg over the pommel and slid from the saddle. He gave a short salute. "A pleasure, Miss O'Donovan." He was all smiles. "Nagel, there are some men who want to meet you back on the airfield."

"Me?"

"I know. I'd have thought they'd have wanted to meet Miss O'Donovan. But they specifically asked for the 'officer on the big gray horse'. So it's gotta be you."

"Who is it?"

"Those three lieutenants from France. They're waiting for you. Go ahead. I'll see that Miss O'Donovan gets back to her party."

Nagel felt Rose move behind him just a little. "That's all right, Sarge. I'll see she gets back. I'm going that way anyway." Pulling his horse behind him he took Rose's hand and hurried away.

Once they were out of earshot, Nagel asked, "What's wrong, Rosie?"

"I just didn't like the way he was looking at me. He seems nice enough. If we were in the bakery around other people it would be fine. But out here in a field where no one can hear? I want to stay with you."

"I'll get you back to the edge of the airfield. Then I'll need to mount back up and ride to wherever these lieutenants are. But you'll be close enough to see Millie and Dylan from there."

"Okay."

He held her hand until they were beside the candy

striped canvas. Rose raised on tiptoe and kissed his cheek quickly, and scurried off to where their friends were waiting. Tadhg stuck his foot in the iron, grabbed a handful of mane, and swung up into the saddle.

*****

"Now remember Luisa. Rounded tones. Enunciate every syllable. Antonina, don't try to sing over your sister. You're each singing different notes. It's not a competition."

Monsieur Marcel Duprey, formerly Gerhardt Weissmann, wondered why he thought teaching music would be a good idea. Here it was, Sunday, and he had to give a make up lesson because the girls had missed their day during the week. He had two voice students, sisters, who were trying their damnedest to outdo each other.

"But Mr. Duprey, she's singing harmony. They're supposed to hear me more."

Lord, he wanted to slap them both. "No, girls. You are singing a song. You are learning the Ave Maria. Listen to this." He turned to where Silviane Gareau, formerly Sophia Davies O'Fallon, sat at the keyboard. "Madame Gareau, will you play the first four bars please?"

Madame did as she was asked.

"Now, ladies. Tell me which note is the melody."

The sisters looked at each other and shrugged.

"Now. Let's try this one more time. If you cannot perform amicably, in proper harmony, you will have to go back to your mother and tell her the price has gone up and you will take your lessons separately."

The girls looked at each other in panic. "No sir, please Mr. Duprey," Luisa, the older of the two, told him. "Our brother's already taking piano lessons from you. Mama wants to send our brother Marc for violin lessons. She's saving up to buy one for him."

"How old is Marc?"

"He just turned ten last month."

Duprey scribbled down an address on Baltimore Street and gave it to Luisa. "You give this to your *Maman* and tell her Mr. deGroot will make her a price on a half-sized violin for Marc. Make sure he knows I sent her so he gives her a good price."

Luisa clutched the paper to her breast. "Thank you, Mr. Duprey. I'll make sure Mama gets it as soon as we get home."

"Now may we go through this once more?"

Madame Gereau had a suggestion. "*Monsieur* Duprey, it seems the girls are listening to each other rather than the music. What if Luisa stands in the parlor and Antonina can stand in that corner over there." She pointed to a spot on the far side of the dining room.

"An excellent idea Madame. Ladies, if you would take your places please?"

The girls did as they were told. Each held her page of music. At Duprey's direction they watched him, and took their cue from the piano. This time it went much better.

"Very nice, ladies. Antonina, is your brother practicing his piece?"

"Yes sir."

"*Bon.* Now, you girls go home and practice very hard, and we shall see you again next week."

The girls skipped out the front door and down the steps.

Duprey went after them and closed the front door and locked it. "Thank God that's over." He flopped down on the sofa, pulling off his glasses. "Last time I heard that much squawking there were two roosters tied together and tossed over a clothesline."

"You do know we're going to have to have a Christmas recital for the little darlings. We'll set up chairs in the parlor, their parents will come with their aunts and uncles to see how much they've learned. Then they will send their friends to the wonderful *Monsieur* Duprey."

He groaned, making Sylviane laugh. She left the piano and walked over to sit beside him. To the outside world, Madame Gareau was his housekeeper and occasional accompanist. In reality they were partners in everything. Or as much as they could be partners. She was a person of color and he caucasion, and the State of Maryland still retained their draconian miscegenation laws.

Several years ago she had been involved with a brash Irishman, Rory O'Fallon, who had taken her to Pennsylvania where they could marry. They'd still had to keep their relationship a secret in their home state, but she felt honored he had thought enough of her to make her his wife. Then Rory was hanged for murder, leaving her alone.

Mrs. O'Fallon had fallen in with two brothers who were abusive. She met a rather charismatic older gentleman, Landry Glass, whom the world considered white, but whose birth certificate said otherwise. He took advantage of her generosity, took her money, then tried to throw her over for a younger, lighter-skinned woman. Sophia wasn't having it. She fed him a slightly deadly dose of mercury chloride.

Since meeting the man she had known first as Gerhardt Weissmann she had made her own fortune. The two of them had worked in concert robbing wealthy people during weekend house parties. When the police had gotten wise to them they had changed their names yet again and had opened a posh hat shop downtown. The pair had made money hand over fist in that endeavor. Unfortunately, it had fallen apart when they became a bit too brazen. Sophia was almost arrested at the Flower Mart, but she'd managed to get away. She and Gerhardt had been reunited and had set up housekeeping under their new assumed names.

Gerhardt, now Marcel Duprey, had discovered the home Landry Glass had bought with Sophia's money was still vacant. Glass' son had inherited the house off Parkside Drive and had been trying to rent it out. No one had been interested. Gerhardt had offered to buy the house for the same price Glass' father had paid. When the younger Glass had balked, Gerhardt had lowered his offer, and added a threat or two. The younger Glass had tried to cheat Gerhardt on the agreed-upon sale, and had later been found face down in Herring Run.

The two were partners in crime and held each other in great affection.

"So we really have to keep doing this? Can't we just go off somewhere and pick up where we left off?"

She pulled off the scarf she wore as a turban in her role of housekeeper and shook out her hair. "You know we need to lay low. Let's stick this out until summer. Then maybe we can go to Overlea or Belair and start over."

"Why can't we go to Virginia?" He put his arm around her shoulders, pulling her closer.

"We could. But those horsey set people are worse than that bunch in Timonium. They think their position is their God-given right, and their shit don't stink."

He laughed at her coarseness. "What's for supper?"

"Lamb chops. With potatoes and spinach."

"Come on. I'll peel."

*****

Lieutenant Norman Prince and his friends Lieutenants Thaw and Genet, stood talking and smoking on the edge of the airfield. They had already flown their first turn in the airshow, demonstrating the aerial acrobatic ability of the Nieuport 11 Bebe. They would fly again later, but for now they were standing about. Prince threw down his cigarette when he saw Officer Nagel riding their way.

Nagel rode up to where the three men stood. Once he had their attention, he snapped a salute and waited for it to be returned before he slid from the saddle. "I understand you wanted to see me, Sir?"

Prince stepped forward. He was resplendent in his uniform, with tall leather boots, jodhpurs, and leather jacket. "I wanted to see you, Mr. Nagel. To thank you for what you did earlier. That was damned brave."

Tadhg reached up and patted The King's neck. "All we did was catch three stupid girls before they could get any stupider, sir."

"And to do it, you rode right into the backwash of a running propeller. Have you any idea how close you came to disaster?"

He shook his head. "No sir. I trust my horse. I told him where we needed to be, and he got us there."

Prince started to put his hand on the other side of the animal's neck. The King shied a little.

"I'm sorry, sir. He was mistreated before I met him. He doesn't trust many people."

"But he trusts you?"

Tadhg scratched the horse behind his jaw. "We trust each other, sir. It's a long story."

"Maybe one day I'll hear it. So, would you like to go up with one of us?"

"In your plane?"

The lieutenant chuckled. "Unless you'd rather go

up in the observation dirigible."

"I'm on duty here for at least another four hours, sir."

"When you're off duty, you stable your horse, and come back here. We'll take you up so you can see how things look from five thousand feet."

"Yes, sir. Thank you sir. Where shall I meet you?"

Prince pointed to the hangar at the end of the field. "Over there. We'll keep a plane outside. So long as it's not dark yet, we'll take you up."

"Thank you, Lieutenant. I'll see you then."

Tadhg mounted and rode to the bleachers where Dylan and Millie were sitting with Rose. They had managed to claim seats at the end of the risers. Dylan leaned over and asked, "Everything okay?"

Tadhg turned his mount so he could observe the field. "That was weird. Those three Americans in the French uniforms..."

"The flyers?"

"Yeah. They wanted to thank me for riding to their rescue. The one I was talking to wants me to go up in his plane with him after the show's over."

"You mind if we hang around to watch?"

"Not if Lieutenant Prince doesn't."

"Go back to work."

"How's Rose?"

"Ask her yourself."

"Rose?"

She peeked around Dylan. "I'm fine. Go back to work." Her voice sounded weak, and he saw she was huddled in a blanket.

"Dylan, you don't need to stay. Get Rose home. She's freezing to death."

Shay put his hand over Rose's. "Millie, does she have a fever?"

Millie laid the back of her hand against the girl's

forehead. "Dylan she's burning up. We'd better go now."

Tadhg didn't like this. "I can find a doctor or call an ambulance."

"No." Millie was adamant. "We just need to get her home."

Dylan jumped down from the bench, held up his arms to Rose. Tadhg moved him aside and nudged his horse closer to the bleachers. He took her in his arms, blanket and all, and set her before him across the saddle. Dylan helped his wife down.

Johnny Allen rode up. "Everything okay Nagel?"

"Sargeant, this is Dylan Shay with the Bureau of Investigation and his wife. They brought Rose down today. She's burning up with fever. We need to get her to a taxi so they can take her home."

Allen nodded. He pushed his horse into a crowd that was gathering to watch the show from the ground. The King followed the black horse, carrying his precious burden to wherever his master deemed a place of safety.

*****

Sister Gabrielle Lane Pennington relaxed on the *recamier* in her dressing room at the new Howard Theater in Washington DC. Compared to Nashville's Ryman this place was a palace.

She was doing her first show tonight. If she did well she had an option for any part of the next two weeks. This was the first time she had played to what was obviously a mixed race audience. The theater was owned and managed by a black man, and he refused to segregate his audiences.

Barnaby Fogg knocked on the door then opened it without waiting for an answer. "These came for you." He was carrying a huge spray of yellow roses. They must have cost a fortune this time of year.

"Is there a card Barney?"

Fogg pulled off the card and read. "It's signed 'Your Brother in Christ'. Any idea?"

"Not me. Maybe he'll show up after the show. How's Buford?" Buford was a two hundred pound Irish Wolfhound who resembled a werewolf and could look vicious on command. As soon as Sister Gabrielle gave him the high sign he would lie down and roll over for a tummy rub. The rubes ate it up that this wonderful spiritual leader could calm the wild beasts with a wave of her hand.

"Buford is in with Larry having supper. They're both partial to veal chops."

"Good. Tonight I'll do Daniel. Tomorrow Acts. If things get to jumping, I may break out Revelations."

"Good. We don't want to use Buford too often."

"We need another gimmick. Snakes won't fly here."

"Maybe you can take a crack at raising the dead."

Chapter Two

One of the hardest things Tadhg Nagel had to do was to hand Rose over to Dylan when they reached the taxi rank outside the aerodrome. He wanted to take her home himself and wait for the doctor to arrive. Instead he remained at his post and finished out the day. By the time all the visitors had left the field it was too late for any sort of flying demonstration or to get a late train back to Baltimore. Once again he and Johnny Allen would bed down with their animals.

In the few minutes he had in between he did manage to seek out Lieutenant Prince. "It looks like I'll have to miss going up in your machine Lieutenant."

Prince didn't make the mistake of approaching the horse this time. "You don't have to miss it, Officer Nagel. Come by at dawn. We always try to go up then. It's good practice."

Tadhg knew they couldn't get a train back until almost ten in the morning. "I'll be there, sir. Thank you."

The lieutenant stepped a little closer. "I saw you carry the young lady off the field. Is she your girl?"

"Yes sir. She was suddenly taken ill. I asked her friends to get her home."

"But you didn't have to carry her off across your saddle like Sir Lancelot." His grin could have been thought lascivious, but Nagel chose not to see it that way.

"No sir. But I figured that's the only chance I might get to behave chivalrously so I'd best take advantage."

"Spoken like a proper gentleman." He changed the subject. "Come see us early so we can talk then one of us will take you up."

Tadhg saluted. "Yes sir. Thank you, sir." He wheeled his horse and rode away, trying to steer remaining tourists away from the precious airplanes.

Prince returned to his two friends. "Well, what do you think?"

"He seems a good enough fellow," Genet answered. "And he can't do any worse than Thaw here the first time he went up."

Prince laughed. "Which time? When he flew straight into a barn, or nosedived directly into the ground at full speed?"

Thaw wasn't amused at the reminder of his early mistakes when he tried to join the *Aéronautique Militaire*. He hadn't been the only one. But he took their ribbing good naturedly. "Just don't put him at the controls without any instruction."

Prince clapped his friend on the shoulder. "But if we did that, we wouldn't have nearly so much to laugh about."

Genet turned to leave the field. "Come on. I'll buy you both a drink, and we can talk about Thaw's screw ups some more."

Tadhg managed to find a telephone at the local sheriff's office. He got permission to call Baltimore and tried to get a call through to *Zofia's Cakes and Tarts*. He waited around as long as he could but there was no return call from the operator. Finally he returned to the barn and bedded down his horse. He hoped to be able to get a call through first thing in the morning.

*****

Dylan carried Rose through the alley to the cellar door behind *Zofia's Cakes and Tarts*. Millie had already decided they would take her into what had been the young men's dormitory and was now vacant in Tadhg's absence. Mary and Siofre had taken time to clean the place and change the bed linens in case the rooms were needed. He laid Rose on the bed, and waited for Millie to pull the covers over her.

"I'll go up and call the doctor. Should I call Marsh or Wollaston?"

"Wollaston first. If he's not available, get Marsh."

"Do you need me to bring anything back?"

"Holler upstairs to Katy and tell her Rose is sick, and you and I are going to stay downstairs until we hear from the doctor. We don't need to take anything upstairs to the babies."

He nodded and headed up the stairs.

Millie ducked out the back door and knocked on the door of the ladies' quarters next door. Siofre opened it. Millie stepped back so she wasn't in direct contact with the girl. "Rose is sick. I've got her in the next room. Can you toss out some nightgowns and a robe for her please? Just set them out here on the step and I'll pick them up. We don't know what she has, and we don't want anyone else to catch it."

Siofre ran to do as she was asked. She returned with the requested items shortly and laid the folded garments on the top step.

"You and Mary are going to be pressed into service in the bakery I'm afraid. And please get word to Hannah in the morning that she'll need to take the girls down to Katy's so Dylan and I can bathe and change."

"I can run upstairs and get you some clothes."

"No, hon. I don't think we'll be getting much sleep tonight anyway until we find out what's wrong with her. We're waiting for the doctor." She picked up the clothing and disappeared into the adjoining dormitory.

By the time Dylan returned the shivering Rose had been dressed in a flannel nightgown, her hair braided, and she was resting under multiple blankets and quilts on the bed.

Dylan handed Millie a plate of leftover meat he had found in the icebox upstairs. "Edmond will be here in half an hour. He said he's leaving as soon as he can get his pants on." He nodded toward the plate. "I thought you might like something to eat."

"I'm starving. But right now I'm going upstairs and make some tea."

"You should run into Katy. She said she's going upstairs and get us some clean clothes."

"I told Siofre to tell Hannah to take the girls down to Katy in the morning so you and I can get bathed and changed. We don't need to be around anybody for now, not until we know what this is and who's had it."

Dylan gave her a quick kiss before she dashed upstairs.

Millie returned a little while later with a market basket holding clean clothes for both of them, a bar of soap and a towel. On top she had put four cups, and she carried the teapot in her other hand. She set it on the small table in the other bedroom.

"One of the cups has sweetened condensed milk in the bottom. I figured we could use that for now. Is Rose still awake?"

"Not the last time I looked."

She fixed tea for them both and sat on one of the empty beds. They sipped tea and nibbled on cold mutton and pork. After a while 1 they heard Dr. Wollaston's knock on the back door. Dylan hurried to answer it.

Edmond Wollaston had done exactly as he had said he would. He was wearing his trousers and shoes, true enough. His shirt was collarless and buttoned crooked, his suit coat wrinkled as if it had been on the floor in a corner. He had left his overcoat at home even though the temperatures outside had dropped dramatically. "Where's my patient?" he asked as he pushed his way into the room.

"She's in here." Dylan led him into the middle room, where Rose was dozing under a mound of covers.

Wollaston sat on the edge of the bed. "Miss O'Donovan?"

Rose stirred restively. "Tadhg?"

The doctor looked up at Dylan, who told him, "That's her young man. He's working in College Park today. We went down to see him when she was taken ill."

The doctor nodded. "Miss O'Donovan, I'm Dr. Wollaston. We met a few times I believe. You're very ill. I've come to see what's wrong with you."

Rose opened her eyes and started to sit up, but groaned and fell back against the pillows.

"That's all right, Miss O'Donovan. You stay right where you are. But I need to examine you to see why you became so ill."

"Okay." Her voice was tiny.

"First things first. Let's get these covers out of the way."

She grabbed at them. "No! Cold."

"I won't keep them off for long, I promise. But I have to see what's wrong with you."

Millie sat on the opposite side of the bed. "I'm here with you Rose. I promise, the doctor won't take long then you can cover up and get warm again."

"Okay."

Wollaston asked, "Rose...do you mind if I call you Rose?"

She shook her head.

"Rose, when did you first start to feel sick?"

"Never felt sick. Just so cold. We went to the airshow to see Tadhg...Officer Nagel. We walked a ways, and all of a sudden I was freezing. I thought it was the wind off the airfield. I went back to sit in the bleachers, but it was all I could do to sit up. Tadhg had to carry me to the cab, and Mr. Shay had to carry me to the house."

"No sore throat, no pains anywhere?"

"No sir."

He put his hands on her throat under her jaw and felt very gently. "Maybe we don't have to uncover you. Mrs. Shay, do you have any pickles or lemons?"

"I do, upstairs."

"Would you go get one, please."

Millie dashed off to do as she was asked. Wollaston headed to the bathroom to wash his hands, and gestured for Dylan to follow.

"Dylan, have you had mumps?"

He had to think about it. "Yeah. When I was about seven. We were still in Ireland."

"How about your brother?"

"I know he had them. He was really little at the time, and the doctor was afraid we'd lose him. And before you ask, he's sleeping upstairs in our spare room."

"Good. Do you know if Mr. Dougherty's had them?"

"No idea. Why?"

"Because when men who have started puberty contract mumps, they stand a chance of becoming sterile. You and Mr. Dougherty already have children, but your brother doesn't." At Dylan's horrified expression, the doctor had to reassure him. "No no. It doesn't make you impotent. It just removes the necessary...seed to procreate."

"So you mean we'd shoot blanks."

The doctor was still laughing when Millie returned with an orange. "Katy must have used up all the lemons. Will an orange work?"

"It will. Can you cut it into wedges?"

Dylan pulled out his pocket knife and cut a section from the orange. Wollaston took one and handed it to Rose. "I want you to bite into this and chew it up really well."

She took the orange wedge and bit out a chunk of the pulp. It only took a few seconds for her to grab the side of her jaw in pain. Wollaston held out his hand. "Go ahead and spit it out. It's okay." She spat the orange into his hand.

"Well, I'd say that's settled. Miss O'Donovan you have the mumps. Provided you rest, have nourishing food, and stay warm, you should make a full recovery. But there are still some things we have to watch."

Millie sat on the edge of her bed again and took Rose's hand in her own. She looked over to her husband and saw he was standing against the dresser, eating the remains of the orange.

The doctor went on. "First off Mr. and Mrs. Shay, I'm afraid you are all in quarantine for the next ten days or so. Rose, you haven't had contact with the children have you?"

"No sir."

"I know you work in the bakery. Is anyone else in the bakery ill?"

Millie answered. "Not that I know of."

"Good. Most importantly, you have to tell the Doughertys they may not be around you during quarantine. And you must be kept away from your children. It will be hard, I know. But children that young don't need to catch the mumps."

"Doctor, do you think we could move up to our flat if the girls and Rhys went down to Katy's? We've got no kitchen down here. It's not fair to make Katy send food down to us all the time. Not with all she'll have to do extra."

"I don't see why not. But when Miss O'Donovan goes outside she has to be well bundled. So I wouldn't recommend moving until the warmest part of the day tomorrow."

"Doctor," Rose croaked from the bed. "What about Tadhg?"

"What about him?"

She blushed. "We were really close at the air show. Will he need to be quarantined too?"

"Only if he hasn't had the mumps. But he doesn't need to be around you any more than he already has. It is possible that it can be carried by a healthy person to someone more vulnerable. When he gets home, ask him if he's had them." He bent down and whispered something. Rose blushed and shook her head. "Good. Now then, I'm going upstairs and I'll let Mrs. Dougherty know what's going on. She's probably going crazy."

"Thank you Doctor. Could you ask Katy to please send Rhys down with some breakfast as soon as she starts putting it out. She'll know what to do."

"Certainly." He shrugged into his jacket, and picked a piece of cold meat off the plate. "Mm. This is good."

"Tell Katy to feed you. It will give her something to do while you're talking."

"I'll let Miss Dombrowski know about this." He named the public health nurse. "I'm afraid she'll have to put a sign on your outside door."

"I don't care. Will we still be able to run the store?"

"So long as no one else falls ill, I don't see why not."

"Thank you, Doctor. Will one of us need to sit up with Rose tonight?"

"I don't think it's necessary. You'll be in the next room?" She nodded. "Leave the door open so you can hear her, and maybe check on her in a few hours. If her fever goes any higher, which it shouldn't, she may have to have an alcohol bath. But for tonight, sleep is what she needs most."

Once Wollaston left, Millie asked Rose, "Do you want something to eat? Some tea? It's still warm."

"Some tea maybe. No lemon though."

"Good. Let me get it for you. We've got some leftover meat. You want a piece of that?"

She shook her head.

Millie went to get the tea. When she brought it back, and handed it to Rose, she asked, "What was it the doctor asked you when you got all flustered?"

"He wanted to know if there was any chance I could be expecting."

"And of course you said no."

She whispered, "There have been a few times, if Tadhg wasn't such a gentleman..."

"I understand, honey. We've all had those moments."

Rose handed back the now-empty cup. "Can you turn off the lights now?"

"Sure, honey. You want to go to sleep?" She nodded. "Come on, Dylan. It's time to turn in."

He threw the orange peel in the garbage and headed into the room he would share with his wife. Millie took her nightgown from the basket, tossed the nightshirt to her husband, and went into the bathroom. When she returned she found him sitting on the edge of the bed looking at a flimsy dime novel. "What'cha got?" She sat beside him.

"Whose bed was this?"

"This one? Mulalley's. Why?"

He showed her the cover. "I found this stuffed under the mattress."

She covered her mouth to stifle her laughter. "That little devil. He's been reading *Lady Fanny and the Boys*. I wonder where on earth he got it."

"You act like you've read it."

"Most abbeys have libraries, darlin'." She giggled. "There were a lot of hours to spend when we weren't entertaining. There's only so many times you can listen to the professor play the same song on the piano. And the girls get tired of each other's company. So we read. Blaze had a fairly decent collection. A lot of this crap, but she also had some poetry. The real thing, not just naughty rhymes. On Sunday nights, the girls used to sit around and read to each other. We even memorized some. Katy can recite *The Cremation of Sam MacGee*."

He put an arm around her. "Can you recite any of them?"

"I know some Poe. Most of the poetry I know is songs. But you know that."

"When we're out of quarantine, I plan to wear out that player piano downstairs one Sunday."

He got up to put out the light, then pulled the door almost closed between their room and the one where Rose was sleeping. Millie had already pulled back the covers. He climbed in beside her. "We're doing well on Sunday lunches, aren't we? Do you think it would be worth it to get a license to have music on Saturday nights? No alcohol. But we could move the tables in the department dining room and make it a dance floor."

"We'll talk to Katy about it. You keep the books. You know how much we have every month now. But it would mean you and Mike would have to be here every Saturday night to keep order. You know as soon as you get couples dancing somebody's going to get their back up over some imagined slight."

"Tomorrow. Now hush and come over here."

*****

Tadhg fed his horse, then sprinted across the airfield to the hangar. He found Lieutenant Prince sitting on an upturned keg drinking coffee, his feet up on an empty box. His jacket was unbuttoned, his hat pushed to the back of his head. Tadhg had to wonder if he had been up all night.

"Good morning Lieutenant. I hope I'm not too late."

"Not at all. I feel foolish calling you 'Officer Nagel'. What's your name?"

"Tadhg Nagel, sir."

Prince set his cup down, stood up and offered his hand. "Norman Prince." The two men shook hands. "There's a jacket and helmet over there. You need to put them on. It gets damned cold up there."

Tadhg shrugged into the leather jacket and looked at the helmet. He wasn't quite sure what to do with it, so he watched Prince put on his own gear.

"Help me push this out onto the field." Tadhg and Prince each grabbed one wing and walked the plane out onto the open grass field. A mechanic came out of the hangar, looking half asleep. Prince climbed up into the rear seat then waited for Nagel to climb into the seat behind him.

Before starting the engine he leaned to Tadhg and said, "Don't touch anything. There are controls back there too. Stick your hands in your pockets and keep them there."

"Yes sir."

Prince yelled something in French at the mechanic. The man gave the propeller a spin, and the engine backfired loudly then caught. It revved for a few minutes until it reached whatever Prince considered appropriate speed. The mechanic pushed the plane forward, and they taxied down the field.

Tadhg was afraid they were going to fly straight into the stable. Before they got anywhere near it the front end of the plane lifted off, and they were airborne. Tadhg Nagel had never felt anything so exhilarating or so terrifying at the same time. It was glorious! He wanted it to go on forever.

The lieutenant pulled back on the stick, and they climbed higher and higher still. At the top of the climb the officer turned the plane in a narrow arc, stalled the engine and aimed straight for the ground.

Nagel was in a panic. This man was trying to kill him. The ground was getting closer, things growing larger as they plummeted toward the earth. Then Prince hit the starter, pulled up and they climbed again. This time, the pilot performed a series of barrel rolls, made a wide bank and came around again, bringing the plane down for a smooth landing.

Tadhg jumped from the plane. He was grinning like a fool.

The lieutenant jumped down beside him. He put his hand on the young officer's shoulder. "Intoxicating, isn't it?"

"My God! That's better than...better than..."

"Thaw says it's better than sex. But I don't think he's doing sex right."

Nagel doubled over laughing.

Once he was able to catch his breath, Prince asked, "Don't you feel like you need to puke or anything?"

He shook his head. "Watching my first autopsy did that. Not this!"

Prince made a face. "How would you feel about flying one of these?"

"Me?"

"Why not? Most of the men in our unit never even saw an aeroplane before they climbed in the cockpit. I know you have a regular job. We'll be here for the next few months. We're supposed to be taking back a shipment of parts. Captain Thénault told me if I could find a couple more men who already knew how to fly we could use them if they were interested."

"You could?"

"I already discussed you with Genet and Thaw. We all think you have what it takes."

"What's that?"

"Balls of steel."

"Huh?"

"We watched you almost ride into a spinning prop to save those three stupid chits. And I bet that's not the first time you've ridden to the rescue."

"Not exactly. I did ride down a robber the year before last. I had to bull-dog him off a wagon box in the middle of Preston Street."

"What I thought. How old are you?"

"Twenty-seven. Why?"

"Just wondered. We've got a couple men who are only nineteen. That young lady you were with. Are you planning to marry her?"

"Eventually. We're trying to save up enough money for a place of our own. Right now we both have rooms at the bakery where she works. It's a long story."

"Where exactly is this bakery?"

Tadhg gave him the address. "Since you'll be around you really should come into the City for the day. They're open for Saturday suppers, and the second Sunday of the month they have a big family style lunch. I usually try to help out on the weekends, particularly since two of the boys who were working there moved to Boston."

"If you decide to join up, marry her before you ship out. At least that way if anything happens she'll be taken care of."

Tadhg nodded, knowing exactly what the lieutenant meant. Flying had to be one of the most dangerous things a man could do.

Prince went on. "You'll need to come down here at least one day a week. Can you manage that?"

"I can catch an early train on Sunday and a late one home Sunday night. Is that enough?"

"Should be, if you're a fast study. We'll take turns taking you up. You do know how to read and write?"

"Yes, sir," Tadhg grinned. "It took me a while to catch up after I left Ireland, but I went to City College and got a diploma."

"City College?" A cop with a college degree was rare.

"It's a public high school. I didn't have the money to go to Catholic school, but I was able to go to night classes at City."

"How old were you when you came over?"

"Fifteen or sixteen. My mother had remarried and there was nothing to keep me. So I lied, got on a boat and made it here. I worked in the City stables until I turned twenty-one and could join the force."

Prince checked his watch. "You'd best go get your horse and head to the depot. I'll see you here next Sunday morning."

His smile threatened to split his face. "Will I need to bring anything with me?"

The lieutenant looked him over. "Some clothes you won't care about if they get ruined. Sometimes we get sprayed with oil. That's one reason for leather coats. They're easier to clean off. That, and they offer a little more protection than plain cloth."

"I'll be here." Tadhg saluted one last time, shook the young officer's hand, and loped off across the airfield to where his horse was stabled.

*****

Sophia was cleaning the kitchen when someone knocked on the front door. She was wearing her Sylviane Gareau outfit. She brushed her hands down her apron, checked to make sure her hair was under her turban and went to answer the knock.

She peeked out the window and saw a boy around ten. A potential student. She pulled it open. "May I help you?"

The kid was short, chubby, carrying a violin case under one arm. "My mother sent me. My teacher died, and Mother said the man here teaches."

"Come in please. Have a seat. I"ll get the *maestro*." Gerhart had taught her that word. It did sound much better than "professor".

Gerhardt was sitting at the kitchen table, working on his schedule, trying to make sure he didn't take too many students a day. It was wearing to teach nothing but beginners with zero musical knowledge and sometimes less talent.

"Excuse me, *maestro*. A young man is here about lessons."

"*Merci, madame.*" He closed his book and carried it with him to the parlor where his potential pupil waited. He took a seat in a wing chair opposite the sofa. "Now then, young man. How may I be of service?"

The boy was in awe of this man, who looked as if he belonged conducting a symphony orchestra or playing a piano concerto. "I took lessons for two years with Mrs. Clark. She died last week. Mother says I have to keep up my studies so I should ask you about taking lessons."

Finally a kid who wasn't a blithering idiot. "What's your name?"

"I'm sorry. Barton Wattermann."

"And I'm *Maestro* Duprey. Now let me hear what you can do."

The kid stood up and set his case on the sofa where he had been sitting. With great care he removed his instrument and bow. The first thing Duprey noticed was the boy had a full-sized instrument, rather than the three-quarter size that was appropriate to his age and size.

"I don't have any music with me. Is it okay if I play from memory?"

"Certainly. I only need to hear how you play."

The boy plucked each string experimentally to check the tuning, shouldered his instrument and began to play.

Duprey had expected something simple. Scales, some easy pieces. Instead, the kid played Vivaldi. Not a written part from one of the *Four Season* concerti, but what had to be a transcription for solo violin.

After a few minutes, Duprey said, "Stop!"

"Did I do something wrong, *Maestro*? I have a hard time finding solo pieces. I bought a copy of *Four Seasons* for chamber orchestra and rewrote it. Did I get it right?"

"Barton, do any other members of your family play an instrument?"

"My sister started taking piano at school, but no one else."

"Amazing. And you've only taken lessons for two years?"

"Yes sir. Mrs. Clark said I was too little before."

"Come with me." He took the boy into what they treated as their music room, and put the score to the Bach-Gounod piece on the piano. "Madame Gareau! Will you come in here please."

Sylviane hurried in. "Yes?"

"Will you play the Bach please?"

She sat at the keyboard. She knew Duprey wanted to be able to pay attention to how the boy played each note and couldn't do so if he played himself.

Sylviane began to play. The boy came in at just the right place, kept the metre perfectly, played each tone perfectly. By the time he played the "amen" at the end she had tears in her eyes.

Duprey sat down on the bench beside Sylviane. "Barton, this is Madame Gareau. She helps me with lessons sometimes and accompanies our students when necessary."

"Pleased to know you, Madame."

This kid was no dummy, for sure. Sylviane would have bet money, looking at him, that he got his behind kicked a lot for playing a fiddle when the boys he went to school with were out playing ball. So he took refuge in music, and probably read a lot.

"How often were you taking lessons with Mrs.

Clark?" Duprey asked.

"Once a week. For an hour."

"How much did your mother pay Mrs. Clark?"

"A dollar a lesson. That's what she said, anyway."

"Well, Barton, I want you to come twice a week, for an hour. But I'll only charge you fifty cents a lesson. You'll have to pay extra for music and supplies. Do you think that's all right with your mother?"

"Probably. But what days? I have to help her out at the store after school."

"Which store?"

"Mother has a shop on Harford Road. She sells dry goods and notions."

"And you help her?"

"Yes sir. I have to help her stock shelves, and sometimes I have to deliver things to ladies who order them."

"What days can you come?"

"Tuesdays and Thursdays, right after school?"

Duprey checked his schedule. "What time do you get out of school?"

"Half past two. School's up on Harford Road, so I could be here by three."

"Good. Do you take your instrument to school with you?"

"I do." Suddenly the boy stared at the ground. "But I get beat up for it."

Duprey picked up his own violin from the sideboard and handed it to Barton. "Try this."

The boy accepted the instrument and played a few experimental notes to get the feel of it and played the same Gounod melody as before, this time from memory.

"Leave your violin at home. You'll play this one when you come here. I can't have my best pupil showing up with a black eye, now can I?"

"Best?" The boy's eyes were wide.

"Yes. Best." Duprey rarely felt any sort of empathy to another person, other than what he felt for Sylviane. But the kid reminded him of his youth and being abused by the other boys in that posh boarding school to which his father had sent him and his half brother. "If your mother needs to talk to me you have her come see me anytime. But for now, you need to get home and help your *maman* in her shop I bet. Oh, and you bring that score for the *Four Seasons* when you come back. I'd like to see how good a job you did with your transcription."

"Yes sir. Thank you. I'll see you Tuesday."

The boy packed up his instrument and hurried out the door.

Duprey was still sitting beside his housekeeper/accompanist on the piano bench. She asked, "Why on earth did you cut him a deal?"

"Because, *liebchen*, that boy is the best I've ever heard. He's a genius, possibly another Mozart. He needs someone to guide him and I can do it."

She gave his hand a squeeze. "He reminds you of yourself when you were that age, doesn't he?"

"He does. When the old Count sent me to school with my half brother, I tried to fit in. All it got me was beaten. That was how I learned music myself, to stay off the football pitch. It didn't help much. My brother and his pals caught me between the music master's rooms and my dormitory. They broke my instrument and left me as you see me." He gestured to his groin. She knew his manhood had been permanently damaged during his school years, but he had never really gone into all these details with her.

She laid her head on his shoulder. "That doesn't make any difference to me." She squeezed his hand again, offering what little comfort she could.

"I know, *liebchen.* But I wish I could be more for you."

"But if all that hadn't happened we wouldn't have found each other, would we?"

"If I had finished school there I never would have been apprenticed to a locksmith. I probably would have wound up back on *Herr Reichsgraf*'s estate as a gamekeeper, or maybe even a butler if he thought I looked good enough in a suit. And I would have been miserable." He raised her hand and kissed it. "Now, I have that Pizelovic boy coming to abuse the keyboard in half an hour. Do we have time for coffee?"

"Come on. There's crumb cake too."

Chapter Three

Tadhg came into the kitchen door of *Zofia's* near the close of lunchtime. He looked around, peeked into the dining room. He grabbed Tommie Bennet, one of the cooks. "Where's Rose? I don't see her. Or Millie either. What's wrong?"

Tommie was up to her elbows in hot soapy water. "Talk to Katy. She's out front doing take away."

Tadhg shrugged out of his uniform jacket, his collarless shirt sufficient to show he was off duty. He went into the bakery and found Katy behind the counter wiping out the remains of the day's meal from the glass case. "Katy, where are Rose and Millie?"

Katy straightened up and looked into the room. Only a few stragglers waiting for Annie to serve them remained. She pulled Tadhg back into the kitchen. "They're in quarantine."

He dropped into a chair. "My God! What's wrong? Has the doctor been?"

Katy sat beside him. "Yes the doctor's been. He was here last night. She has mumps. She'll be fine. But it can be dangerous for someone who hasn't had them sometimes. So, the doctor wants to know. Have you had the mumps?"

"I did. I probably picked it up on the boat coming over but I didn't get sick with it until I was here. I really thought I was going to die. Then all of a sudden, I got better."

"And how old were you then?"

"Fifteen or so. Why?"

"Just wondered." She didn't mention what the doctor had said about mumps sometimes leaving a man sterile. Because Millie and Dylan were with her all day. They're all in quarantine for the next seven to ten days, until her symptoms are all gone."

"Can I see her?"

"The public health nurse will be by later today. Ask her."

"I need to talk to Dylan, too."

"That's still part of quarantine. Ask Miss Dombrowski. She'll tell you yes or no."

Tadhg started looking around the kitchen for something to eat. Katy told him to sit down and said she'd bring him some meat pies. He poured himself some coffee, sat down and took the plate from Katy.

When Tadhg was done he scraped the crumbs into the trash and handed Tommie his plate. Normally he would have gone downstairs to get changed. Today he didn't want to take a chance on missing the Public Health nurse. So he sat, nursed a cup of coffee, and kept an eye out for the young woman on her bicycle.

He heard her set the bike up against the back of the building before he saw her. He hurried out the door, pulling on his uniform jacket as he went. She had her foot on the bottom step when he called to her. "Miss Dombrowski!"

"Mr. Nagel, is it?"

"Yes, ma'am. May I speak with you a minute before you go upstairs please?"

She followed him into the kitchen.

"Katy...Mrs. Dougherty told me Miss O'Donovan is in quarantine with the Shays. May I see them?"

"Have you had the mumps?"

"Yes, ma'am. I was with her Sunday when she became ill. In fact I was the one who carried her off the field ."

"Let me go up and see her first. If she feels like having company you may go up. But you'll have to keep at least six feet away from each other. No touching. Understand?"

"Yes ma'am. How is Rose?"

"I saw her earlier today right after Dr. Wollaston called me. They were downstairs in what I believe was your room last night. This morning, Mr. Shay had moved her upstairs. His brother is downstairs now so they can have the flat to themselves. Miss O'Donovan wasn't feeling too badly this morning, but sometimes people get worse in the afternoon."

"She's not in any danger, is she?"

"Not if her temperature is controlled and she doesn't get another infection on top of this. Yet another reason for quarantine, Mr. Nagel, so you don't take anything contagious to her."

"I understand. I'll be right here after you see her."

Two cups of coffee and a pastry later the nurse found him in the kitchen. "Mr. Nagel?"

He stood as soon as he heard her.

"Miss O'Donovan is tired, which is to be expected, but she says she doesn't feel too bad. She'd like to see you, but she asks if you could give her fifteen minutes."

Tadhg knew that meant she wanted to try and run a comb through her hair and maybe put on a clean nightdress. "Of course."

"Now, when you get upstairs there's a chair sitting in the doorway. You may sit in that chair, but you go no closer. Otherwise I'm afraid you'll wind up in quarantine with them."

He grinned. "That wouldn't be too bad."

"Yes it would. I don't think Mrs. Shay would want an extra person upstairs getting in the way. Besides, someone will need to carry groceries upstairs, to run errands and other things. I realize you have a full time job. But you're home at a decent hour in the afternoon. So you'll have plenty of time to do for Miss O'Donovan and your friends."

He nodded.

"When you're done upstairs you need to wash thoroughly, to put your clothes in the laundry, and sponge off your uniform. Any time you go upstairs, you need to wash and change after."

"Yes ma'am."

"I'll be back tomorrow about this time." She picked up her canvas nurse's bag. ", Mrs. Shay asked if you could take her some things when you go upstairs. She said she'd like some meat for supper, milk and butter."

"I'll have to check with Katy and see what I can take."

"Go see to that. By the time you're done it should be safe for you to go upstairs."

He heard the back door close as he hurried to find Katy.

Ten minutes later, he was climbing the back stairs to the Shay flat, carrying a basket filled with the requested supplies and a few other things. He knocked on the kitchen door.

Dylan had been waiting for him and pulled the door open. Tadhg set the basket on the table in the warm kitchen and began unpacking. "Katy sent you up a dozen of eggs, some pork and mutton tailings. She said Millie could make stew. And there's potatoes, cheese and some sausage. Do you think you'll need anything else?"

"Not until tomorrow."

He put the empty basket by the back door so he could pick it up on his way downstairs. "Can I see Rosie now?"

Dylan looked over his shoulder at the door. "Not yet. Millie's still helping her get ready."

"That's okay. I need to talk to you anyway."

"What about?"

"About the airshow." He pulled out a chair and sat without being asked. "Those three lieutenants, the Americans in the French army. One of them took me up in his aeroplane this morning."

"He took you up?" Tadhg nodded. "Damn. How was it?"

"It was wonderful. One of the flyers says it's 'better than sex'," he whispered. "Lieutenant Prince says that's because he's not doing it right."

Dylan's reaction was the same as Tadhg's had been on the airfield. He was still laughing when Millie came in from Rose's bedroom.

"Anyway, Lieutenant Prince wants me to take flying lessons with them on Sundays, and to join the American unit in the French air corps."

Millie felt herself sag against the door frame. No, Tadhg could not go to war. He was just a baby. Never mind that he was older than she and only two years younger than Dylan. She still saw him as the rookie officer who blushed at everything she said back when he was walking the beat by the cat house in Fells Point.

Dylan told him, "We'll talk about it later. Go on in and see Rose. She really wants to talk to you."

It was all Tadhg could do not to run to the guest bedroom. He stopped when he came to the chair sitting just inside the door. The curtains were open letting in the afternoon sun. Rose lay in the sunbeam, the light glistening off her strawberry blonde hair. The vision took his breath away. He sat down in the straight back chair. "How are you feeling, sweetie?"

"Not bad. Just tired. And I can't seem to get warm."

"Good. Because you have to get better really soon. You and I have to have some serious discussions."

"Is something wrong, Tadhg?"

"No, sweetie. Nothing's wrong. But we need to talk about things, and I want to be able to hold your hand when we talk."

"Because if you're holding my hand I can't hit you?"

That tickled him. "No. Because I like to hold your hand. But I promise, it's nothing for you to worry about."

"You promise?"

"Cross my heart and hope to kiss a pig."

Now it was Rose's turn to laugh. "I don't think Michael would like that much."

"So, how'd you manage to get the mumps, anyway? I thought that was something kids get?"

"I don't know. Oh, wait. I was at church a couple of weeks ago. There was a family with a mess of kids sitting next to me and the little one fell asleep on me. I didn't think anything of it at the time. I bet he was sick and gave it to me."

"How long does the doctor think you'll be stuck up here?"

"He said a week to ten days. I have to wait until the fever goes away for three days, then I'm safe to go out in public."

He nodded. "Put this down in your diary. On Friday next you and I are going out. Just us.'

"I don't want to wait that long."

"Then you'll have to get better faster. I'll be back tomorrow. Can I bring you anything? Is there something special you'd like?"

"Ice cream?"

"You want ice cream, honey? I'll walk down to the Arundel and get you some."

"No, not the Arundel. Read's. I want a chocolate ice cream soda. Take Inga with you to make sure they do it right. Ask Inga if you need to take a glass or something with you to get a take away."

"I'll get you one, honey. Right after lunch. I've got some things to do in the morning."

"Thank you." Her voice grew tiny. Tadhg knew she was getting tired.

"I'm going to go now. I need to talk to Captain MacFarland tomorrow. Also stop at a few other places. But I'll be by after lunch with your soda. I promise."

He turned to leave the room, and heard her sigh as she pulled the covers up to her neck.

*****

The theater in Virginia was a wonder. Over a thousand seats and every one of them filled. Fogg had made a sweetheart deal with the owner to get the place. Rather than pay a fixed price they only had to pay a quarter of what was in the collection plate. If the crowds kept up she could play here for the next year.

Oh it was a little inconvenient to have them showing movies before her performance. That's what Sister Gabrielle Lane Pennington was doing. She wasn't preaching the gospel or holding service. She was giving a performance. So every night the Howard theater would run a motion picture or two, depending on the length, starting at six. Then at half past seven

Sister Gabrielle would step out onto stage with a local choir and Larry Wardworth at the piano. She would sing, preach, buzz the rubes and Barnaby Fogg would pass the plate.

This theater was truly a miracle. The rubes paid their nickel to get in to see the film, stayed for the free preaching, then dropped twice, or three times that much into the plate. All it took was a few broadsheets spread around town, and she could play here until Christmas, when she was booked at the Hippodrome in Baltimore.

Sister Gabrielle was a little worried about returning to Baltimore. There was a chance she was still hot there. After all, she and Larry Wardworth and the rest of her crew had jumped bail after they were caught by that nosy red haired copper who had sneaked into her service like he belonged. Of course, if Larry hadn't been so stupid, grabbing that girl and keeping her around rather than sending her straight off to Myrtle's, none of that would have happened. She might still have her tabernacle on Fait Street.

Ah well, it had worked out in the end. The only way she could make more money was if she had a press.

Tonight, she was going to do something really spectacular. Tonight, Sister Gabrielle Lane Pennington was going to raise the dead.

They'd been working on it in her hotel room for the past week. Buford, the wolfhound, was a quick study. She used to think that arithmetic dog they used for the poison gag was good. He had nothing on Buford. Tonight Buford would die on stage, then she would raise him up. All it would take is a horse doctor willing to declare him dead, then the word from Sister to make him undead.

Tonight she would become Sister Gabrielle Lane Pennington, Miracle Worker.

She and Barnaby left their hotel room late in the day. They wanted to get to the theater while the movie was running. Larry brought Buford with him packed in a cage, the dog snarling and growling like some rabid thing.

When the time came, the choir from First and Third Baptist Church were filling the risers. Buford was sitting patiently in the wings with Larry Wardworth. Larry would hand the dog over to Barnaby Fogg directly, so he could accompany sister on the piano. Then their drama would begin.

Larry Wardworth took his seat at the keyboard. A few arpeggio to make sure his fingers and the keys were in sync, then he played the first few notes of their opening hymn.

The ladies' choir began, *"To God be the Glory, great things He hath done. So loved He the world that he gave his own son."*

Sister Gabrielle made her entrance during the first verse tonight. She had a lot of ground to cover, including a planned resurrection and all. She sang, *Who yielded his life our redemption to win. And opened the life-gate that all may go in."*

At Sister's gesture the faithful in the audience began to sing along with her. When they got to the last line, *"And give Him the glory. Great things He hath done,"* Sister opened her Bible on the pulpit and turned to the lesson of Revelations ending with "The dead in Christ will rise first."

She gave a good sermon on the topic, discussing how the dead only sleep to be awakened at the angel's call in the end days. That was Buford and Barnaby's cue.

The great brute began to bark and growl in the wings. As soon as Fogg dropped the lead the dog leapt out onto the apron, snarling and lunging at Sister Gabrielle. Sister raised her hands and began to pray just as Fogg came onstage.

"I'll save you, Sister." Fogg fired the pistol he carried at the dog. Buford yelped and dropped as if he'd been poleaxed, a red splotch on his side.

"Brother Fogg, what have you done?"

"The dog, Sister. He must have gone mad."

"But Brother it's not the animal's fault. It's man's. He was mistreated. Look at him, the poor, tortured creature. Now he lies dead at your hand. It's not fair to the poor beast."

"It's too late now Sister. Besides, it's only a dog."

She shook her head sadly. "But is he not one of God's creatures, Brother? And does the Lord not take notice even of the sparrow that falls? No Brother. We must save this pitiful animal."

She raised her hands and began to chant softly. Then she knelt beside Buford's still form and laid hands on him. Her chanting continued until the dog took a deep breath, whined once and jumped to his feet. The dog began to lick Sister Gabrielle's face as she hugged his neck and praised the Almighty for His mercy.

Sister spent the rest of her time on stage with Buford by her side, sitting patiently as he waited for her next command.

She knew this would be the last time they could use the dog here. But it didn't matter. They would take in enough money to keep them in good whiskey and better hotel rooms for the next two months.

When Sister gave the altar call more than two-thirds of the audience came forward. She had an arrangement with the ministers of the local churches to provide "Christian Counselors" to speak with those who answered the call, and to provide baptism to any who asked. Fogg had even had cards printed to give to every person answering with a Bible verse and a "personal quote" by Sister Gabrielle printed on it.

Gabrielle decided they needed to leave town in the morning. She couldn't possibly top tonight. She'd talk to Barnaby about finding a little country place to rent for a couple of months. Someplace where Buford could run and play, where they could work out some new gags for the rubes when they got to Baltimore.

She'd been thinking about this for a while. Maybe she could try the spiritualist gag for a while. She'd have to discuss it with Barnaby.

*****

Tadhg hated leaving Rose Sunday morning before the sun was up, but had no choice. She still wasn't well enough to come out of quarantine, and he had promised Lieutenant Prince he'd return.

The train to College Park had been almost empty. At least he got to ride in the day coach rather than in the stock car. The smell was slightly better in the day coach, but the seats were no more comfortable.

It took him some time but he managed to find a taxi to take him to the aerodrome. It cost him two bucks each way. He really needed to get a bicycle to get back and forth from the depot if he had to keep making this trip. He'd have to check to see if the station master would let him leave the bike here for the week.

The sun was peeking over the eastern horizon when he got to the hangar. The place looked dark at first. Nice. He came all the way down from the City, only to get stood up. Tadhg wandered around the hangar, poking here and there, until he came upon a door at the back of the building. He knocked.

"Wait a minute, goddamnit." Somebody inside was stumbling and swearing inside. The door swung open.

Norman Prince stood in the open doorway clad only in long underwear. His hair stuck out in all directions. Even his normally neat mustache looked wrinkled.

"I'm sorry, Lieutenant. I can come back another time."

"Don't be stupid, Nagel. Come in. Give me a minute to get my pants on and we'll go get some breakfast."

Nagel closed the door behind him, trying to keep out the cold . The interior of the room was almost as frigid as outside. The only difference was the wind.

Prince stepped into his trousers, pulled on his shirt and ran a quick comb through his hair. He didn't even bother looking in the mirror to ponder shaving. Then again, it was Sunday. If Tadhg hadn't had to go out, he wouldn't have shaved either.

"The mess hall's open by now. Let's go find some coffee." Prince led the way to a long wooden building behind the hangars where a few men were sitting at long tables.

The aerodrome at College Park had been built by the Army to train the fledgling flying corps. It was the only one in the state with the exception of a few private airfields. As the country prepared to defend itself from the German threat, arms manufacturers were increasing production. More food was being put up in tins than in previous years to be laid by for emergency use, and the military was quietly adding volunteers.

Three enlisted men stood at attention as Lieutenant Prince passed. He made a dismissive gesture. "Oh, sit down and eat."

Nagel followed Prince to the service counter where they both drew off cups of coffee. Prince grabbed a plate and took a couple of biscuits and some ham from the serving tray. Nagel did the same, curious to compare these biscuits to those he got at home. They found a table, and sat on opposite sides. The lieutenant took a reviving swallow of the steaming coffee.

"So, Nagel, how'd you wind up in the mounted police? Isn't that usually reserved for old cavalry soldiers?"

Tadhg took a bite of the biscuit, finding it dry compared to Katy's. He looked around for some jelly. "It started a couple years ago. I was sent under cover..."

"You were a spy?"

"For the Bureau of Investigation. Yes sir. It started when my cousin and his friends were brought over from Ireland. They were only seventeen. Some crook told them he'd pay their passage and they could work it off. After four months of hard work none of them had put a dent in their debt, and they owed four times more than they'd earned. My cousin got hurt and was sent to a hospital in Baltimore. He got in touch with me. When we were clean shaven we looked enough alike that I was able to take his place on the work crew.

"My job was teamster. I drove wagons hauling rails and ties to job sites and carrying men back and forth. The foreman took a dislike to me because I wouldn't let him bully me or beat the horses. He refused to listen to anything and frightened the team, hoping they'd run away with me. I calmed them down and we rode back to camp.

"When I had the information they needed it was time for me to get back to the rail head. The only way to get there was on horseback. That big gray horse had taken a liking to me and would let me do just about anything I wanted with him. There wasn't a saddle in camp large enough to fit him. So I put a bridle on him, swung up on his back and rode out in the middle of the night.

"The foreman followed us and tried to kill me. He had a shotgun. When he shucked it my horse reared. I fell off in the mud, and the gray backed into the foreman's horse. The foreman went down with his mount. The horse got up and shook it off. The foreman's neck was broken. The gray took a load of buckshot in his arse.

"I met up with the two men from the BoI at Aberdeen. They decided to take the foreman's body back for autopsy and the gray as evidence."

"So you kept him?"

"It took a little finagling. And I had to get special permission from the Department. After getting my arm busted in service to the Bureau, and being given a medal and everything at the Democratic Convention the chief would have given me anything I wanted. And I wanted The King."

"Is that his name?"

Nagel shook his head. "Well I started calling him Brian Boru. But some of the coppers who aren't Irish thought that was sort of snooty so they started calling him The King. Probably because he's the biggest horse in the stable."

"What about this cousin? Is he keeping your girl company back in town?" Prince was grinning, needling Nagel the way men do.

Tadhg pushed his plate aside. "He was murdered a few months later by the man who sold him into peonage."

"Christ, Nagel. I'm sorry. Did they get the bastard?"

He nodded. "The City hanged him. That was the only hanging I was ever glad to attend."

"Were you the one who arrested him?"

"Not this time. It was Mike Dougherty about a year later. Mike caught him carrying a box of pornographic pictures as the bum was waiting for a streetcar."

Prince got up and refilled their coffees. When he sat back down he said, "You mentioned riding down some thieves?"

"Oh that. Two crooks had stolen a dozen gowns from some fancy fashion show. The eejits tried to make their escape in an ice wagon. The horse was just an old plug but the driver tried to outrun us. I rode up beside the wagon, stepped off onto the box, and coldcocked him."

"Naturally you got credit for those two arrests."

"Three."

"How'd you do that?"

"One of the thieves' girlfriend ran out and started beating on me. I used my handcuffs on her and cuffed her to the wagon wheel. They're still in jail. She has another year to do. Her friends got fifteen years each."

Norman Prince sipped his coffee in silence for a while. Then said, "You've done a lot so far and you're not even thirty. You sure you want to do this?"

"Lieutenant, I've been looking at what's in the newspapers. I read about the Germans sinking American ships. I hear how the Bosch are sending arms to Ireland in order to split the British front. I still have family there. Ireland is my homeland. Hell I talk to my horse in Gaelic. I don't want my cousins and friends to die because the Kaiser thinks it would be fun to get rid of his cousin the King."

"You know you could join the British Army and they'd be glad to have you."

Nagel shook his head. "As cannon fodder. With a name like Tadhg Nagel, I'd be one of the first ones over the top and one of the first to die. I want to make a difference, Lieutenant, but not by dying for some general's vanity campaign."

Prince only nodded. "Tell me Nagel. Can you shoot?"

"Revolver, rifle, shotgun. I had to qualify with a revolver on the force."

"So, you ready to go up?"

"Yes sir." Nagel followed Prince out into the morning sun. Thaw and Genet had moved all three planes out of the hangar, and were suiting up.

"I'm going to let you go up with Soda."

"Sir?"

Thaw tossed Tadhg a leather coat. "They call me Soda. My name's Bill." The two men shook hands. "Tadhg, right?"

"Yes sir."

"Alright, Tadhg. We're going to take the aeroplane up. You'll sit in the front, I'll sit in the rear. All I want you to do right now is watch what happens to the stick and pedals in front of you."

Tadhg had already noticed those controls on his first flight. He had been so panicked about not hitting the ground he hadn't really paid a lot of attention. "So I ride with my hands in my pockets again?"

"Unless I tell you to take over. Come on. I'll explain what these different doo-hickeys are supposed to do."

It took a good half hour for Tadhg to grasp the few controls in the larger Nieuport flying machine. Not because they were complicated, but because Thaw insisted on giving an anecdote about every member of the American unit of French Aircorps and how they managed to crash a plane by misusing the control in question. Tadhg knew the man was trying to frighten him. It didn't work. "So the stick steers and aims the plane up and down. The pedals control the rudders and the speed. Keep my hands in my pockets until you tell me otherwise. If I need to puke, lean over the side of the cockpit. I think I got it."

Prince was grinning at Thaw. "I told you."

Thaw climbed into the rear seat, Tadhg into the front. Both men pulled on their helmets. The pilot pressed the starter and at his call of "Contact!" Genet grabbed the propeller and gave it a spin. It backfired but didn't catch, so he repeated the procedure. Prince ran back and pulled the chock blocks from under the wheels and they started to taxi forward.

Tadhg anticipated the feel of the plane taking off. But he had not expected Thaw to yank the stick straight back, pulling the plane almost vertical. They took off nearly straight up. Thaw executed a series of loop-the-loops and spiraled down, finally bringing the plane down on the field, only bouncing it twice.

The lieutenant cut the engine, and Nagel jumped to the ground. "Whoo-Hoo!"

Prince looked at Thaw grinning. "Told ya."

Genet put his hand on Nagel's shoulder. "Now that the college boy here's had his fun, let's see if we can show you how this thing really works." The two climbed into Genet's aeroplane, Thaw spun the propeller and they were off.

By prior agreement, Nagel would take over once they were airborne. He would fly some basic maneuvers, straight, climb, descend, bank left then bank right. He was ready.

They were off the ground, leveled off at about five thousand feet. Genet leaned forward and shook Nagel's shoulder. Tadhg felt the ship shift a little to the left as Genet released the stick. Nagel took hold of his own control and guided the Bebe 11 into a gentle bank to the left and leveled off. They circled the field, and, at Genet's direction Nagel pulled back on the stick slightly to climb another thousand feet or so and leveled off again.

Charles Genet gestured that Tadhg should bank to the right and begin his descent. Three laps of the field, and they were nearing the ground. The lieutenant shook Nagel's shoulder again so he could take over the landing.

As he did before, Nagel was the first one out of the cockpit. "You were right, Lieutenant. That is better than sex!"When he realized what he'd said he blushed to the roots of his russet hair.

*****

Millie sat on the edge of Rose's bed, reading the Sunday American. They were reading stories aloud to each other, laughing at some of the personal advertisements.

"Listen to this one, Rose. 'Bobby -- come home. All is forgiven. Love Mom.' Then two spaces down, 'Bobby -- Mom's lying. Stay where you are. Dad'. Can these be real, do you think?"

"Oh, about as real as some of the men in the lonely hearts ads. Do we really believe the 'rich man seeks understanding wife' is a man with money wants a wife for his old age? Or is he a creep who wants to get her alone in a dark corner knowing she's needy enough to be reading the lonely hearts ads?"

Millie threw the paper over her head. "Rose, are you sure you never worked like Katy and I did? You sound about as cynical."

"I'm sure," she laughed. "I guess I've been hanging around here too long." She folded the paper she'd been reading. "Is the doctor or Joanne coming today?"

Millie shook her head. "Edmond said he'd been here first thing in the morning. How are you feeling?"

"Like I'm going to lose my mind. I want to go outside. I want to see people. I want to see Tadhg."

"You know he had to go out today."

"He didn't say where he had to go. I worry when he does things like this. The last time he disappeared he wound up at that railroad camp."

"I wouldn't worry about that. I'll make sure he comes up to see you when he gets home. He should be here for dinner. You feel up to sitting at the table tonight?"

"I even feel like putting on clothes. I'm sick and tired of wearing a nightgown day in and day out."

"Then come with me." Millie helped her out of the bed and took her through to her own bedroom, where she pulled out a housedress. "It's nothing special but it's not flannel and you don't need a corset." She laid her hand across Rose's forehead. "At least you haven't had a fever for two days. Maybe tomorrow the doctor will spring you."

"Good. Would you be angry if I couldn't go back working right away?"

"Honey, I don't expect you to. I remember having mumps when I was about ten. I went back to school, but I felt like death on a soda cracker for about two weeks after."

Rose pulled the nightgown off over her head, pulled on a borrowed shift and the housedress. Millie was right. It wasn't anything special but it surely did feel better than a nightgown.

"Have you got a shawl I can borrow?" The dress may be more comfortable, but without proper undergarments Rose still didn't feel secure.

The paisley shawl Dylan had given Millie on the birth of their daughter Chiara lay across the *recamier*. Rose knew how special it was and made it clear she had no designs on the piece. Millie went into a drawer and found a green wool shawl Rose could wear around her shoulders, or pull more tightly and tie behind her back if she needed both hands to work in the kitchen.

Rose sat on the slipper chair in front of the dressing table. "What can I do to help with supper?"

"Well I'd tell you to set the table but Dylan's been hiding in there working on the books."

"Can I help you in the kitchen?"

"Sure. You can peel some potatoes."

"Good. I can sit down to do that."

Millie got Rose set up at the kitchen table with a knife, a bowl and a bag of King Edwards and went to check on her husband. She found him still at the dining room table with a collection of register tapes, a pad of paper and a ledger in front of him. She noticed he had an almost empty bottle of beer on the table. "Is it that bad?"

"I asked the girls to keep track of what's selling and what's left over. We really need to change some menu items."

She sat beside him. "Like what?"

"It seems like no German food is selling much at all. Oh we move some things. Sauerkraut and *Weisswurst* always sells but not as much as it used to. Mike told me there's been some assaults on people with German names and German accents. I think we really need to eliminate any German names from our offerings."

"What if we use the Polish name for the same thing?"

"There's a Polish name for it?"

"*Kapusta.* We can get kielbasa instead of *Weisswurst.* The only thing we can't have is *Sauerfleisch.*" She looked at his stack of notes. "How are we doing otherwise?"

"The number of customers is down just a little. But the dining room is making up for it, and the Sunday lunches are putting us over the top again."

"You mentioned an entertainment license. Can we afford it?"

"Not now. But you know what we can do?"

She was almost afraid to ask. "What?"

"It sccms we have the same people here every Sunday we're open. What if we make it a subscription? That way we could have music and dancing, because it would be members only."

"Before we do that I think we need to see how our customers feel about it. Think about those families who bring granny here on Sunday. Would they want to come to dance or would they prefer a quiet meal?"

"We'll take a survey next month."

"Did Tadhg say anything to you about where he went today?"

Dylan started gathering up his papers and tucking them inside the ledger. "Mm-hmm."

"Well?"

Dylan checked his watch. "He'll be here in about half an hour. Ask him then. But I think he'd like to tell Rose first.

Chapter Four

Marcel Duprey, with his longish hair brushed back from his forehead, his vanDyke beard and his horn rim eyeglasses, walked briskly down Centre Street. He found the shop he sought and turned in.

The music store in the middle of the block near the Peabody music school had a little bit of everything. Today he wanted to buy some more music stands, two violins, bows and cases. If they had what he needed he'd get some sheet music, too. Otherwise he'd walk two more blocks to the publisher's storefront.

As far as the City police were concerned his alter egos, Gerhardt Weissmann and Madame Pascal, were dead and buried, a similar body having been found in an alley by the harbor. Nobody was looking for a middle aged music master.

"Good afternoon Mr. Duprey. How's that piano working out for you?"

"Very well Mr. Lewis. Have you got a tuner you could send me? We're planning a recital in December and I'd like to have everything perfect."

"Certainly, Mr. Duprey. I'll see to it myself. When would you like me to come round?"

"The first week in December will work well if you can fit me in."

"I'll call you and let you know what time I have available if that's all right."

"Perfectly. Now, I need a three-quarter size violin and a full size one, with bows and cases."

"Any preference?"

"The full size one, I'd like something nice. I have a new student. The boy is a genius Mr. Lewis. I plan to recommend him to Peabody in fact. The kid's twelve and made his own transcription of Vivaldi. He's been playing two years on a pawnshop fiddle that's not fit for kindling. I'd like him to have something decent."

"That's very nice, Mr. Duprey."

"After listening to beginners screeching in my ear all week long this kid is a pleasure."

"Let me go upstairs and see what I can find."

Duprey browsed through the small selection of sheet music arranged on a rack by the door. He found a few suitable beginner pieces, and some things for the Wattermann boy. On another rack, he found a stack of music manuscript paper. Good. He could work with Barton on some music theory. It would also work to make handwritten copies of single pieces for the beginners.

Lewis returned from the second floor carrying two cases. He set them up on the counter and opened the smaller one first. "This is a standard beginner's instrument. I took it in trade when a kid graduated to a full size. Three dollars, including the case and the bow."

Duprey nodded, and Lewis closed the case and set it aside.

He pulled the other case closer. "Now this, this is something special. Oh, it's not a Guarneri or a Stradivari. But it has rich round tones, a good feel. It was brought in by a widow. She left it on consignment. The woman's in dire need of funds and I told her I'd do what I could for her."

Duprey knew that was a ploy. If it had come in on consignment recently it would have been downstairs in the showroom. "May I?" He picked up the instrument and checked the tuning, then took the bow and played a few sample notes. The tone was nice. It was German made, fairly new, but a well-known luthier. All that was left was to make a deal without giving away the house.

"How much, Mr. Lewis?"

"As I said, the widow is in dire need of funds."

"Then she should have sold it outright. If you give me her name, I'll be happy to call on her directly." Duprey's smile was pleasant, but it didn't quite reach his eyes.

"Oh, I'm sure there's no need for that, Mr. Duprey."

"Of course, Mr. Lewis. How much."

"Fifty, Mr. Duprey."

"Hogwash, Mr. Lewis." Although he was still smiling Lewis was beginning to be afraid. "I'll give you thirty for both instruments, cases, bows, sheet music and paper, and throw in two sets of strings."

"Mr. Duprey, really!"

"Yes, really, Mr. Lewis. I can go to any store in town and get the same sheet music. I can order the small violin out of the catalogue for fifty cents more. And I have a feeling that destitute widow died ten years ago, otherwise you wouldn't have had this one upstairs. It would be down here, hanging on a peg over your head like those two violas."

"You said thirty, Mr. Duprey?"

"Thirty."

"Give me a minute to wrap up the music for you."

*****

"I'm sorry I fell asleep before you got home last night." Rose was sitting at the dining room table with Tadhg. He was on his way to work and stopped in to see her before he left. He was getting used to seeing her in a nightgown and wrapper.

"That's okay, honey. You needed to rest, as sick as you've been. And I was late. I didn't mean to be, but there was a breakdown on the tracks and we had to wait for it to be cleared."

"You never did tell me where you went."

He stared down at his coffee cup. "I was invited to go up with those French flyers in their aeroplanes."

"Really? You got to go up? Was it wonderful?"

"Lieutenant Thaw says it's better than..." He caught himself. "It's better than anything."

"Did you do anything else?"

"Lieutenant Genet let me fly his plane."

"You flew?" she squealed.

"I didn't take off or land. But once we were up, I took the stick and flew around the airfield, then spiraled down so Genet could take over and land."

"That sounds glorious. I don't blame you for spending the day down there."

"I'm going to have to go every Sunday for the next few months."

"Months? Why?"

"So I can learn to fly."

"You want to fly? Why?"

He mumbled something.

"Tadhg? I couldn't hear you."

"So I can join the *Aeronautique Militaire*."

"You want to join the French Army?"

He shook his head. "I want to fly. I want to do something to stop Germany from destroying the world. I can't go to England and join the army. I'd be dead within a month. The French are putting together a unit of American flyers. I've got a chance to be part of that."

Now she was staring into her cup. "If it's what you want to do."

He emptied his cup then came around to sit beside her so he could put his arm around her. She started to pull away, but he wasn't having it. He held tight, and pulled her closer. "To hell with the quarantine. If I haven't caught it yet, I'm not going to. Now I need to ask you something really serious. Can you listen for a minute?"

She nodded, brushing tears from her face.

"Why are you crying, sweetie?"

"Because you're leaving me."

"Honey, I'm not leaving you. That's what I wanted to talk to you about. I don't want to leave you. I want to marry you. I'll have six months before I'll qualify. I'd like us to be married before then. I'd like to get married next week but that's not fair to you."

"Why not?"

"Don't you want to have a church wedding and everything?"

"I don't care."

"You don't care about marrying me? Or you don't care about a church wedding?"

She was mumbling again, then said, louder, "Get the license when you're downtown today. Will Father Toolen marry us without bans?"

"I don't know. But I bet Father Dougherty will. If I have to, I'll appeal to the Archbishop for a special license."

"Can you do that? I mean, we're not at war yet. You're not in the army."

Tadhg was quiet for a long moment. "I am, though. Or at least I will be as of next Sunday when I get my uniform. I'll have to wear it when I'm on the airfield. Norman Prince says I'll be an *Aspirant*. That means cadet. Once I finish training, I'll be a *Sous Lieutenant*. Second lieutenant."

"So you'll be an officer."

He nodded. "And I won't be in the trenches."

"Tadhg?" she whispered.

"Yes, sweetie?"

"Where will we live?"

"I talked to Dylan last night. Rhys will move up here. You and I can have the basement flat for now. We'll need to get a kitchen put in. I can call the gas company tomorrow and set that up. Do you mind working for a while? While I'm gone you'll have something to do, and I know Dylan and Millie will look out for you."

"Call the gas company. As soon as we have a kitchen, we can get married. But not until."

"I'll get Mike to go down and threaten them again." When the families had moved into their current flats it had almost taken threats of violence to get the plumbers from the gas company to come out and do their kitchen installations. "Now, kiss me so I can go to work."

Edmond Wollaston arrived an hour later. He had gotten used to coming up the backstairs and having coffee in the kitchen with Dylan before seeing his patient. This morning he was surprised to see Rose sitting in the kitchen with her hosts.

"I see someone's feeling better this morning."

"Good morning, Doctor. I feel much better today. I haven't had a fever since Friday night. I'm ready to start tearing down the plaster if I can't get out of the house."

"We can't have that, can we?" He noticed she was dressed, albeit in a house dress. "Let's go take a look at you and we can decide what comes next."

Millie went with them into the guest bedroom where Rose had been sleeping. Wollaston palpated the lymph nodes in her neck and found neither swelling nor tenderness.

"And no fever since Friday night?"

"No sir."

"Good. Let's do this. No more quarantine. I'll see Miss Dombrowski knows. You can go out, but you have to be careful you don't overdo. You know what that means?"

She shook her head.

"That means you can't go to work for the next week. You've lost weight since you've been sick. You're still weak. I want you to sit around, read trashy magazines and eat cookies. Spend time with your friends."

"But my friends will all be downstairs working."

"So go down and sit at the table while they work. You can peel potatoes or something. So long as you're sitting. Got it?"

"Yes sir. Can I sew?"

"You mean sit and embroider something? That would be fine. But a sewing machine, no. It would put too much stress on your body, I'm afraid. I know it sounds strange, but I see a lot of women who work in sewing factories with back and neck pains caused by strain and stress."

"Can I go shopping?"

"If someone goes with you, and you take a taxi there and back." He grinned. "We can't have you falling out on the streetcar. Why all this sudden interest in sewing and shopping?"

Rose sat on her bed and blushed. Millie finally answered. "Because she's getting married soon. She's going to need a trousseau."

"In which case, my best wishes, Miss O'Donovan. I assume your intended is that young officer I see hanging around?"

She nodded.

"As I said, you can shop, but you have to have someone with you. And sit down as often as you can. I really don't want to get a call telling me you collapsed on Howard Street."

Millie had been sitting beside Rose on the bed. She stood up. "See, I told you to order out of the catalogue. Then we can just go down to Washington Boulevard and pick everything up. Siofre can make any adjustments you need. Now we just have to figure out when the gas company can show up."

Wollaston was collecting his things. "I'm going to leave you a prescription for an iron tonic at Read's down on the Avenue. You'll need something to build you up."

Rose made a face.

"I know, it tastes like burnt rubber. But it's good for you."

"Can't I just eat liver?"

"Do you like liver?"

She nodded.

"Then eat it at least once a day for the next week. About the time you get sick and tired of it you probably won't need it anymore."

Millie asked, "So I can see my daughters again?"

"Yes. I would highly recommend it. I saw your nurse in the backyard with them when I came in. The poor girl seems at her wit's end."

*****

Gabrielle Lane Pennington stood in the kitchen in the old house Larry Wardworth had rented on Assawoman Bay in Ocean City. The place was out of the way, with no nearby neighbors. Perfect for the evangelist to use for a rest before starting a new revival campaign. right after Christmas in Baltimore.

She was watching the Irish wolfhound, Buford, through the kitchen window at the animal Larry Wardworth had found for them to use in their act. The dog was running circles around Fogg, obviously happy. Fogg would say something, or wave his hand and the dog would suddenly drop down as if stricken by a bolt. Then he'd jump up, shake and start his happy run again.

Sister Gabrielle opened the back door. "Are you going to kill that dog all day or you going to come in and eat?"

Fogg put something in his pocket, called Buford and the two of them headed for the back door. Barnaby kissed Gabrielle's cheek as he passed her. Buford trotted into the kitchen and flopped down in front of the stove.

She had to maneuver around the big dog to get their food on the table. "You really do need to teach him to lay someplace else."

"Honey, he's bigger than I am. He can lay anyplace he wants."

"Can't you at least get him to move?"

"You move him."

She tried. "Buford! Move."

The big shaggy beast looked over his shoulder at her, groaned and rolled onto his other side.

Gabrielle started to laugh. "Well he did move."

"Give the boy a break. He's worked hard all morning."

"At what? Chasing a stick?"

Fogg shook his head. "I'm working with him to respond to a cricket rather than a hand gesture. That way, no one can say we're signaling his behavior."

"You mean the clickers the floor walkers use?"

"Of course. Did you think I meant a bug?"

She put the food out on the table. "That's a good idea. But don't wear him out too much. I don't want him really dropping dead on stage."

"He's still a puppy. When he gets tired he'll do what he's doing now." Fogg got up got a third plate and dished out some food for the dog. He put it down on the floor. The dog jumped to his feet and started eating.

"Oh, for that you move!" Gabrielle sat down and began her own dinner. "How are you doing with advertising the Hippodrome show?"

"I haven't started much yet. I wanted to talk to you about it first." He noticed the dog had already finished his food and was eyeing what was on the table. "No you don't. You've had yours already." He took the cricket from his pocket and gave it a click. On cue the dog collapsed in a heap. Fogg finished his meal, turned and gave the cricket two quick clicks. The dog jumped, shook it off, and sat, waiting to be praised. "See? I told you he learned something new."

"Amazing. Buford come here, boy." The dog trotted around the table to his mistress and sat by her while she fed him food from her own plate.

Fogg pushed his empty plate away. "I want to start a newspaper campaign, I think. One ad a week, on Sundays. Start it four weeks before your first appearance. Something like 'Would you be free from your burden of sin,' then the second line the following week, until all four lines run. Then the day before you open, reprint the entire stanza, and announce your revival meeting at the Hippodrome."

"Can you put the announcement without having my name on it? I'm still nervous about getting nabbed over that screw up at the Tabernacle."

"Don't worry. I'll make sure you see everything before it runs."

"When do we open?"

"New Year's Eve. I got the same deal we had at the Howard. Three-quarters of the take. We can stay as long as we like."

"Wonderful." She put her plate down so Buford could finish it. "Where's Larry? It's not like him to miss a meal."

"He's out getting papers. He heard something today he didn't like and wanted to verify it before he said anything."

"What?"

"Myrtle Purcell is in jail. She gets sentenced today. Apparently they put her in with some of the girls she sold before. They beat her half to death and put her in a wheelchair."

Gabrielle shook her head in pity. "It's a shame. Any idea what will happen?"

"They'll probably send her to Springfield State Hospital." He made a *tsk tsk* sound. "That was a good income, too."

"I don't know, Barney. That was a lot of risks to take. We're doing better with this revival gag."

"Larry had an idea."

"Hmmm?" Buford laid his head in her lap and she busied herself giving his ears a good scratch.

"Larry thinks we could have some pretty girls with us, maybe as singers, maybe something else. When they're not 'serving the lord', they could be servicing some of the preachers in order to get into their churches."

"I don't know, Barney. That's awful chancey.

There's got to be more ways we could make money without risking arrest."

"Honey, you don't notice the way some of those good Christian men look at you. I've heard that you can always tell the church elders because they pretend not to know each other at the cat house."

*****

Madame Gareau opened the door to admit Barton Wattermann. The boy was carrying a leather folder of some sort. "Good afternoon, Barton. Go on through to the music room. Maestro's waiting for you."

The kid almost ran into the next room and skidded to a halt when he saw his beloved teacher sitting in a wing chair with a violin case across his lap. "Come in Barton, come in. What did you bring?"

Barton set his portfolio on top of the piano and flipped it open.

"Ah, this is your score for *Primavera*. And did you bring your own transcription?"

"Yes sir." He pulled out another handwritten page from the back.

Duprey reviewed what Barton had written. The first thing he noticed was the boy had to make his own manuscript paper, drawing the five staff lines with a pencil and a straight edge.

"This is very good, Barton. Did you learn to do this from Mrs. Clark?"

"No sir. I figured it out on my own. I just played around until it sounded right."

Marcel Duprey couldn't believe his luck getting this kid as a student. The boy really was a prodigy. "Barton, I have some things for you. Look on the side board. You'll see some sheet music. Bring that over here, please."

Barton did as asked and returned the stack of music to the top of the piano.

"Look through them, and pick out a piece you'd like to try."

The boy started leafing through, stopping when he came upon a complicated composition by Paganini. He pulled it out and handed it to his master. "This one, please."

Duprey smiled. "You sure?"

"Yes sir."

"Well you can't possibly play it on my poor instrument. It's not worthy. So I want you to play this one." He handed over the case in his lap.

Barton accepted it reverently. He didn't know exactly what sort of instrument it held, but given the age of the tattered case it had to be something special. He pulled the violin from its cradle and held it to the light. "Oh, Maestro! It's a Heberlein, isn't it?"

"It is."

"And I can use this?"

"No. You may have it. You are an exceptional musician Barton. I don't want you hindered by an inadequate instrument. Now tune it and try it out. See how you like it."

Young Wattermann plucked the strings experimentally, adjusted the tuning pegs just the tiniest bit. "Maestro, may I check it against the piano?"

"Of course."

His fingers touched the keys. Barton compared the sound to the notes from the strings. Once he was satisfied he shouldered the instrument. It took him a moment to get it in a comfortable position. Duprey could have sworn the boy was actually sniffing it, taking it into all five of his senses. A few experimental notes and he began to play Schuman's *Träumerei* from memory.

"Lovely, Barton. Just lovely. Have you played any more of Schuman's *Kinderszenen*?"

"No sir. I've never heard of it."

"I'll see if I can find you the full set of scores. There are fifteen or so pieces. Quite nice when played properly. And you play it very well."

"Thank you, Maestro."

Duprey got up and got his own violin from the side board. "Madame Gareau, would you come assist please?"

Today she would only be turning pages. She wasn't good enough to play anything by Paganini, the violinist some had considered to be possessed by Satan given the speed and dexterity of his playing.

She started to set the music up on the stand when Duprey stopped her. "Now Madame. Today for Barton's first official lesson, we're going to have some fun. You have the music for *Cascades?*"

"The Shubert or Joplin?" She was smiling, figuring he'd demand what was considered an exercise piece.

He surprised her again. "The Joplin, of course. As I said, we're going to have some fun. Madame Gareau, I want you to play this through once so Barton can hear it. Then I want you to play the left hand only, he and I will play the treble line."

"Yes Maestro."

Barton listened intently as Sylviane played the piece through the first time. The composition wasn't as fast as many ragtime pieces, nor as difficult as some others. The boy took in every note, seeming to absorb it through every pore.

Sylviane finished, and Duprey asked, "Any questions, Barton?"

'Yes, Maestro. What kind of music is that?"

"That, Master Wattermann, is Ragtime. The new music of the people. It's every bit as complicated as Bach or Paganini, but some people look down on it, because of its origins."

"Origins, sir?"

"These pieces are mostly written by colored people, young Barton. They're played in clubs and music halls rather than in conservatories and concert halls."

The boy looked to Sylviane and back at Duprey. "That doesn't seem fair."

"Barton, come around here so you can see the score. Don't try to play every note on the sheet. Remember, we're only playing the treble line. Madame is playing the bass. If you miss I note, I'll pick it up, and if I miss one, you catch it. Think we can do it?"

"Yes, sir. I think so."

Marcel Duprey's smile was as wide as his student's. "Madame. If you please."

Sylviane began the bass line, and Barton played the upper notes of the treble scoring, while the music master played the lower. They managed to finish at the same time though there were some missteps and some missed notes. By the time they were done Barton was actually giggling.

"That really was fun Maestro. How come Mrs. Clark never had me play anything like that?"

Duprey sat in his chair looking as though his back or his knees were bothering him. He was only twenty-seven, but to the outside world, he looked closer to forty. "There are some people in this world, Barton, whose minds are so closed they can never allow any fun into their lives, or into anyone else's. Everything is work, work, work until you are so beaten down you can't think about anything else."

"Is it wrong to work hard Maestro?"

"Of course not. But it's also not wrong to take time to play. Music is supposed to be fun, to give pleasure. I know you've played some Bach. Have you ever played any Mozart?"

Barton shook his head. "Mrs. Clark said it wasn't serious enough."

"Madame, look in that stack and see if there isn't a copy of *Rondo alla Turca*."

Sylviane did as she was asked.

"Barton, this is a lovely piece. You come back on Thursday afternoon. When you come back, I want you to have transcribed this for violin. Mozart was one of the greatest composers ever born. But he didn't get the respect he deserved in his life, because he had a sense of humor and liked to play around with his music. When you first came here I told Madame you could be another Mozart if your talent wasn't beaten out of you."

"Really Maestro?"

"Really. Let me play this for you the way it's written, then you can take it home and transcribe it. Add some things if you think it needs it. There's always room for embellishments."

"You'd let me do that?"

"Of course. One day very soon, with your mother's permission, I'll take you to a real concert so you can hear how professional musicians play."

"You'd do that?"

"Of course. How do you expect to get into Peabody if you've never been to a concert?"

The kid dropped down on the piano bench. "Peabody? Really? For really reals?"

"Yes, Barton. For real. But I don't want you trying to make your own manuscript paper. You take this." He got up and pulled half a dozen sheets from the stack. "If you need more, tell me, and I'll see that you have it."

"Thanks, Maestro."

This must have been like Christmas and birthday all rolled into one for the kid. "Barton, how is your mother doing at her shop?"

"Well, I told you she sells dry goods. But with stores selling cheap clothes ready made she says it's hard sometimes. She says her customers can buy something from Braeger's cheaper than they can make it."

Duprey nodded. "I imagine so." He checked his watch. "You'd best head home. You take that violin with you and practice. I'll see you Thursday."

Barton Wattermann dashed out of the house clutching his treasures.

Sylviane sat on the arm of his chair and kissed the top of his blond head. "That kid thinks you're Santa Klaus."

"It makes me feel good to do something for the boy." He slipped his arm around her waist. "Is there anything you need at a drygoods store?"

She smiled at him. "Are you planning to go make a purchase?"

"I thought I should introduce myself to the woman. Otherwise I'm afraid she'll stop her son from taking lessons. She may think I'm strange, giving the kid lessons twice as often at half the price. And giving him an expensive instrument."

"Was that really an expensive violin?"

"It is. It was made in Germany about twenty years ago by a man called Heberlein. As you heard, those instruments have a marvelous tone. For such a new one they bring a nice price. I only paid thirty for all the music, the Heberlein and the little Sears fiddle. The Heberlein is worth over five hundred, easily. But the music seller on Centre Street doesn't know his arse from his elbow. First he insulted me, then he gave me some story about the violin being on consignment from a destitute widow. He was trying to effect a fast sale."

"And you only gave thirty for the lot?"

"I did."

"Well since you saved so much money on music and all, I think we can afford a few luxuries from the drygoods store. I'll make you a list."

She pushed herself off the arm of the chair. "Any more students tonight?"

"No. I've got two thirty minute piano students tomorrow. But we're done for the day."

"Good. I'll go put supper on."

"And I need to go through some of these new scores. I'm not familiar with all of them. I don't want to embarrass myself in front of my students."

Chapter Five

Millie and Katy were sitting in Millie's kitchen with their four children. The kids were sitting on the linoleum playing with Millie's pots, banging them with wooden spoons and making an hellacious racket. Millie adored every second of it.

"Katy, are you sure you don't mind taking Rose over to Washington Boulevard tomorrow?"

"Why should I mind going shopping? Rose ordered everything she wanted. Now it's just a matter of picking it up and letting Siofre make any alterations."

"Has she spoken with Callum or Father Toolen yet?"

"She spent last night on the phone with Callum. He was at Ma's last night for supper. He said he'll talk to Father Toolen and get the use of St. Catherine's just like he did for us. They can waive the reading of the bans because Tadhg's in the army, even though it's the French army."

"We're going to have to shut down again for Wednesday and Thursday next week."

"I don't care. Dylan and I already decided. We're going to give them Thursday, Friday and Saturday at a nice hotel somewhere. Tadhg's got to be back at the aerodrome Sunday and he'll have to be back at work Monday."

"That's nice. Michael and I haven't decided what to give them yet. He did get the gas company to show up this morning to install their cooker."

"That was fast."

"They probably remember the threats Dylan and Michael made last time."

"Where's Rose now?"

"Last I saw she was downstairs, showing the girls the dress and things she picked in the Monkey Wards book."

"Friday night I'd like to have supper for everyone. Family, staff, down in the dining room. Sort of a wedding announcement for the happy couple."

"Do you think it would be appropriate if Michael and I gave them a bed for a wedding gift?"

"Why not? We gave you one. Hildy bought us a new mattress. And it doesn't have to be fancy, either. We'll give them a table and two chairs."

"Then let us go halves on the hotel."

"Deal.

"Come on. Help me fix supper and we can send these monsters off to their nursemaids."

"What are we fixing?"

"I was thinking pancakes, bacon and eggs."

"Good. And we'd best talk to Rose and Tadhg before we make any dinner plans. Maybe they don't want the fuss."

"Oh okay. You take all the fun out of things."

*****

Tadhg parked his bicycle against the side of the hangar and went inside. Norman Prince was already going over his aeroplane, checking the struts and canvas. He looked up when he heard Nagel come in.

"Nagel, look in that box on the workbench. Everything should fit. You'll have to wait a few days to get your hat, bars and insignia."

Tadhg pulled open the box and took out a jacket and trousers like those the other officers wore.

"There's puttees on the bottom. Your riding boots from the Department will be acceptable, too. Wear the shirts you have on under the jacket until you can get some new ones."

Nagel stepped to the side of the workbench, dropped his trousers, pulled on the new pair and the jacket. Amazingly everything fit well. He pulled out a leather belt and holster. "What's this?"

"For your side arm. You'll be issued one when you arrive in France."

"I have my own."

"Your service weapon?"

He shook his head. "No sir. That one belongs to the Department. I have my own. A .38 revolver."

"Do all cops have extra guns?"

" On undercover assignment I learned not to not be without a weapon of some sort. I carry one of these, too." He pulled a lead-filled sap from his discarded trouser pockets.

"What on earth for? You've had occasion to beat someone into submission?"

"Not for third degree, I promise. I went with my girl to a church meeting a few months ago, and found one of our friends who had been drugged and was going to be sent to a brothel out of state. I managed to get Rose out of there, got some other officers there. But when we went in to raid the place I found myself utterly unarmed. I had to borrow a blackjack. After that I bought my own. Works a lot better than a nightstick and it doesn't leave so much of a mark."

"How is the lovely Rose?" Tadhg had shown them all her picture when he was at the field the previous week.

"Much better. Would you, Thaw and Genet be available to come into the City next Thursday?"

"Thursday? Maybe. Why?"

"Because we're getting married. I'd like to have you all there."

"Tell me when and where. We'll be there."

"St. Catherine's in Highlandtown, at eleven in the morning. No nuptial mass, just the service. Then the reception at *Zofia's Cakes and Tarts*."

"So we'll get to meet all those people you talk about."

Tadhg blushed, a little embarrassed that he had been running on about his friends. "I'll need to wear this uniform for the wedding. Will that be a problem?"

"Not at all. You're entitled to wear it. I'll try to get your insignia before the wedding and bring it with me. Maybe Thaw still has his you can borrow."

Nagel finally got his puttees on, bloused his jodhpurs and adjusted his belt. "What are we doing today?"

"Today we're going to go over the parts of this beast, and you're going to learn how to recognize a problem before it makes you crash. Then we'll discuss what to do when something goes wrong in the air."

For the next three hours the two men went over the aeroplane meticulously. Tadhg proved himself when he found a frayed cable on the rudder Prince had missed. The lieutenant handed him a clipboard with a checklist for their mechanics. "I know it's in French. Our mechanics are all French. There's a sketch of the Bebe. Take your pencil and draw a circle where the problem is. They'll do the rest."

"So I don't have to fix it?"

"Oh no. That's the best way to irritate the mechanics. And you never ever want to irritate your mechanic."

"Ahhh. Like making the cook angry."

"Exactly. So, do you think that cable is sturdy enough to fly one more round or should it go to the shop?"

Tadhg went back to the rudder and manipulated it several times. "It doesn't seem to be weakened. For a simple, what did you call it, 'touch and go'? For that, it should be fine. For more complicated flying I'd rather it went to the shop."

"Very good." He took the clipboard to the three men who were playing cards on a barrel head just outside the hangar door. Tadhg didn't understand what they said but it was obvious Prince wanted the cable repaired now, not later.

"Come on," Prince said when he returned. "Let's go get some lunch. The cook's making shit on a shingle."

Laughing, Nagel asked what that meant, since it sounded disgusting.

"Dried beef in a bechamel sauce, over bread."

"Oh! Creamed chipped beef. We have that all the time at the bakery. Except we have it on biscuits."

"Will that be on the menu for your wedding breakfast?"

"I don't know. I think they may be making it, but it will be served in little pastries."

"They can pull all this off in a week?"

"They serve two hundred meals a day, sometimes more. Some of it people eat there, others carry it with them. I just hope Rosie feels up to dancing by then." Prince looked confused, so he explained. "We have a player piano, and some of our friends play and sing. Parties there are always good."

"Then, by all means, the three of us shall be there. Do they allow alcohol?"

"I planned to buy a couple cases of wine and a keg of beer."

"That should be enough for us. We'll bring something.
"

*****

Barnaby Fogg sat with Larry Wardworth in the small bar nursing their beer. It had been a long week, sitting in the middle of nowhere, playing happy families with Sister Gabrielle.

Larry wanted to go back on the road and start picking up girls to turn some extra dollars. It wasn't a good idea to be sending girls to cathouses now. So why shouldn't they run their own abbey?

Barnaby Fogg was also tired of sitting on his hands. He needed to do something, to work the advance on the show. He needed to be out hanging posters, chatting with promoters, anything that would increase their attendance.

Instead Gabby wanted to play house. Cooking, cleaning, playing with the dog, even rearranging the furniture. She was even talking about making new curtains for the parlor.

The two men agreed. They needed to get back on the road, and soon. They just had to convince their boss.

"We need a new gimmick, Barney," Larry said. "The dog's a great gag. The 'slain in the spirit' gag is good. But we can't do that every night. People will catch on.

Fogg drained his beer and signaled for another round. "Did you see those women marching back and forth outside?"

"The 'lips that touch liquor will never touch mine' bunch? Yeah."

"Not them. The suffrage marchers. They're demanding equal rights for women. Why can't we do that?"

Wardworth was aghast. "You want Gabby to preach about letting women vote?"

"Oh no. I want her to preach against them. Think about it. Women all over the country are leaving their families to march up and down the streets. They get beat up by cops, get arrested, and are making spectacles of themselves. Sometimes a wife's arrest keeps her husband from getting a job. Gabby can push the idea of women leaving their homes, and how it isn't what the Lord intended for his most perfect creation. I really think we need to try it out down here. See how it goes. Then we can work our way up the Eastern Shore to Delaware, then be in Baltimore in time for the January run."

"That's a good idea. Do you think she'd buy it? Even though she's a suffragist herself?"

"I'll work on her. Grab the bartender when he comes back. I need to take a bottle home. Make yourself scarce for a few hours, will you?"

"Sure. You think three hours is enough?"

"If you want to stay gone till breakfast I won't argue." Fogg's grin was lascivious. "You need some cash money?"

Wardworth reached into his pocket and checked his roll. "I've got enough for what I have planned. How soon do you want to try out this new gag?"

"I was thinking of starting next Saturday. That would be good. We'll do a week at a local church. Then we can move north for another week."

"Let me check out the local churches and see which one would be more open to take on a new revival. Then I'll have a lovely evening with some of the local talent."

Fogg spotted the bartender headed their way and signaled to him. "Let me have a bottle of brandy if you have it."

He checked under the bar. "I don't have but half a bottle. I've got Bourbon and rye. Will either of those do?"

"Bourbon."

The bartender put the bottle up on the bar. Fogg thanked him, paid and carried it out the door. It was a good walk back to their house and it was cold. He'd be ready for a shot by the time he got home.

He got to the front door and turned the knob. Buford started snarling and growling. Fogg reached into his trouser pocket, found the cricket and gave it a click. The dog stopped immediately as Barnaby came through the door. "Good boy, Buford." He scratched the dog's head with his free hand.

Sister Gabrielle Lane Pennington sat in a wing chair in the parlor, wearing a cotton nightgown and flannel robe. She had been waiting for him.

Fogg dropped the bottle on the settee and went to her. She took his hands, allowed him to pull her to her feet and kiss him.She looked around him at the settee. "You brought a bottle."

"I did. If you get two glasses, we can have some."

She ran her hands up his chest. "I don't want any. Not right now. I'd rather go upstairs."

"You would?"

"I would. I'm cold." She held out one bare foot. "I thought if we went upstairs you could warm them up for me."

Dayam! This was going to be easier than he thought. "You go on upstairs. I'll be up as soon as I grab some glasses and something to nibble on."

She leaned up and bit his earlobe. "I've got something to nibble."

"Then I'll just get glasses."

"I'll wait." She laughed lightly, seductively to Fogg's ears.

She sat on the edge of the chair, giggling. Barnaby ran to the kitchen, grabbed two glasses, came back and handed them to Gabby. He picked up the bottle, took her hand and led her up the stairs to the room they shared. Oh if only some of their congregants could see them now. Some of the things he had planned were probably preached against in their Sunday sermons.

*****

Rose was frantic. She and Katy had taken a taxi all the way to Washington Boulevard to pick up the dress she'd ordered, stopped downtown to pick up the lingerie and undergarments from Hochschild's and went to Hutzler's for shoes. While Rose was trying on different styles, Katy excused herself and disappeared for a good half hour. Rose wanted to collect her purchases, get another taxi and go home. And Katy was nowhere to be found.

She paid for her shoes and sat down while the clerk wrapped them up. Finally Katy reappeared. She was out of breath, her hair starting to come down from its pins. "You all right? You look like you tried to run home."

"I forgot something. I had to run around the corner. But I'm back now. What'd you get?"

Rose pointed to the black patent leather with the white kidskin topped laced boot. "I thought I could get some decent wear out of those. What do you think?"

"They're lovely. And they have a good heel. You think you can dance in them?"

Rose leaned in closer. "That's another reason I got them. To protect my toes. Tadhg likes to take me dancing but he's not very good."

Katy laughed. "I'm glad Michael doesn't have that problem. Maybe Tadhg just needs more practice."

"We go dancing once a week at the Knights of Pythias. He still can't get it right. I don't care though."

"There will be a lot of dancing next week. And singing, and music. I suspect Callum will be on the piano most of the night, until he gets a skinful and he breaks out his fiddle. Then Michael will take over playing."

"Will Michael's family be there?"

"Well, would you like them there, honey? It's up to you and Tadhg."

"I like his mother. You know she came to see me when I was sick. She tried to teach me to knit but I dropped more stitches than I made. I gave it up as a bad job."

Katy hugged her. "I can crochet, so can Millie. But knitting? That's not happening."

"I think I'd like to get with Siofre about some embroidery on my nightgown."

She whispered, "You can, of course. But don't expect to keep it on too long. Not if your Irishman is anything like mine." She started collecting the parcels.

Rose gasped. She whispered, "He won't want to see me...that way, will he?"

"Let's go up to the tea room. I think we need to have a talk."

Kate asked the clerk if they could leave their parcels behind his counter, and they took the elevator to the sixth floor. This was where Katy and Millie had taken their lunch before Katy and Michael married in February three years ago. It was also where they had poached their best waitress, Betsy.

A hostess greeted them at the entrance. Katy asked, "May we have a quiet table where we can talk?"

"Certainly madam. Come with me." She led them through the room filled with women of various ages taking a break from shopping, husbands and children. She seated them at a table in the far corner. "I'll have your waitress over in a minute."

They sat and waited for their server. Katy ordered tea, surprised they now offered tea by the pot, whereas before it had been only by the cup. She also requested a basket of sweet rolls. They were brought momentarily and Katy was able to get down to her talk with Rose.

Katy poured tea for them both. "Rose, honey, do you know what happens on your wedding night?"

Rose blushed up to her russet hair. "Not really. I know we'll go off together, and sleep in the same bed. I know something will happen and it will hurt at first. It must be something awful nice though, otherwise I wouldn't get those...funny feelings when I'm with Tadhg."

"Have you ever seen a naked man?"

"No! Of course not."

"Rosie, Rosie, Rosie. Your education has been sorely lacking, I'm afraid. Do you even know how a man and a woman differ?"

"They're stronger than we are. I know they can do things we can't."

"They may be physically stronger, honey, but that's about all. We're the ones who carry and raise the children, who keep the house, who cook the meals. Can you imagine if men had to do what you and I do on a regular week?"

That made her laugh. "I see how Dylan's been since he was hurt and stuck in the house. Millie was ready to slip laudanum in his tea."

"Exactly. But that wasn't what I meant. Do you know how you get your curse every month?"

She nodded.

"So you know how your lady parts are made. That's good. Do you know how babies get made?"

"I know a man plants a seed."

"Uh-huh. And where does that seed come from?"

"I never thought about it."

Katy was racking her brain trying to figure out how to explain this to the girl without shocking her out of her socks. "You've changed Declan and Donagh's diaper when they were younger, didn't you?"

"I did."

"You know how boys have willies and girls don't?"

"Yeah."

"Well, those parts grow as the boys get bigger. Some are larger than others, but there's no right or wrong size. And his parts and yours are meant to fit together like two parts of a puzzle. Some things I can't explain without scaring you to death. But I promise once you and Tadhg are together everything will be fine. The most important thing to remember is you don't have to be perfect, you only have to be there. You can respond. If you don't like something he does, tell him. If you do like something ask him to do it again. And you can touch him, too. Nothing is out of bounds, I promise."

Poor Rose looked like she was either going to pass out or throw up. "I don't know if I can do that." She could barely whisper.

"Rose, honey, I'll have Michael and Dylan have a talk with Tadhg. We have to make sure he knows what to do. Not every man does. He may have never done it before either."

"Really?"

'Sweetie, some of these good Catholic boys don't do anything until their wedding night. Some of them get so drunk they couldn't find their arse with both hands if they were tied in a sack. So we'll make sure only the guests get pie-eyed."

Rose finally took a swallow of her tea that was cold now. "Katy, I don't even know what to do when we get to the bedroom."

"Well, you're going to have your wedding dress on. First thing you do is go into the bathroom and put on that pretty nightgown you got. Nothing else. By then Tadhg will have skinned out of his suit, put on his robe and will be waiting for you. He'll take you in his arms, and you just let nature take its course."

"And that's all?"

"That's all." Katy picked up a roll from the basket, broke off a piece and dunked it in her tea. "I'm really glad you got the dress you did. Did you hear about Maria's wedding?"

She shook her head. "I remember Maria's wedding. I thought that black dress was odd until she told us the story."

Katy nodded. "Faithful unto death is a nice sentiment. But I still wouldn't want a black wedding dress. But that's me. You remember all the buttons on that dress way down past her waist?"

"I was the one who had to help her button it. I never used a buttonhook on a dress before."

"Well, Tomás wasn't patient enough to unbutton her gown. That was when Maria found out he carried a knife in his boot."

"Oh no!" Now Rose was laughing out loud. "He cut her out of her dress? For real?"

"For real. I saw the cuts on the buttons after she sewed them back on."

"I'm glad mine buttons in the front." Rose took a bite of the roll she had selected. "But you know, it is sort of exciting."

"You'll be just fine, honey." She refilled their cups. "You know I forget sometimes you didn't come from the same place Millie, Tommie and the rest of us did."

"What do you mean?"

"Well, you know where we all started."

"You mean in the...house on Warren Street?"

"Well Tommie and Annie didn't come from there, but they were in same situation. So was Maria. For that matter only you, Hannah and Betsy haven't been...uh...nuns in an abbey. If you have any questions, you can ask anybody there. Although I wouldn't ask Hannah. She was married, but her husband wasn't worth the powder and shot to blow him to hell."

"Katy?"

'What sweetie?'

"Thank you. I feel better now. I was...not really scared. I know Tadhg wouldn't hurt me. Not on purpose. But I didn't understand. Not really. You explained everything so I could understand. Thank you."

"You're welcome. Now finish your tea. We need to get back before the traffic gets too bad."

Katy paid their bill, they headed back to the shoe department to collect their parcels and went out to find a taxi.

Once they were seated in the back seat of the Ford, Rose started to giggle. Katy looked. "What's funny?"

"I was just thinking about calm, serious Tom Ribiero carrying a knife in his boot and cutting off buttons."

That set Katy off. She started giggling too. The driver just shook his head, thinking he shouldn't pick up crazy women anymore.

They pulled up in front of the bakery. Lunch was over. Millie was cleaning out the case. "About time you got back," she told them in jest.

"You know it takes time to buy out the stores. You remember how it was when I got married and when Mary Faith got christened."

Rose still couldn't believe everything was happening so quickly. "Millie, are you sure you don't mind if I use your bouquet?" Millie and Katy both carried bouquets of silk roses.

"Rosie, if I minded, I wouldn't have offered. Now let's go upstairs and see what you bought."

They made their way to Millie and Dylan's third floor flat. Rose went to the room she had been using and would continue to use until she and Tadhg married. Dylan said he felt better having two floors between her and Tadhg this close to their wedding. He remembered Michael Dougherty sneaking up the stairs to Katy's room after they had all attended the opera. That had been only a few weeks before Michael and Katy's wedding.

Rose took out her wedding dress first. It was a suit, mint green, with darker green soutache embroidery on the skirt and repeated on the jacket, and a white shirtwaist with frothy lace at the throat and cuffs. The next box contained a Juliet cap with a short veil. Katy had insisted she wear one. Neither she nor Millie had felt entitled given their previous occupations.

Katy pulled the lid off the box that held Rose's new nightgown. Millie lifted it from the box. It was a delicate confection of white lawn and lace, not really appropriate for this weather, but ideally suited to a wedding night.

Rose took it and laid it on the bed. "See, Katy. I wanted to put some green embroidery around here." She pointed to the neckline, "so it would match my dress. Do you think I'm being foolish?"

Millie sat on the bed. "Let's see your wrapper."

Rose opened another box and pulled out a wrapper of fine silk that was a perfect match for her green wedding dress.

"Rather than embroidering on it, what about putting a green ribbon in your hair? You'll want to leave it down anyway. I'll show you how to tie it, and you can even put a piece around your throat. But I wouldn't sew on that."

"All right. If you say so."

"Put all this away. I need to go play with my girls for a while and get supper started. Will Tadhg be home for supper do you think?"

"He said he has to talk to Captain MacFarland today. Did you see his new uniform?"

"I did. Katy, are you all eating with us?"

"Are we invited?"

"You are. Provided you bring something."

"What are you fixing?"

"Oyster stew, boiled cabbage and bacon. You got some potatoes and something for dessert?"

"There's leftover crumb cake downstairs. And I have a *Schmierkase* in the icebox."

"Perfect. Come on. We've got oysters to shuck."
*****

"That's right, Stefan. Nice and even. One-two-three-four. Keep time with the metronome." The kid hit a clinker, stumbled, and started over.

"No, no, no." Marcel Duprey slapped the top of the piano making his pupil jump. "If you hit a wrong note you just keep playing. As far as anyone knows it's supposed to sound that way and you meant to do it."

"Why? I thought I was supposed to play it right?"

The Maestro smiled sadly. "You are. And you will. But even the best make mistakes sometimes. The trick is to not let them know it. Remember, when we have your recital you will be accompanying your sisters and Isaac for one of your pieces."

"Isaac?"

"Isaac Pick. He's an alto right now. He and your sisters will be singing the Ave. And you have to play your part evenly and cleanly. They sing the melody, you're playing the rhythm. Understand?"

The boy nodded.

Since he'd been working with Stefan, Duprey had discovered the kid really wasn't stupid as he'd first thought. He had merely lacked exposure to any sort of music other than hearing the organ at church.

Tomorrow Marcel Duprey planned to remedy the problem for all his students. Peabody Conservatory was having a concert. It had taken some doing, but Duprey had managed to get passes for all ten of his students. He had to promise that Barton Wattermann would audition for the violin master there.

Sylviane Gareau would be going with them to help corral the children. No one was looking for them as far as he knew. So long as he wore his hair long, kept the glasses and his beard, no one would easily recognize him as the German count or the French *modiste*. No, now he was the French music master giving piano, violin and voice lessons to a bunch of kids whose parents couldn't really afford it, but who were trying to give their children a chance. No, no one would expect the crook and conman to have any sort of altruistic motives.

When Stefan's lesson was done, Madame Gareau came in to play for Stefan Pizelovic's sisters, Luisa and

Antonina. The pair had actually improved, but not quite enough. Marcel wanted to speak to their mother about letting them have separate lessons so they could get some individual attention. As it was, they spent more time giggling than they did singing. He'd have to work out a new payment plan with her. As it was she was already paying a cut rate for having three children taking lessons. There were ten other children in the family and he figured he'd eventually wind up teaching them all.

Stefan sat in the parlor waiting for his sisters, making faces at them behind Duprey's back. When Antonina began to giggle, the Maestro looked over his shoulder. "Stefan! Come in here."

The kid dragged his feet getting to the music room. He acted like he thought the Maestro was going to cane him.

"Sit down beside Madame."

He sat.

Maestro clapped his hands to get the girls' attention. "Now, Madame will play through once while you sing. Then you will do it again while your brother plays. Stefan, you will turn pages for Madame."

Apparently he had everyone's attention this time. Madame played. The girls sang. It wasn't too bad. "Very nice ladies. This time Stefan shall play for you."

After the first ten bars, Maestro clapped his hand. "No, Stefan. Don't listen to your sisters. Only play what's on the page." He went to the sideboard,retrieved his baton and handed it to Madame Gareau. "Madame, point to every bar as Stefan plays so he doesn't lose his place."

They began again. The boy did much better. They ran through it one more time before the end of the lesson. "Remember, everyone has to be here at noon tomorrow. We're going to the Peabody Institute tomorrow to hear their students play."

Stefan was still sitting at the piano. "Are we taking the streetcar?"

"Oh, no. There's a bus coming to pick us up. So eat lunch first, then come here. Tell your parents you'll be home in time for supper."

"A bus? Really?"

"A Ford bus. We have it for the afternoon. We'll ride there and back on it."

"Wowzer! I seen one of those. They're boss."

"They are. So be here at noon, or we'll leave without you."

"Yes sir!"

All three kids ran out the front door. Duprey locked it behind them. He flopped down in the nearest chair. Sylviane followed him in and sat in the chair opposite.

"Are you sure you want me to go tomorrow?"

"I've already spoken to the organizer of the concert. You'll be sitting with us as my assistant. Put on your prettiest dress, wrap your hair in a pretty matching scarf and we'll be just fine."

"Do you know where we'll be sitting?"

"In the sixth row. You sit on one end, I'll sit on the other with the children in between us. When the concert ends we'll go to a practice room, and Barton will play for the violin master."

"Does he know?"

He nodded. "He's been vacillating all week about which piece to play. I told him to play his own transcription of something."

"He did so well with *The Cascades*. How do you think the school would react to him playing Scott Joplin?"

"Barton should ask what they'd like him to play. They may want him to cold read a piece. So we'll let the teacher there decide."

"Good. No matter what they want, I'm sure Barton will do well. Do you think the rest of them will behave while he plays?"

"They better."

She was grinning. "What are you going to do? Tie them to their seats?"

"I'll make them sit on the bus in the cold."

"Meaning I'll need to go sit in the cold with them."

"No. They'll sit with the bus driver who will have permission to slap them silly."

"Good." She leaned back and closed her eyes for a few moments. "I'm tired. I think I'll go upstairs and lie down for a while. Do you mind?"

He stood up and held out his hand. "Not if I can go with you."

Chapter Six

The three flyers came up on the train the evening before Tadhg and Rose's wedding. Their intention was to take the young man out and get him drunk, but Michael and Dylan were already a step ahead of them.

When they reached Mount Royal train station, Norman Prince called the bakery. The women were in the commercial kitchen preparing food for the next day.

Katy answered the ring. "Lieutenant Prince! This is Catherine Dougherty...No, Tadhg isn't here. He's with my husband and some friends. They're at a pub downtown. If you'd like to join them...Certainly. It's the *Limping Pig* downtown by the Central District police station. The cabbie should know where it is...Certainly. And when you're done downtown you make sure Michael and Tadhg bring you back here. We've got room for you three downstairs...No, you won't bother us at all. And if you get too loud, we've got three coppers in the house to settle you down...Good to talk to you too, Lieutenant. See you tonight."

Maria was sitting in a rocker Michael had brought down from their nursery. Her three month old son, Benito, had just fallen asleep in her arms. "So you're having extra houseguests tonight?"

"I guess." Katy went back to par baking biscuits for tomorrow. At Rose's suggestion everything would be put out buffet style, so that all her friends and fellow employees could relax and enjoy themselves. "I can't believe Tadhg asked me to fix creamed chipped beef for the wedding."

Rose told her, "Why not? It's his favorite. He told me the cook at the aerodrome makes it, and yours is better."

"Really? I never thought about it." She put the biscuits she had just cut on a sheet, slid them into the oven and checked the time. "So, we're having the chipped beef, lamb, roasted vegetables. Do you want to start with Scotch Barley soup or something else? I've already got the stock done in the ice box."

"I saw the tinned oysters in the icebox. I thought we were having oyster stew?"

"We could. I'll have to cut the oysters into quarters so they'll go far enough. Is that what you'd like?"

"I think so. I think Tadhg's friends will be impressed with that too. That's important to him."

"Then we'll have oyster stew. Betsy, you sure you're okay with leaving the wedding early to start the food?"

The older woman looked up from where she was washing dishes. "I am. Everything is already measured out. All I have to do is turn on the stove then put it in the pan at the right time."

"Millie and I will be here as soon as we can, and we'll finish everything up. Everybody can pitch in and put the food out while the men are making their stupid toasts."

Millie asked, "Are Michael's family coming?"

"We know Callum will be here, and Ma Dougherty. I figure everybody but Sister Sister will show up. She's teaching at a school in Arbutus now."

Inga Rottmann was cutting vegetables and arranging them in a pan around a large leg of lamb that would be put in the oven early in the morning. Tears glistened on her cheeks. "What's wrong, Inga?" Millie asked.

She sniffed. "Nothing. I'm cutting onions."

"No you're not. You finished them half an hour ago. You're cutting up potatoes, parsnips and carrots. Now what's wrong."

"Rose is leaving."

Rose walked around the table and put her arm around her friend. "Honey, I'm not leaving. I'm going to be right here. I'll still work with you every day. I'll just be sleeping on the other side of the wall now."

"But Tadhg won't want to stay here forever."

"No, he won't. But he's going to France in January or February. Now where else would I be, with my husband five thousand miles away? You can even come over and stay with me while he's gone."

"You sure?"

"If Millie and Katy don't mind."

"Of course we don't," Katy told her. "Although since the gas company put in the cooker we really need to charge you a little rent for the flat. You think you can afford two dollars a month for the utilities?"

"A month? That's not enough, Katy. Not nearly enough. Two dollars a week is fair."

"You've been living here for how long now?"

"Almost two years."

"Did we ever charge you rent?"

"No."

"So why should we charge you now?"

"But..."

"No buts. The only difference in cost to you and Tadhg being married is the cost of gas you'll be using to fix your meals. But you won't be eating up here so often.'

"Thank you."

The bride changed the subject. "How late do you think they'll be tonight?"

"I figure they'll close the place. So it will be after midnight. And you'll be upstairs in bed."

"Can't I..."

"No, you don't want to see your groom the night before the wedding. After you see him with a skinful you may decide you don't want to marry him. Besides, he'll have three drunken flyers with him, who are going to sleep downstairs. You really don't want to have to face them until after they've had some hair of the dog and about half a pot of coffee."

*****

Prince, Thaw and Genet found Tim Kelly's *Limping Pig* with no trouble. They were surprised when they walked in and saw a dozen uniformed police officers standing around holding pints of beer.

"Lieutenants! Come in." Tadhg spotted the three where they stood inside the door. "Lieutenant Prince, Lieutenant Thaw, Lieutenant Genet, these are my friends, Dylan Shay, Michael Dougherty, Tomás Ribiero." He went on to introduce the rest of the men in the room, ending with "And our landlord and host, Tim Kelly."

Kelly pulled three pints and set the glasses on the bar. "Gentlemen, welcome. I'm glad you could make it."

Thaw took a long swallow of his beer. "Nagel, had we known this many people were going to see you off, we would have brought more whiskey."

Kelly looked offended. "What's wrong? Ain't my beer good enough for you?"

Thaw drained his glass and handed it over to be refilled. "Nothing's wrong with your beer. We brought up a case of whiskey for the reception tomorrow. I can see we may need more."

"Never fear. We'll have more than enough to drink. Tadhg's already ordered a keg of beer, a case of champagne and three cases of wine. Even with a houseful of Irishmen we should be able to manage. And if we need more, all it takes is a call to my son, and he'll personally bring reinforcements." Sean Kelly looked up from behind the bar where he was drying shot glasses and gave a mock salute.

Tom Ribiero was the first to offer his hand to the flyers. "Lieutenants, I'm glad you could come. Officer Nagel speaks very highly of you. It's good to know you're not all figments of his imagination."

Prince noticed a man in a Roman collar leaning on the bar. He leaned over to Michael and asked, "Who's the guy in the dog collar?"

Mike looked over his shoulder and grinned. "That's me brother, Callum. Father Dougherty. He's the officiant tomorrow. We had to invite him tonight otherwise he won't play piano for us during the reception."

Genet actually groaned. "Don't tell me he'll be playing hymns at the reception?"

"Hey, Callum!" Father Daugherty brought his beer as he strolled to where his brother stood.

"Aye, Michael?"

"Tadhg's friends here seem to think you'll be playing hymns tomorrow for the reception."

The priest grinned. These boys must be Protestants. "Hey Tadhg, who was that man you worked for at that railroad camp?"

Tadhg knew exactly what he was about. "You mean *Muirsheen* Durkin?"

"That's the one." There was a piano against the wall. "Mike, you want to give me a hand?"

"Sure. But I haven't played it in a while." Mike took his seat on the stool and checked the action of the keys. They were loose, like most barroom pianos. Not that it mattered. He'd play a few chords,the cops in the room would join in and nobody would hear him anyway.

Callum set his glass on top of the piano. "Whenever you're ready."

The younger Dougherty played the opening notes. Callum clasped his hands comically before him, elbows bent, toes pointed out, the vaudeville image of an opera singer.

> *In the days when I was courtin',*
> *I was never tired 'resorting,*
> *To the alehouse and the playhouse and many's the house beside.*
> *I told my brother Shamus*
> *I'd be off and be right famous*
> *And never I'd return again 'till I roamed the whole worldwide.*

The other men in the room were laughing and clapping at the good father's euphemistic mention of the whorehouses. They all joined in to sing the refrain. By the time Callum had sung all five verses, even the flyers had joined in.

Dylan handed his glass over to Kelly to be refilled. "That's one of the cleaner ones he knows. We had a crab feast for July Fourth year before last. Between Father Dougherty and our wives, there was no person who hadn't gotten an education."

"Your wives?" This was the one story Prince hadn't heard. Tadhg didn't think it was his to tell.

Shay gestured for the lieutenant to follow him to a quiet corner.Most of the men here knew Millie and Katy's history, but it was not one he broadcast unnecessarily. "Back in 1911, when the state made prostitution illegal, Millicent Stanley and Catherine Dudek were arrested in a raid on a brothel. They took that opportunity to make new lives for themselves. That was the day I met them. A few weeks later they opened their own business. No, not what you're thinking. They opened a little bakery in Highlandtown, where they sold Polish pastries and hot lunches. Michael and I became regular customers.

"The girls were in constant danger from the man who had forced them into that old life. He had broken into their store several times. It wasn't safe for them to remain there, but they had nowhere else to go. Fortunately, I had been planning to ask Millie to marry me anyway. We just moved the date up a bit. I proposed on July fourth, and we were married on the fifth.

"Michael's story is pretty much the same, only it took him a few more months to convince Katy his intentions were honorable."

"Damn. And you're happy?"

"Quite. Millie and I have two little girls, Mary Faith and Chiara. Mike and Katy have twin boys, Declan and Donagh. Special Agent Ribiero's story is similar. He and his wife, Maria, have a new baby."

"I hope I get to meet your wives tomorrow."

"You definitely will. The reception is in our dining room. They're cooking the food as we speak. And I've been told you're to come home with us to spend the night."

"We can't put you out."

"You're not putting us out at all. You'll be sleeping downstairs in the men's quarters."

"You have a barracks?"

"Up until recently we had some young men working for us. Our wives insisted we make a place for the employees to live because of the hours they're open. We have separate quarters for male and female employees. Right now, Tadhg is the only one in the men's quarters. Once they're married it will be his and Rose's flat. In fact we just had a stove put in for them. And while they're getting married tomorrow two rooms of furniture will be delivered as wedding gifts."

"And your wives are making money like this? It's not just a hobby?"

"Hobby? Katy's up at three every morning starting breakfast. She bakes about four hundred biscuits every day, twice that many on Fridays and Saturdays. She starts the gravy, then goes back upstairs to sleep a few more hours. That's when the other girls come up and start rolling and cutting out pastries, cooking meat and frying dough. All that before they open at seven. That's when Millie opens the front door and starts serving breakfast. At noon they do it all again. It's not just take away.We have a full dining room, plus a private room where the police force eat their meals. On Saturdays we have supper service. So yeah. They're making money. What Mike and I make goes in the bank."

"I think I need to find a wife like you've got."

"I don't know, Lieutenant. It's not for the faint of heart."

"You mean braver than going up in a canvas and balsa wood motorized kite against the Bosch?"

Dylan drained his glass. "Let me put it this way. Several months ago I was on assignment in West

Virginia. Millie told me not to go because she had a bad feeling. I went anyway. I got stabbed in the shoulder. I'm still not on full duty yet. I wasn't afraid of the guy with the knife. I wasn't afraid of the surgery to fix the damage. I was terrified of telling Millie what happened."

"I can't wait to meet her."

"And she wants to meet you. So do some of the girls who work in the bakery. Including Rose's best friend, Inga Rottmann. She's been really upset about Rosie getting hitched. I know she'd appreciate a little attention."

"Inga, huh?"

"Pretty little girl. Around nineteen or so. Lots of almost white blonde hair, big blue eyes. But she's shy as a new kitten. She had some trouble last year."

"Trouble? Not another rescued inmate?"

Dylan shook his head. "No, but it was a near thing. She was drugged and held in some phony church until they could ship her off to an abbey. Tadhg got a citation for her rescue."

"Our young groom is quite the hero, it seems."

"He is. The department hates to lose him, but the Captain sees your acceptance of him as an honor to the department as well."

"We'll do everything we can to get him back home in one piece."

"That's all we can ask. That and make sure he writes home regular. It about killed Rose when he took that assignment in that railroad camp. He couldn't write to her and was gone for a good month. Rose went with us to pick him up.He comes walking into town, leading that monster horse of his and another with a dead man slung over the saddle. Tadhg's arm was hanging, useless. That was when we moved him in with us."

"He'll be back with us Sunday. Bring Rose down for the day. She can watch him go up. He landed on his own Sunday and did well. In fact, much better than any of us did the first time we tried landing solo."

They heard Genet and Thaw starting to sing in French. Prince went to make sure they didn't get much more drunk. It wouldn't do for them to show up at the wedding tomorrow so hung over they couldn't make their eyes focus.

Two hours later, two taxis pulled up on Luzerne Street at Baltimore. Seven loud, drunken men piled out and followed Dylan to the kitchen door. He didn't need to use his key, which was a good thing because he couldn't have found the keyhole.

Millie, Katy and Maria were sitting at the big kitchen table. Dylan went straight to his wife, pulled her to her feet and kissed her right in front of their friends, God and everybody. "Millie, me darlin', these three reprobates are Lieutenants Prince, Thaw and Genet. Don't try to tell them apart. They're interchangeable"

"Jaysus, Dylan. You're tighter than a boiled owl." At least she was laughing when she said it so she couldn't be too angry. And she kept her arm around his waist as they stood in front of the sink.

Tomás Ribiero was on his knee in front of his wife, whispering to her in Spanish while she giggled and tried to fend off his wandering hands. "Tomás, not now."

He pulled her out of her chair. "Come on. Let's go home."

Katy turned in her chair, ignoring her husband for the moment. "Tomás, you and Maria are spending the night in our guest room. You can't be taking Benito out in this cold."

"Come on then, *querida.* I'll take the baby and we'll go upstairs." He tried to grab her hand again.

Maria turned away and went to the stove. "Sit down, Tomás. None of you have eaten since lunch, have you?"

Mike said, "Kelly had some pig's knuckles."

Katy looked at Tadhg, who was teetering on his feet. "A fine supper for a strapping boy. Now sit down. We've got some sausage and gravy leftover from supper. Millie, hand me a pan of those par bakes. We'll have food up in ten minutes."

They quickly got the men to the table. Coffee was poured, and food placed on the plates. The flyers didn't seem interested in food, until they tasted it. Then it disappeared in no time.

Thaw wiped his chin and hiccoughed. "Madam, those were excellent comestibles." He managed to cover his mouth as he belched.

"Thank you, Lieutenant." Katy was busy picking up empty plates and putting them in the sink. "Tadhg, why don't you take your friends downstairs so you can get some sleep. You've got to be up at a reasonably respectable hour and dressed for church. If you need your uniform pressed for tomorrow, bring it up. Frances will be happy to do it up for you."

Tadhg was almost asleep in his chair. Prince grabbed him under one arm and pulled him up. "Come on, Nagel. It's time for all good boys to be in bed. And us too."

That struck Thaw and Genet as hilarious, and they both slapped Prince on the back, which made him fall forward. He dropped his hold on Nagel, who wound up with his butt on the floor. That made all the men guffaw even more.

Tomás appeared to be sobering up some. "Maria, if we're sleeping in Katy's spare room, where's Rhys sleeping?"

"In their parlor. He'll get his room back tomorrow." That seemed to satisfy him.

"Dylan," Millie asked, "Do you think you can show Tadhg's friends where they'll be bunking tonight without rousing the neighbors?"

Dylan managed to get the men on their feet and out the back door. Millie heard him use his key to open the door to the downstairs flat and come back inside.

Katy took charge now. "Maria, take your husband and your son upstairs. Mike will lend you a nightshirt."

"But I haven't..."

"I don't care if you don't wear a nightshirt at home, Tomás Ribiero. In my house you will. I have no desire to get a glimpse of your naked arse running into the bathroom two hours from now."

Dylan and Michael started to head for the stairs but Millie stopped them.

"No you don't. You two can stay down here and help us clean up. Otherwise you'll wind up waking up the kids and we'll never get to sleep. We've got to be up by eight to start cooking."

Michael groaned.

*****

"*Liebchen,* I'm going to be out for the day." Gerhardt Weissmann was sitting on the dressing table bench as he tied his shoes, while Sophia made their bed.

"Is anything wrong?"

"No, not at all. I have to go to College Park. There are some flying machines there that require my special attention."

"Aeroplanes? What do you know about them?"

"Flying? Nothing. But I do know how engines work, and I know they won't fly if they have a bag of sand poured into their fuel tanks."

"And why do you care if they fly or not?"

"Because these aeroplanes are being used against my Fatherland. The more that are stopped, the fewer German soldiers will die."

"Can I do anything to help?"

"No. Just be here when I get home. I'll be in late tonight. I'd appreciate some good hot soup when I get home."

"And fresh rolls. I'll have it ready." She came around and took his coat from the wardrobe. "Make sure you check the train schedule. They've been changing the later departures for some reason. I read about it in the *News Post* this morning. People are complaining like mad, too."

"I'll make sure I check with the ticket agent before I leave the depot."

She helped him on with his coat, and fetched a muffler from the peg on the wardrobe door. "Did you make this?"

"I did. I got tired of seeing you with your coat collar turned up, shivering."

He kissed her as she tied the woolen scarf around his neck. *"Danke, liebchen."*

"Gerhardt, how do you know those aeroplanes won't be watched?"

"Because, *liebchen,* the flyers are in Baltimore for a few days, and the mechanics will be stupid drunk for the next two or three days. It will be an easy matter to slip onto the field, do my mischief and slip out before anyone knows what's going on."

"Since you'll be out all day, I think I'll take the opportunity to do some shopping. I'm tired of ordering everything from the local grocer."

"Be careful. And if you get the chance, stop by deGroot's."

"Why?"

"He's holding something for me. It just needs picking up. I haven't had a chance to get there."

She nodded. "I'll do it. Do I need to stop anywhere else?"

"Remember I showed you the German store by Lexington Market?" She nodded. "They're closing, and the prices are cut in half. See if there's anything you'd like there before it's gone."

"I hate this is happening. All because of a stupid war five thousand miles away."

"Do you need some money?"

"I've got plenty. Unless you want something special."

He shook his head. "Just bring home something fun. And chocolates."

The train ride to College Park only took around half an hour. What took the longest was getting to the aerodrome. He didn't want to take a taxi in case the driver remembered him. He wore a knitted cap pulled low over his forehead so his blond hair was covered. He might be recognized by his beard, but this morning he had taken no time to groom it. His mustache was unwaxed, his cheeks unshaven. No one would pay him any attention. He should be able to slip in and out of town unnoticed.

The sun was high when he reached the airfield. Three French-made aeroplanes stood on the field in the shadow of the open hangar doors. There should be four mechanics on hand: one supervisory and one assigned to each machine. They were nowhere in sight.

Gerhardt knew he had to work fast. He dropped the satchel he carried and pulled out three two pound sacks of sand.

A step ladder stood against the wall of the hangar. He carried it to the first machine, climbed two steps and poured the contents of the sack into the fuel tank. He moved quickly, repeating the maneuver on the two remaining aeroplanes.

He returned the ladder to its original place, collected his empty sacks, and started his long walk back to the depot. He made a point of not hurrying. He was a man out for a walk. The last thing he needed was to draw attention to himself.

On the way back to the depot, he ditched his sandbags in a culvert along the side of the road. He made short work of the apple he had grabbed at the house before he left. He ate as he strode down the road, then chucked the core into the weeds.

His shadow was long by the time he got to the ticketmaster's office. He bought his passage back to Baltimore where he intended to take a streetcar back to their house off Parkside.

Yes, today had been a perfect day. Now to sit back and wait and see what happened.

Sophia Davies O'Fallon, now Sylviane Gareau, took the streetcar on Belair Road that would take her downtown. She got off a few blocks from Lexington Market, then walked over. She went to the market first, collecting fresh winter produce she couldn't get at her local grocer, then on to the butcher to find some pork and veal. One of the stalls had freshly killed rabbits. She thought Gerhardt would like it, so she got a nice plump one instead of the veal. He'd asked for soup tonight. There were dried peas in the pantry at the house, so she bought some sausage.

Her market basket was filled, but she still wanted to stop at the German store. Sure enough, the windows were covered in butcher's paper, with "going out of business" written on the glass. She pushed the door open and was surprised to see no one in the shop.

The plump storekeeper stood behind the meat counter, leaning on his elbows and staring at nothingness. Sophia made a beeline for him. "Good morning, Mr. Thiebes. I'm sorry you're closing."

He perked up, hearing someone speak politely to him rather than calling him vile names because of his ethnicity. "Mrs. Gareau. A pleasure to see you, even under these circumstances."

"I'd like something special for breakfast, Mr. Thiebes. What do you recommend?"

The shopkeeper looked down the case, obviously honored to be asked his opinion. He grabbed a piece of pork sausage, put it on a piece of paper and onto the scale. "*Bauernomelett*. Meat, onions, potatoes, all folded into an omelet. And don't forget the fresh rolls. The baker just put those out. Take enough so you can make a bread pudding for dessert tonight."

"A very good idea, Mr. Thiebes. Thank you. Do you have any *spek*?" She asked for the German version of prosciutto.

"I do. How much would you like?"

She gave him her best smile. "It depends. How much is it?"

The price he quoted was less than a quarter of the normal price. "Let me have two pounds then Mr. Thiebes. You know how he likes it sliced. May I look around for a bit?"

"Certainly. My wife put out some Christmas things if you're interested. You may never see them here again."

She wandered down the narrow aisles, looking at the various blown glass ornaments and advent calendars. She stopped when she found three candle driven Christmas carousels.

Frau Thiebes was wandering around, dusting and straightening. Sophia called to her. "Excuse me. What can you tell me about these?"

The German woman, almost as broad as she was tall, hurried over. "These are Pyramids, *Weihnachtspyramide.* We put them out for Christmas. This one is the Christmas story." She pointed to a five tier structure of light natural wood, with small painted figures on each level. "On the top are three angels. Then the shepherds and their sheep. Under them are all the animals from the stable. At the bottom are the most important, the Holy Family. We put candles here, and here," She pointed to the cups around the base. "The heat from the flames makes the fan on the top turn."

"I'm afraid to ask how much these cost."

"Do you like these, Mrs. Gareau?"

"I do. And I think Mr. Gerhardt would enjoy one very much."

Mrs. Thiebes counted on her fingers quickly, then quoted a price that was pennies on the dollar.

"Mrs. Thiebes, I couldn't possibly pay that little. I'd feel like I was cheating you."

"Mrs. Gareau, if you don't buy it I'm afraid we'll have to give it away, or put it in our own attic. I would be very happy if this went to someone who would appreciate it, and be gladdened by it over Christmas."

"In which case, Mrs. Thiebes, I'll take it. And two boxes of candles please."

Sophia went back to the meat counter to collect her purchases and stopped to get some good chocolates to take home.

She had to buy an extra mesh shopping bag, as her market basket was already filled and was weighing heavily on her arm. She paid Mrs. Thiebes for her treasures, thanked her and asked the little woman to please let them know if they opened a new shop elsewhere.

Her next stop was only a few blocks away. Sophia walked up to Baltimore Street to deGroot's Pawn Shop. This time she went in through the front door as any other customer would.

The Dutchman looked up at the sound of the bell over his door. "Mrs. O'Fallon. It's so good to see you. You must be here to pick up that parcel for your friend."

"I am, Mr. deGroot. And I need to make a purchase of my own."

"What can deGroot get you?"

"Gerhardt's coat is very plain and not very warm. I'd like to get him something nice, with a fur collar maybe. Do you have anything that nice in stock?"

The little man's face lit up. "Come in the back." He took her into the back room, the place where she was accustomed to doing business. He pulled out a box from a stack, set it on a long table and pulled off the lid. "Look at this, Mrs. O'Fallon. Sealskin, with a fur collar. I believe it is close to the right size for him. What do you think?"

Sophia took the coat in her hands, rubbing the soft sable collar against her face, smelling the skins to make sure they were cured properly. "How much, Mr. deGroot?"

"If you prefer, I have a nice cloth coat with the same kind of collar."

"How much for the sealskin?"

"I could show you how much this would cost at the furrier's on Howard Street, but I won't insult your intelligence. You probably already guessed this came off the back of a truck somewhere in Canada. I got a dozen in last week, brought down from Montreal. I can let you have this for twenty."

"I have two requests."

"Yes?"

"Can you wrap it up for me, and can you hail me a taxi? I have too much to carry home on the streetcar."

They made the deal. There was already a parcel waiting, wrapped in brown paper. "Your Gerhardt told me to tell you that you are not allowed to open this. You are to take it home and put it in his wardrobe."

"It won't explode, will it, Mr. deGroot?"

"Certainly not, Mrs. O'Fallon. But one doesn't ask about Christmas gifts. It's not polite."

So Gerhardt was buying her a Christmas gift. Now she was doubly glad she got the coat. And the pyramid. "I shall follow his instructions to the letter, Mr. deGroot. Thank you."

Once the money had changed hands and he'd wrapped her parcel, he went out on to Baltimore Street and hailed a taxi. A Yellow Cab pulled up to the curb, and deGroot gestured for her to come out. "How much to Parkside, between Belair and Harford?"

The driver gave him the off-the-meter fare. DeGroot handed the driver the fare that Sophia had already given him. The driver started to balk when he saw the complexion of his passenger. Then he noticed she was holding a dollar bill in her hand. The Dutchman told him, "You get her to her front door, and the dollar is yours. Put her out anywhere else, and we'll have your hack license."

Sophia climbed into the back seat with her

parcels, waived to the pawnbroker and they were off to Herring Run.

Chapter Seven

Tadhg woke his bride with a sweet kiss early Sunday morning. "Time to get up. They're throwing us out of here today, and I've got duty."

Rose groaned and tried to turn over. He pulled the covers off her, laughing. "Come on, Rosie. I've got to get you home, and I have to get the three lieutenants out of Millie and Katy's hair."

The newly minted Mrs. Nagel finally sat up and swung her legs over the side of the bed. "Whatever made them decide to stay this long? I thought they'd be gone by Friday morning."

"So did Dylan. He swears they're hanging around for the food. I think Chaz Genet's sniffing around Inga."

She laid her cheek against his bare shoulder. "I hope you told him to be gentle with her."

"I did. And Dylan's keeping an eye on them." He sat for a moment, enjoying the feel of her touch against his skin. "Now get dressed or I'll wind up back in that bed and we'll never get to College Park."

"We?"

"That's right. Dylan and Millie are going to ride down with us today. You can watch me go up today. I'm supposed to solo."

"Solo? What's that?"

"It means I don't have to have another pilot in the cockpit babysitting me. And it means I get to take off and land on my own."

"Oh, Tadhg! Isn't that dangerous?"

"Sweetie, it's no more dangerous than riding a six foot tall horse down Broadway in the middle of the day."

"Well all right then. But it doesn't mean I can't worry about you."

"Fair enough. Now get some clothes on, woman. Michael and Dylan only gave us this room until this morning. I don't want to give the manager of the Emerson Hotel a reason to complain to the department because a copper is refusing to vacate their room."

"All right," She pouted. "Hand me my wrapper."

She slipped on her wrapper and ran into the bathroom. Tadhg had already been up for an hour, had washed, shaved and packed his own clothes. He was already wearing his trousers and boots. He put on his clean shirt and pulled up his braces. He'd leave his jacket for very last. There was something about this uniform that felt very good to Tadhg. It wasn't that much different from that which he wore every day with the department. But somehow, wearing the uniform of a foreign nation felt more important, and gave him the feeling that he was on the verge of something that could change the world.

Rose came back into the bedroom, wearing the same dress she'd worn for their wedding. Tadhg took the opportunity to pull her back into his arms for just a moment. "You're bag's on the bed. I was afraid to pack for you in case I put in something you'll be wanting."

She hurried to pack her one change of clothes, night clothes and under things. She was glad she had listened to Millie and hadn't brought a lot. Millie and Katy had both said she wouldn't be leaving the room much. They'd been right.

"I'm ready," she announced.

Tadhg shrugged into his uniform jacket and fastened the shoulder belt. "Come on then Mrs. Nagel. Let's get back to Millie's and have breakfast. After that we'll go to the train."

"This will be nice, being able to ride down with you."

"You can't go every week. I had to get special permission this time. They really don't like people on the airfield for training because of stupid things happen."

"Like what?"

"Like when Bill Thaw tried to take off the first time and taxied straight into the side of a barn. Or when he landed the first time on his own he flew straight down into the ground, nose first. Broke the plane into stovewood, but all he got was a sprained knee."

"Tadhg, you're not making me feel better, you know."

"I know. And I'm sorry, sweetie. But it's something I've got to do. You know America will be in this war sooner or later. If I go now with the *Aéronautique Militaire,* I'll be an officer. If I wait to join the American army, I'd be the lowest private. I've got no education to speak of so I would have no chance to go higher than corporal. By the time I ship with the French out I'll be a second lieutenant. It means I'll be able to provide for you. For us. You know how much a private makes in the US Army? Less than seven dollars a month. I'll be making almost ten times that much, plus getting flight bonuses."

"I think I understand, anyway." She gave him a

quick hug. "But I still get to worry. Millie told me that's my prerogative."

He grabbed both bags, tucked one under his arm, and took her out to the elevator.

They had stayed in a lovely corner room in the Emerson Hotel downtown. Tadhg had ordered room service every morning for breakfast, and they had eaten in the hotel dining room every night for supper. Rose never wanted their time together to end, even though she understood it had to.

Tadhg settled up the room service bill at the desk and asked the doorman to hail them a taxi.

The three flyers were already dressed and sitting at the big table in the kitchen with cups of coffee. Tadhg thought they all looked rather rough, but didn't dare say anything. Rose didn't even notice.

She went right to where Katy stood at the stove and gave her a hug, then went to Millie and did the same. The three women smiled at each other over Rose's newfound knowledge.

Tadhg was already sitting at the table when Rose handed him a plate of gravy and biscuits with bacon. The three men sitting with him sniggered when they saw Rose trail her fingers across Nagel's shoulders. Tadhg glared at them.

Genet looked at Nagel over the rim of his cup. "I don't have to ask how your weekend was."

"No you don't." Tadhg answered. "But from the looks of you three, I don't have to ask how yours was either."

"Why didn't you tell us how many bars were around here?" Thaw groaned.

"That's Baltimore. A church every three blocks and a bar on every corner. I didn't expect you to investigate every one of them."

Prince watched Nagel shoveling food. "The food

here is awfully good. The army will break you of that. Make you appreciate this more."

"I'll be able to get packages from home, won't I?"

"You will. But it may take so long to get to you the stuff will be inedible."

Katy put a platter filled with bacon on the table as Michael and Dylan came in. "Tadhg, how do you feel about fruit cake?"

"The kind you make? It's good. Why?"

"Because those things will last for years. And cookies and bourbon balls. We can send you all of those whenever you like. And don't forget candy. You'd be surprised how creative we can be when the time comes."

None of them noticed the tears that gathered in Rose's eyes at the talk of Tadhg going overseas.

The Shays accompanied the Nagels and the three French flyers to College Park. Prince, Thaw and Genet were loud, laughing at private jokes and chattering in French. Rose sat quietly, holding her husband's hand, her head on his shoulder. Dylan and Millie chatted with Tadhg about their children, and they speculated when Dylan would be permitted to return to full duty with the BoI since his injury.

Tadhg didn't have his bicycle today. He'd be taking his wife and friends back with him in a taxi. It took some doing to secure two taxis that time of morning, but they finally managed to make it to the airfield.

The mechanics were sitting, drinking coffee when the flyers arrived at the field. Lieutenant Prince called something to them in French. The four men in white coveralls pushed a plane out into position, and one moved into place at the propeller.

"You ready to solo, Nagel?" Prince asked.

"Now?"

"No time like the present. So kiss your wife and go get into your kit."

Nagel was only too happy to do as he was told. He pulled Rose into his arms and gave her a wild, fast kiss that left her breathless and had the three lieutenants applauding. He released her and ran to the hangar to collect his coat and helmet.

This was what he had been waiting for, the chance to go up on his own, to take off and land without someone in the second seat guiding him, ready to take over if he made a mistake. Nothing had ever been so important to him. Not even his recent wedding could take the place of this. Although now he knew Thaw was wrong. Flying was not better than sex. A close second perhaps, but not better.

It took the mechanic three spins to get the propeller to catch. Tadhg's orders were to fly to fifteen hundred feet according to the plane's altimeter, circle the field twice, then bring the plane down for a landing. The mechanics would refill the castor oil in the engine's crankcase, and then he was to take the plane up a second time and practice touch-and-go landings.

The engine sounded a little rough to Tadhg, but he thought perhaps that was the temperature. The morning was cold, so cold he could see his breath. It was no wonder the powerful motor was having a hard time kicking over.

He taxied to the end of the field, turned, then began his acceleration to take off into the wind. There was a slight stall, a hesitation as he pulled back on the stick, but the plane began to lift off as it should. As he climbed the ship's handling seemed sluggish, but Tadhg hadn't been up often enough to really be able to make a judgment. He shrugged it off and continued to climb.

Nagel followed instructions. He flew higher, all while banking to the right, circling the field. He kept an eye on the altimeter to make sure he did indeed reach fifteen hundred feet.

The aeroplane had reached fourteen hundred feet when the engine coughed, sputtered and cut out. All three of his trainers had covered engine stalls with him in the past. It was a relatively simple matter to get it restarted. If it worked as it should, the motor would restart, the propeller would spin again, and all would be right with the world.

But it wasn't. And it wouldn't. No matter what Nagel tried, the motor was dead. He still had control of the wings. Genet had taught him how to bring in a glider. That's what he did now.

On the ground, Prince and Thaw had been watching carefully and spotted that Nagel was in trouble. From this distance there wasn't much they could do other than pray that the kid remembered what they'd taught him.

Rose and Millie had no idea what was going on. They only knew that the racket from the sky was suddenly gone, and all was quiet, except for the voices of the men on the field.

Dylan Shay knew something wasn't right. He excused himself from where he had been sitting with his wife and friend and ran to where Lieutenant Prince stood. "Something's wrong. Is there anything I can do?"

Prince never took his eyes off Nagel's plane. "Be ready to grab the ladies when he comes down. They won't need to see it."

"Nagel's going to die, isn't he?"

"Not if he's lucky. Pray that he is."

"What's wrong?"

"His engine died and he can't restart it."

As they watched, Tadhg Nagel brought his plane down onto the field. He pulled back on the stick just as the front wheels touched down, but without the engine speed behind it, he didn't have enough power to raise up the nose to the tail's level. He rolled almost to the end of the airstrip, pulled hard on the flaps to turn the machine to the right, rising up on one front wheel before it bumped down. He was finally able to pull it to a stop.

Genet was there with the stepladder. He set it up against the side of the plane, climbed up two steps and pulled the dipstick for the oil reserve. It was a little low, but looked fine. He called something to a mechanic in French. The mechanic brought Genet a bamboo pole with a sponge attached to the end. He ran the rod into the gas tank. He pulled it out and handed it down to Norman Prince, their superior.

Prince ran his fingers over the end of the sponge and felt the grit. "Son of a bitch! Someone's put sand in the tank."

Millie had finally let Rose go onto the field. The girl ran the length, hampered by her skirts. She grabbed her husband's face between her hands to make sure he was all in one piece.

"Oh, Tadhg, I was so scared! What happened?"

"Someone did something to the plane. I don't know who or what. But it made the engine stop. But you saw what I did, didn't you, honey? You saw how I brought the plane down without the engine and didn't crash or anything?" He sounded like a little boy who had just caught his first fish.

"Who would want to do something to your engine? It doesn't make sense."

"I don't know. But if it was done purposely it's sabotage, and it's a crime. I need to talk to Dylan." He kept hold of her hand as he walked over to where

Special Agent Shay was discussing the matter with Lieutenant Genet.

"...all three engines have been sabotaged. The mechanics deny seeing anyone around the machines while we were gone."

Dylan asked, "Were the aeroplanes outside the entire time or were they hangared?"

"They should have been inside. But you saw when we arrived, they were sitting out on the field. The chief mechanic claims they just wheeled them out anticipating our arrival, but I don't believe them. Not with the depressions in the field that were under the wheels."

Dylan left Prince and went to Tadhg. "Nagel, there's skullduggery afoot." Millie was the only one to notice her husband was grinning at the thought of being able to do some meaningful work. "I need you to take the ladies back to the City, get hold of Ribiero and Dougherty, and file a report with them about what happened. Then get Tomás down here on the next train. Whoever did this has committed treason."

"Treason? How?" Nagel asked.

"It's an overt action against an ally in time of war. I know we're not at war yet, but we are nonetheless their partners in this. Now off with you. And tell MacFarland you may be needed down here to assist with the investigation."

Nagel turned to Lieutenant Prince. "Permission, sir?"

"May as well. Unless you want to sit here and clean valves and pistons with a bucket of kerosene and a rag."

Tadhg saluted, took the ladies by the elbows and hurried them off the field.

"What's happening?" Millie was confused. "Why don't we stay?"

"You heard Dylan. He has to investigate why someone poured sand into the three engines. It's a job for the Bureau. We go back to Baltimore, I tell Tomás what happened, and he comes back here. Millie, Dylan wants you home where you'll be safe, and I'm sure he'll want you to pack his bag. Tomás can bring it down with him."

"All right. But I don't have to like it."

The hour it took to get back to Baltimore was the longest of their lives. Dylan had telephoned from College Park, so Michael met them at the Mount Royal station in the Bureau's Nash.

No one really talked until they were back in Katy's cozy kitchen warming themselves with coffee.

Michael had alerted Tomás as soon as Tadgh had called, so both Ribieros were already there.

The three men excused themselves to go to the parlor, leaving the women to discuss things on their own.

Tadhg didn't waste any time. "Somebody sabotaged all three aeroplanes while we were gone. I took one up and before I hit fifteen hundred feet the engine just died."

Tomás didn't understand. "How does that make it sabotage? Motors give out all the time."

"But they don't have sand poured into the gas tank every day. This wasn't a little, like you'd pick up in a dust storm. Somebody dumped in a bag of the stuff. It was sabotage. Dylan said it is a federal matter and you should get there before the army louses it up."

"Won't the army investigate?"

"They won't do much, even though it happened on an army installation, because the planes damaged are French, . It's up to you two to figure out who did it."

Tomás sighed. "How late is the last train?"

Tadhg had already checked. "Eight. You should have plenty of time to make it."

Katy interrupted, calling them in for sandwiches followed by warm gingerbread.

"Millie, do you mind if Maria and Benito stay here until I get back?"

Maria hated being talked about like she wasn't there. "Tomás, I do not need to have a minder."

"No you don't, *querida*. But your husband feels better when you are not alone. It's also easier to get in touch with our families if you are all in one place."

Maria finally agreed. "So, Katy, do you mind having us under foot for a couple of days?"

"Of course not. And Tuesday we can all take Benito downtown shopping."

All three men moaned at that.

*****

Gerhardt Weissmann brought in the Tuesday morning *News Post* from the porch. He stood in his dressing gown in the parlor and glanced through the stories on the first page, then flipped to page two. Still nothing. Then on page three, there was a small story about someone spoiling three French aircorps ships. Three paragraphs, no more.

"*Liebchen,* come look." Sophia hurried in from the kitchen, drying her hand on a towel.

"What's wrong?"

"Nothing. I wanted you to see where I was last week."

She read the brief article. "It says the Bureau of Investigation are looking into it. That could be bad, Gerhardt. That the federal police."

He sniffed derisively. "You mean the Federal Keystone Cops? They've been looking for both of us for how long? They had their hands on both of us, and we got away. Now we hide in plain sight and no one even suspects we're not who we say we are." She was standing with her back to him as she reread the story. He put his arms around her waist and rested his chin on her shoulder. "Don't worry, *liebchen*. Nothing will happen, I promise. Now, when are we going to do this recital for our students?"

"Do you think they'll be ready two weeks before Christmas?"

"They should be."

"I do have one suggestion."

"What is it?"

His voice still gave her goosebumps, particularly this close to her ear no matter what they were discussing. "When I was downtown last week, I stopped in a record store just to listen to some new music. You know, for ideas. I heard a recording of some monks singing *O Come Emmanuel.* They sang it in Latin, and they way they sang...One lone voice on the first verse, two on the second, adding voices until they finished. How many voice students do you have now?"

"You know we have five voice students, three piano, and two violin."

"That's perfect. There's five verses. I thought Isaac, your boy tenor who's really an alto, unless he's a baritone, could start. Do you think they could learn the Latin words that quickly?"

"*Liebchen.*" Damn, there went those goosebumps again. "These kids go to mass almost every day of their lives, except for Isaac and Barton. The Latin will come easily. But that is an excellent idea." He kissed the side of her neck. "Maybe we should add another Christmas song. *Adeste Fidelis* maybe. They probably already know it anyway from school."

She turned in his arms and encircled his neck. "Can we talk about this later?" She bit lightly on his earlobe.

He was talking against her neck, right by her ear again. "I have students coming today."

"Not for hours yet." She pulled his shirt collar aside and rubbed her face against the exposed flesh.

"I suppose we could discuss this upstairs."

"Mmm-hmm. Or not discuss it at all."

"I always said you have the very best ideas."

Much later, Barton Wattermann was due for his lesson. He arrived right on time, carrying his new violin proudly. When the *Maestro* asked him about it, he said, "I ran home to get it before I came here. I want you to hear how nice it sounds when I play my piece."

The *Maestro* ruffled the boy's hair. "I'm sure it sounds very nice, but I'd hate for you to be late for your lessons. So, what are you going to play for me today?"

Madame Gareau was already at the piano, ready to provide whatever accompaniment the boy required.

"I've been practicing the Mozart and the Bach. I tried the Paganini, but I'm going to need help with the fingering."

"Very good, Barton. That is the sign of a good student. One who knows when he needs his master's help, and isn't afraid to ask. We'll work on that in a little while. First, play me the Mozart."

Barton surprised Duprey yet again. Rather than the music he had been given, the boy played his own transcription of *Porgi, amor*, the Countess Almaviva's aria from *Nozze di Figaro*.

When he was done, Madame Gareau stood and applauded. "Barton, that was beautiful." A quelling look from the *Maestro* made her sit back down.

"Barton, that was very nice. Have you ever heard the opera?"

"No sir."

"Not even on the Victrola?"

"No sir. We don't have one."

"So you just found the music and transcribed it?"

"Yes sir. Did I do something wrong?"

"Well you played all the notes beautifully and correctly. But you're missing some of the feeling of the song itself." He pointed to the end of the piano bench. "Please, sit." Barton sat. "Barton, this aria is sung by a wife who thinks her husband doesn't love her any more. She sings 'give me back my love or let me die.' It is a beautiful song, but very sad, even though it isn't in a minor key. Do you have the music you copied it from?"

Barton was carrying his bookbag from school. He reached inside and pulled out a bound copy of the operatic score.

"Where on earth did you get this?" Entire scores were ridiculously expensive.

"I got it from the library. They sell books that nobody borrows. I got this for fifty cents."

Duprey thumbed through until he found what he sought. "I see what you did. You played the vocal melody and added some double stops and accents to dress it up. That's very smart. But now, I want you to try something different." He flipped to the front. "This is the overture. The whole score is simplified. Rather than for an orchestra it's written for a quartet. Madame, can you play this part?" He pointed to the cello part. "Barton, you play first violin. I shall play second. We'll see how it sounds."

This was Barton's first time playing anything with two other people. He was used to playing singly, or playing melody, while someone else played the rhythm. He was smiling ear to ear as he shouldered his violin.

He was still smiling when they finished. "*Maestro*, is that what it's like playing with an orchestra?"

"Well, sort of. In an orchestra there can be twenty other people all playing the same notes on the same instruments. This is almost exactly what it's like playing in a string quartet. Everyone plays something a little bit different to make one cohesive sound. That's what music is. Lots of different sounds coming together to make one joyful noise."

They spent the rest of the hour going through the Paganini piece. Duprey corrected the boy's finger placement on the strings, and showed him the best way to bow to get the sound required by the composer.

As he was packing up, Duprey told him, "Barton, we want to have a recital for all our students in December. I know your mother is busy with her shop. Would she be able to come if we held it on a Saturday?"

The boy looked down at his feet. "No sir. We couldn't. Not on Saturday. It's the Sabbath."

Duprey nodded. "Of course Barton. My apologies. Then we shall have our recital on Sunday at two in the afternoon. It shall be the second Sunday in December. Because it's Christmas, the songs will be in Latin. I hope that won't be a problem for Isaac."

"No sir. Isaac's family, they're not observant. They eat pork and everything. Just not on Passover."

"I see. I want you to pick out two pieces you'd like to play at our recital. One on your own, and one with Isaac."

"Uh, *Maestro,* I was looking at the score. There's another song someone called Cherubino sings." He mispronounced the name, but it didn't matter.

"Maybe Isaac could sing that and I could play."

Duprey handed the score back to Barton. "Very well, Barton. This is written for a quartet. Two violins, a viola and a cello plus voice. You must rewrite it as a duet with voice. Can you have it by next Tuesday? I'll have Isaac and Stefan here to practice with you. Do you need more manuscript paper?"

"Yes please."

Duprey went to the sideboard and pulled out six sheets of paper, considered and added six more to the stack. "You'll need to write it out for violin and piano. I'll get a vocal score for Isaac tomorrow so he can practice his part and know the words. You think you're up to it?"

"Yes sir!" He started to pack up his instrument. "When does Stefan come for his lesson?"

"He comes Saturdays, with his sisters."

"I'll have his part ready for him on Thursday then. I've heard him play. He'll need more practice."

The *Maestro* roared, and Barton left, never knowing what had caused the hilarity.

*****

Sister Gabrielle paced the raised floor in front of the pulpit in the First Bible Church of Chester. Tonight was the first night of her revival and she was on a roll.

Tonight she had no need of dogs that died on command or snakes that bit without injecting venom. Tonight she was preaching straight from scripture.

It felt good. Oh she still didn't believe any more than she had done previously. She put on a good show, and that was what counted. That and the take in the collection plate.

Barnaby Fogg sat in the front row, smiling warmly, and calling out an occasional Amen if it seemed like the crowd was cooling.

Now was the time to pull out the big guns. "I ask you, 'Who can find a virtuous woman? Her price is far above rubies.' Who indeed, brothers and sisters? Not in the streets, demanding rights. A woman's rights come from her father and her husband, brothers and sisters. Not from any man-made piece of paper."

About half the congregation was on its feet now. Some of the women looked a little upset with her. One or two men, those whose wives obviously "wore the pants", looked confused.

Sister Gabrielle didn't stop. She went on, mocking the "unnatural women" who demonstrated in the streets, and who wound up spending time in jail. "Women are the bringers of life, the keepers of the hearth, the heart of your homes. Women are not meant to cast ballots."

She paused, leaning on the pulpit with her elbows, her hands clasped before her. "Brothers, have you ever seen women at the January white sales?" She waited while they laughed. "Now imagine those same women trying to elect a president. Unlike the bed linens you buy you can't return a president if you don't like him once you get home."

She continued, calling out men who allowed their women to run their lives, men who weren't the heads of their own home. She even railed against married men who permitted their mothers to run them. "Men are to leave their mothers and cleave unto their wives. A man cannot be the head of his own home if he has two women vying for his affections."

Then she went on to speak to the women, this time in a softer, less strident tone. She instructed the women to go to their husbands with questions, not to other women. If they have no husband, they should go to their fathers or brothers. This is because women are incapable of making such life altering decisions on their own.

An older woman in the back of the congregation was on her feet. "Sister Gabrielle, how can you exhort us thus, when you yourself are a woman, one of the weaker sex? Why should we listen to you?"

Larry had done well, planting this shill in the crowd. Sister Gabrielle smiled her gentle, understanding smile at the woman. "You ask how I can speak as I do. I, a mere woman, up here addressing you thusly. I'd like to introduce you to my husband. Brother Barnaby, please stand."

Barnaby Fogg stood, then stepped up behind the pulpit. "Thank you Sister." He raised her hand to his lips, making some of the ladies in the congregation sigh at the romantic gesture. "My brothers and sisters, you ask why I permit my wife to stand here and exhort you in such a manner. I do so because the Lord has called us both to this ministry. She to speak, and I organize. Does not the Word teach us we are to each use our gifts in the manner which best gives Him glory? Is it not a slap in the Lord's face if we ignore his word? We are to come to the Lord as we are, not asking, but accepting."

That was the cue for the church choir to sing, *Just as I am.*

Sister Gabrielle and Brother Barnaby both stepped back, and permitted the church pastor to make the altar call. Gabrielle couldn't help noticing that Reverend Morgan kept looking at their new soloist who was sitting in the center of their choir. It was amazing how much good will a young lady on her knees could generate from a recalcitrant preacher.

Larry Wardworth had found Miss Velma Roland in Ocean City. At seventeen, the poor kid had been taken down during the season, then had been left high and dry by her pimp on October first when all the tourists went home. She'd been living under the boardwalk, trying to feed herself and not freeze to death. Larry had taken pity, taken her home, then had a sample of her techniques. Wardworth had worked with her for a few days, as he said, to "perfect her style".

It was Gabrielle who had discovered the girl could sing. A bonus! Gabrielle had taught the girl the hymns she would need to know while Larry had played the piano. Barnaby had taken time to play the preacher uncertain about taking on a female revivalist. He told Gabrielle it was the ultimate sacrifice to be serviced by their young singer. Gabrielle actually watched, correcting the girl as necessary, telling her how to use her hands, and how to keep the man from finishing, leaving him wanting much more, but not giving it to him.

"Won't he get mad?" Velma wanted to know. "I been hit before. I don't want to get thumped because he ain't happy."

"He wouldn't dare. You see, Larry will be right there. You take the preacher to a corner, while Larry turns his back. Let him get just so far, then stop. Larry will promise you'll come back later. Then we do our revival, and by the time the preacher realizes he never got to finish, we'll be two towns away."

"So you mean I don't have to..."

"Do you like to?"

"Gawd, no. That's disgusting."

"So you'll always leave them wanting more. And never do anything you don't want to do."

"Really?"

"Really. Do you like staying with Larry?"

The girl nodded. "For now, anyway. He's good to me."

"That's good. But if you ever decide you're tired of him you come to me."

"And you won't get mad?"

"Why should I? The only thing I ask is that you stay away from Mr. Fogg unless I tell you otherwise. Understand?"

Velma nodded. "Sure. Miss Gabby?"

"Yes?"

"Buford's been sleeping in the room with me and Larry. Is that okay?"

"Of course. Buford can sleep anywhere he wants. He's bigger than we are."

That made the girl giggle. "I mean, is it okay for him to be on the bed? Most people won't even let a dog in the house, let alone on the furniture."

"Velma, Buford is a big part of our act sometimes. He's a genius." She leaned in and whispered. "I think he's smarter than Barnaby." That made Velma laugh even harder. "He's made us thousands of dollars. He'll make us even more once we can do our regular shows again. For now he gets whatever he wants."

"Good." This time Velma whispered. " Because I think I like Buford better than Larry."

Chapter Eight

Thanksgiving came. Dylan and Tomás had spent weeks interrogating every person on the airbase, both civilian employees and military personnel. The two men took turns taking the train home every few days to spend the night returning to continue to beat their heads against the wall some more. So far they had learned nothing. Only that a hobo had been spotted walking down the road that Thursday.

After the first week Maria took Benito and went home, taking Siofre with her for company. She still came to the bakery most sunny days when it was warm enough to take Benito out.

Michael was manning the BoI office on his own, and wasn't happy about it. Michael Dougherty didn't like making decisions on his own. He was a decent detective. If he had a specific issue to which he was assigned he would go at it like a dog with a bone. Now he was getting daily briefs from Washington. He opened the mail, entered everything in the log, and filed it so Tomás could review it on his return.

Most of what Mike was receiving was normal, run of the mill stuff. Reports from other field offices about wants and warrants. Then he got the letter.

Normally, they didn't pay a lot of attention to letters from citizens. Most of the time they consisted of one neighbor ratting out another for some imagined fault. This time, it was another matter, a serious matter. It came from a young woman in Delmar, Delaware.

Dear Sir,

My fiance is a minister of the Gospel at the Front Street Church in Delmar, Delaware. Last week, he was approached by an evangelist and her company about having a revival.

My parents hosted dinner for the evangelist, her husband and two of her musicians in their home, along with my fiance. While my mother and I were cleaning the dishes, the piano player and his soprano wife took my fiance into my father's study and tried to convince him to permit them to hold their revival.

My fiance was not interested in their mission, as apparently the evangelist is more concerned in denying women their Constitutional rights (Mr. Covington being a friend to the Suffrage movement.) The young woman who put herself forward as the wife of the pianist and a soprano, attempted to unbutton Mr. Covington's trousers and molest him.

Mr. Covington demanded they leave the house and they did so, returning to a hotel in Maryland. The young woman looked extremely fearful when the pianist grabbed her arm and yanked her out of the house.

I believe you are tasked with protecting women under the Mann Act. I believe this young woman is a victim of such trafficking, of being forced across state lines for lewd and lascivious purposes.

The people who attended dinner at our home are:

Gabrielle Lane Pennington
Barnaby Fogg (who puts himself forth as her   husband)
Larry Wardworth, pianist
Velma Wardworth, the young woman in question.

I may be reached at the above address should you have any questions.

Respectfully,

Lydia Langsdale

Now this was something Michael could get his teeth into . They had been looking for the Good Sister for months, ever since she had jumped bail after trying to kidnap Inga Rottmann.

The first thing Michael had to do was to write a letter to Miss Langsdale. He thanked her for her assistance and informed her that an agent of the

Bureau of Investigation would be calling upon her in the next few days to get additional details.

The next thing was to send a telegram to College Park, to Special Agent in Charge, Tomás Ribiero, telling him they were needed in Delmar urgently on a Mann Act case, and to please respond soonest.

Soonest turned out to be that night at supper. Both Tomás and Dylan were at the Shay's flat with Maria. Michael walked in the door to be told by Katy to get cleaned up because they were going upstairs for supper.

Michael took some time to go to his sons who were in the nursery with their nursemaids. The boys climbed him like a tree and he greeted them fondly. It took him a while to peel them off and to hand them to Frances and Marguerite. Once he changed his shirt he was ready.

Upstairs, Tadhg and Rose were also joining them as they had been instrumental in the original arrest of the Pennington woman.

Supper was already being put on the table when the Doughertys walked into the dining room. Mike took his seat and accepted a glass of wine from Tomás. By silent agreement they did not discuss work at the table tonight. After a meal of baked beans, sausage and biscuits the men retired to the parlor to discuss their BoI business.

Tomás took a seat in one of the wing chairs. Once everyone else was seated, he asked Michael, "What do you think, Mike?"

Michael held up his hand. "First things first. Did you figure out who sabotaged the aeroplanes?"

Dylan answered. "No, but we spent three weeks figuring out who didn't do it. We've left cards all over the airfield, so if they come across something of interest they'll let us know. So what do you suggest we do about this preacher lady?"

"I think we have our Thanksgiving dinner tomorrow, lie around on Friday and take the train for DelMar Saturday morning. She'll be having a revival somewhere and we'll find out."

Tomás looked at the three other men in the room. "Dylan, you're sitting this one out. You too, Tadhg. They know both of you. Mike and I will go and see what we can see."

Mike was sitting on the edge of the sofa. Clearly he had been thinking about this. "Tomás, do you think you could play a preacher interested in booking the good Sister's evangelical services?"

"Will Callum lend me a collar?"

"Nope. Most Protestant preachers don't wear them. I think we should go to a service somewhere Sunday morning in Delmar to get an idea how they talk."

"I don't think that's necessary. Sitting in the Sister's meeting should be enough."

"Why don't you talk to Inga?" Tadhg asked. "She attended Sister Pennington's Tabernacle every week for a while. I bet she'd know."

"Will Inga be at dinner tomorrow?"

Mike said, "She and her granny are supposed to be here. Her grandmother's even trying to learn English. She's gotten some heat for speaking German. She started taking classes at St. Catherine's."

"Then that's what we'll do . Shall we rejoin the ladies before they come in here and beat us with dish towels?"

"We'd better. Millie's been making lemon pies all day long for this one here." Mike pointed to Dylan. "If he doesn't get in there and have a slice I'm afraid he'll be wearing it."

They made it to the dining room just in time for

Maria's coffee and Millie's pie. It was Katy who asked the question. "So for how long do we get to keep you?"

Tomás told her, "Mike and I are going to Delaware early Saturday morning. Dylan and Tadhg are staying here."

Dylan had the presence of mind to tell his wife, "The three lieutenants will be here for dinner tomorrow. I told them you wouldn't mind setting three more places."

"I don't mind feeding them. But we don't have a place to put them up."

"Don't have to. They're already at the Altamont Hotel. I told them to be here at noon."

"Good. They can move tables and chairs."

"Oh, I know they'll love that." Tadhg took another bite of his pie. "Did they happen to say if the aeroplanes will be ready by Sunday?"

Dylan helped himself to a second slice of pie. "The mechanics are still trying to get parts. Talk to Prince tomorrow. I think he may have some news for you."

Rose pushed her plate aside. Prince's "news" could mean anything, including that they were planning to take her new husband away to a war in which he had no part. She adored Tadhg Nagel but hated with every fiber of her being what he was doing.

Maria was equally unhappy at the idea of her husband going after the same people who had been responsible for putting a knife in Dylan Shay.

Neither woman said anything about their fears. Instead they pasted on artificial smiles and behaved as if nothing was out of the ordinary.

Maria asked, "Katy, what can I bring tomorrow? I'll be here early to help out."

Katy ran down the menu. "We're having ham, turkey and dressing, cranberries, Brussel sprouts with chestnut sauce, yams and potatoes. What else do we need?"

"How many are you feeding?"

"God only knows," Katy laughed. "All of us and the staff, all the Doughertys, the three flyers. How many's that? Fifty, a hundred?"

"We are putting everything out buffet style like for Rose's wedding?"

"I hadn't thought about it. But that's a good idea. No, just bring something for dessert.
*****

"Gabby, come on. You don't want to be late."

Sister Gabrielle was trying to get her hat pinned to her short, curly hair without much success. "I don't care if I am. Whose idea was it to go to Thanksgiving dinner at some preacher's house, anyway?"

"The preacher's wife. She's invited the four of us. We don't have any place to be today and you're doing three days at her husband's church. I thought it was a nice gesture for her to invite us to a meal."

"That just means she doesn't know that Velma's been paying her darling husband lip service."

Fogg pulled the hatpin from her hand and stuck it back into the cushion. "Wear a different hat, honey." He picked up one with a ribbon tie. "Try this one. Or put on your cloak with the fur-lined hood."

"Oh, all right. I'll wear the cloak." She went to fetch it. "Tell Larry not to let Velma be alone with the fat old swine. He's had his one taste. He'll not get another."

"I'm worried about Velma. She's still bruised from that young preacher. Larry roughed her up pretty good when she couldn't get Covington to cooperate."

"It wasn't Velma's fault. Josiah Covington has a pretty young fiancee who's probably giving him more than an occasional happy ending."

"I stopped Larry before he did any real damage

but she's still tender. At least he didn't do anything to her face"

"Of course not. He knows to never hit where it shows. Let Velma know she should give the preacher a few shy smiles tonight, but she should cling to Larry the whole time. Can't let the wife know what's going on." She pulled up her hood and tied it under her chin.

"So, are you ready?"

"Let's get this over with." They stopped in the hallway and Fogg knocked on Wardworth's door. "I hope she serves ham tonight. I really hate turkey."

Two couples left the Delmar Hotel together and walked the eight blocks to the Delmar Holiness Church.

Hector Jolly met them at the door. He helped the ladies off with their wraps. Mr. Jolly took the cape from Velma and whispered something in her ear that made her shiver and grab hold of Larry's arm. Gabrielle thought that reaction looked genuine. She'd have to find out later what the old bastard had said.

He took them through to the parlor where the minister's two sons waited. They both jumped to their feet. Jolly made the introductions. "Sister Gabrielle, Brother Barnaby, Sister Velma, Brother Larry, my sons, Enoch and Amos."

The young men immediately gravitated to young Velma although she was clinging to another man's arm. Amos actually whispered something to Velma that made her blush.

Gabrielle didn't like this. It was one thing having Velma get a booking by making promises no one intended on keeping. The girl had been willing enough. But to have her set upon and treated like a whore was too much. She nudged Barnaby, indicating he should rescue the girl.

Fogg took Velma's other arm and placed himself in between the two horny young men and their target. Gabrielle could hear noises in the kitchen. "Velma, why don't you and I go help Mrs. Jolly get supper on the table."

Velma hurried to Gabrielle's side. "Yes Sister. We really should help Sister Jolly in the kitchen"

The two women went into the kitchen where Mrs. Jolly was apparently at her wit's end.

"Sister Naomi, we're here to help." Gabrielle actually felt sorry for the woman. "What can we do?"

The older woman looked up from the stove and pushed her steam-wilted hair from her forehead. She was thin, too thin in fact for all her husband's corpulence. Their sons, while still bearing the slimness of athletic youth, could obviously run to fat very easily. "Sister Gabrielle! You're guests in our home. I wouldn't think of asking you to help."

"You're not asking. We're offering." She smiled her best Christian smile. "We've got five hungry men in the parlor. The sooner we get them fed the sooner we can all get the dishes washed up. And before you say anything we will help you with the dishes."

"But that's not right, Sister."

"Naomi...I may call you Naomi?..Barnaby and I spend most of our year living out of hotel rooms and tents and eating our meals in restaurants. It's a treat for me to actually be in a kitchen and to do women's work."

"Well, if that's what you want, Sister..."

"It is. And please, just Gabrielle. This is Velma."

Naomi Jolly looked at Velma, really studied her. "You're the one my husband said did those...things."

Velma dropped into a chair. She had already discussed something like this happening with Fogg and Wardworth. She covered her face with her hands and pretended to weep quietly.

Gabrielle drew Naomi aside. "What exactly did your husband tell you, Naomi?"

"That she took him in her mouth while she did wicked things with her hands."

The evangelist gasped. "Velma?"

Velma, her face still covered, sobbed a little more loudly and shook her head.

"Naomi, Velma and Larry are newlyweds. Why would she stray from her new marriage vows? And why would she commit such a sin with a man of God?"

Naomi had no words.

"Perhaps Brother Hector told you that to encourage you to do what he was imagining?"

"That's disgusting! I could never do that."

"Perhaps Sister, that's why your husband's eye wanders, even in his mind. Men have needs." She put her hands on the thin woman's shoulders, speaking softly in her ear. "If you'd admit it, Sister, women have needs too. And there's nothing sinful in welcoming your husband to your bed. Nor is there any sin in enjoying his attentions or in giving him pleasure. In fact it is your duty, as a wife, to see to his needs. To *all* his needs."

Naomi Jolly was shocked this woman should speak to her in such a candid manner. "What about my sons? I know Hector told them his story."

"We noticed. Your sons were all over poor Velma. That was why we came in here. I think perhaps Brother Barnaby needs to have a chat with them. Would you allow that?"

"He'd have to. They won't listen to me at all."

"If you'll excuse me, I'll go have a word with my husband." Gabrielle hurried into the parlor and took Fogg aside. She whispered to him, "Jolly told his wife and his sons what Velma did. I've convinced his wife that it was a figment of his imagination. That he was only trying to encourage her to perform the service. She'd like you to have a word with Tweedle Dum and his brother about proper behavior."

"Perhaps Larry and I should take them outside?"

"Perhaps Larry should do it by himself. Promise them some of what their daddy got, but only if they behave circumspectly until after the revival is over. If they keep up like this people will think they're running a whore house instead of a church."

"Can Larry threaten to break their faces if they don't behave?"

"I think that might be a good idea." Gabrielle turned and went back to the kitchen.

"Mr. Wardworth is going to take your sons outside for a quiet word Naomi. There's nothing to worry about."

"He won't strike them will he?"

"Certainly not. He'll merely threaten to. It is, after all, a husband's duty to protect his wife." She sat down beside Velma. "Darling, what did Amos whisper to you?"

Velma had finally stilled her sobs to an occasional sniffle. "He told me I had such a pretty mouth he couldn't wait to try it out." She started sobbing again.

"Gabrielle, I've changed my mind. If Mr. Wardworth feels the need I have no objection to him flattening my son."

Velma didn't mention what the preacher had whispered to her, but Gabrielle would have bet folding money that it was ten times worse than the son's comment.

"Naomi, tell me where the dishes are and I'll set the table."

Mrs. Jolly pointed the evangelist to the sideboard in the dining room. Gabrielle made quick work of laying the table and returned to the kitchen. Seeing the   dry, over-cooked turkey come out of the oven Gabrielle stifled a groan.

*****

On Saturday morning Dylan drove Michael and Tomás to the depot. Tomás wore his best black suit and the whitest shirt Maria could manage, with an old fashioned black string tie. Both he and Michael carried thick, well-thumbed Bibles.

Neither Maria nor Katy had accompanied them to the station this trip. The pair had to appear to be ministers. Two self-righteous preachers wouldn't have two weepy women hanging off them at the platform.

They shook hands with Dylan, wishing "Brother Shay" goodbye, and went in to buy their tickets.

On the train, the two sat side by side, talking quietly. Delmar was a long trip north.Then they had to change trains and head southeast into Delaware. "How do you suggest we find her when we get in?"

Tomás answered, "We go straight to Lydia Langsdale. She'll have kept track of where they are after that letter she sent."

"You think so?"

"Don't you think that if a woman had put her hands on you Katy would be aware of every step that woman took?"

Mike had to catch himself when he started to laugh. "No. I think we'd find her in an alley somewhere with a kitchen knife under her third rib. What about Maria?"

"My Maria is too much of a lady for that. After calling her every filthy name she could think of in two languages, she'd probably shoot me."

"We both chose well, didn't we, Brother Tomás?"

"Brother Thomas, please, Brother Michael."

"I don't remember. Are we supposed to be any specific denomination? We talked about so much in the last two days I can't keep it straight."

Tomás put his book down in his seat and gestured for Michael to follow him out onto the vestibule between the cars. Standing on the cold, noisy platform he answered, "After talking to Inga and Callum I decided we were just Ministers of the Gospel. We have a congregation but no denomination. That means we get to keep all the collections for ourselves."

Michael nodded. "I never thought about denominations taking a piece of the action."

"They pay the preacher his salary, they own the building, and they pay into a retirement fund for the ministers. Religion is big business, son. The Catholic Church is bigger than U.S. Steel, Hearst and Standard Oil combined. And they're tax free."

"So by being gospel ministers we get to keep what we make, we don't pay taxes on the property, and no one will bother us about whatever we do."

"That's right." Tomás grinned. "Like a license to steal, if a man is in it for himself and not for the good of the people."

"Do you think we'll get grief for arresting this preacher woman and her entourage?"

"Probably. But we've got at least two witnesses against them and can probably get more if we work it right. Plus they jumped bail. The State's Attorney is itching to get them into court."

They returned to their seats and rode the rest of the way in silence until they got to their first stop, where they changed trains.

In Delmar they had about a ten block walk to the Front Street Church. The parsonage sat beside the church. The only way to tell the difference between the two was the steeple on top of the church.

Otherwise the two white clapboard buildings looked almost identical.

Tomás knocked on the door of the parsonage. A slight young man with thinning hair, dressed in his shirtsleeves, opened the door. Tomás didn't give him a chance to say anything. "Brother Covington, we spoke on the telephone. Thomas Rivers and Michael Dockerty."

"Yes, yes, of course. Come in brothers, please. Miss Langsdale is already here."

They followed him into the small parlor. Miss Langsdale was an attractive woman whose brown hair was pulled back into a prim bun. She would make the perfect minister's wife.

"I'm sorry for the need for subterfuge, Reverend Covington. I'm Special Agent Tomás Ribiero, this is Detective Sergeant Michael Doughterty. He's with Baltimore City Police, but is assigned to the Bureau of Investigation. If I didn't express our gratitude before, Miss Langsdale, please allow me to do so now. We have been chasing this Pennington woman for almost a year and we always seem one step behind."

The young lady sat with her hands folded demurely in her lap. "You're most welcome Special Agent. I only hope you can get her off the streets. She and her followers are a menace. I've heard stories about them."

Tom asked, "What sort of stories? Other than the young woman enticing men into giving them time in their churches."

"When they played the Howard Theater in Washington there was a dog. He ran out on stage and Sister Gabrielle's husband shot the dog and killed him. She was supposed to have raised the dog from the dead."

Tomás nodded. "I've seen that done. The gun was loaded with chalk blanks. The shell had red chalk packed into it. It makes a red splotch on the dog's fur that looks like blood. The dog plays dead . At some signal it revives, changing from a vicious jungle beast to a silly puppy."

"That's exactly what I heard. My father went to see her when she was there. It was all he could talk about."

"It's nothing but a vaudeville trick, Miss Langsdale. Nothing supernatural or spiritual about it. Now do you know if Miss Pennington is still in town?"

Josiah Covington answered. "She's at the Delmar Holiness Church until tomorrow. I haven't been to see her but some of my congregation have. They were quite impressed. The first night she preached against women's suffrage. But last night she went on about men who stray outside their marriage, and how women can keep their husbands home by meeting their needs. The man who told me about that said it all seemed rather strange."

"Strange in what way?" Mike asked.

"Sister Gabrielle talked about how men had needs, and how it was a wife's duty to meet them. If the husband was any kind of man he would see his wife's needs were met too. Jimmy Stevens, the man I spoke to, said it was all very embarrassing. And the whole time she was talking Reverend Jolly and his two sons were making...kissy faces at that young soprano. The one who...assaulted me."

Tomás nodded. "Reverend Covington, would you mind going with us this evening? We need you to make an identification of the young lady in question."

"I'll be happy to. Will it be necessary for me to introduce you to them?"

"Why don't we wait and see. Do you remember our names?"

"Thomas Rivers and Mike Dockerty?"

"That's right. We're from a church in Baltimore, and are considering inviting them to do a revival. But we're not sure. Do you know where they're staying?"

"The Delmar Hotel. On the Maryland side."

"And they're in Delaware right now. So they've violated the Mann Act right there."

Mike looked at Tomás. "What's the age of consent in Delaware?"

Tomás shook his head. "Seven. It was ten. Then about thirty years ago they lowered it. The state must have some real perverts in the legislature. The best we can do is the federal charge."

"Good enough."

Miss Langsdale stood. "Gentlemen, Josiah's cook has prepared a nice supper for us. Why don't we eat? Then you can go over to the church and meet that whore of Babylon."

Before they ate, Tomás used the telephone to call the Delaware police chief. He arranged to have two officers handy for when they started making arrests. Tomás explained they expected to make four arrests and would appreciate having two extra men there. Possibly a matron also, if one was available. A Paddy wagon too, but he didn't want them to arrive until after the revival had begun.

Their dinner was cheerful. Three men doing their best to entertain a young woman who was extremely interested in everything they did. Tomás and Michael told sanitized stories of the cases they'd worked, leaving out the parts involving blood and gore and the seedier elements of life. Mike talked about catching Noble Riesling in their bakery in the middle of the night. Tomás told the story of how he and Maria had played *Hidalgo* for the phony German count.

The men walked Miss Langsdale to her home and went on to the revival. The fifteen blocks seemed doubly long with the November wind whipping down the wide street. They pulled their hats lower and their collars higher.

They could hear the piano was in need of tuning as they neared the church. Whoever was playing was good. He was doing as well as he could with the Bach Toccata with a dead key on the piano. They stepped into the light and slight warmth of the sanctuary. A man in his forties with artificially darkened hair rushed to meet them.

"Brother Covington! Welcome. May I take this to mean that you have reconsidered our proposition?"

"I'm sorry, Brother Fogg. But I'm afraid my parishioners who were interested have already been here. However, two friends from the City are here for the holiday. I told them about your service, and they both wanted to see for themselves. Barnaby Fogg, this is Reverend Thomas Rivers and Brother Mike Dockerty from the Holy Gospel Church."

"I'm not familiar with the church. Where is it?" Fogg looked suspicious.

"We're new." Michael volunteered. We're down on Warren Street in Fells Point, near Federal Hill."

"Oh, you're in Baltimore."

"Yes, Brother. In Baltimore."

"I thought I was familiar with all the churches there."

"As I said, Brother Fogg. We're new. We only opened our doors a month ago."

"And how did you come to select that neighborhood?"

Tomás said, "May we sit down Brother Fogg?"

"Where are my manners? Please. Sit." The three

sat in a pew near the back of the sanctuary.

Mike went on with his tale, knowing it was one he could remember. "There was a house of ill repute on Warren Street. The police closed it down a few years ago. Since then it's been empty. It was bought by a benefactor for the back taxes. We are putting a church and a school there."

"An excellent idea, Brother Dockerty. Is all you'll have there a school and a church?"

"That's all, Brother Fogg."

"What sort of school?"

"For adults in the neighborhood. We plan to have Sunday school classes. But we'll have classes for the immigrants during the week. Language classes for those who need them. Home sciences. You'd be amazed at the number of young girls who arrive in this country not knowing how to boil water. We have some ladies who are willing to teach. We plan to have a program to set up young men in apprenticeships. We have an elementary school program for children whose parents can't afford the local Catholic school. We've worked very hard, but now we're in need of extra funds. We thought a revival may be the easiest way to get them."

"Easiest, Brother Dockerty? Not easy. But the most lucrative, surely. For how long do you anticipate you'll want Sister Gabrielle's services?"

Mike looked at his partner. "What do you think, Brother Thomas? We really hadn't discussed this."

"I'd like to meet with Sister Gabrielle first. Then I can get a better grasp on what we can expect."

"And excellent idea Brother Thomas. Why don't I take you to meet Sister Gabrielle now?"

Mike leaned over. "I understand you have a young soprano who performs with you. Could we meet her too?"

"If you'd like to. What about Sister Velma's husband? He's playing the piano right now."

"Brother Thomas? Should we meet everyone now? Or should we wait until later?"

Tomás appeared to ponder. He looked over his shoulder and saw the Black Mariah pull past and two plain clothes officers slip inside the sanctuary as if they were coming to the meeting. "Why don't we go now? After all, it would be a special thrill to be able to meet the famous Sister Gabrielle."

"Then come with me."

Barnaby Fogg stood and led the two men down the side aisle. through a side door, and down the street. "I hope you gents don't mind walking a few blocks. The ladies are still at the hotel."

"Oh, the Delmar. Isn't that on the Maryland side?"

"It is."

Tomás had to think fast. The police with the wagon were on the Delaware force. They had no authority in Maryland. He nudged Mike.

"Excuse me, Brother Fogg," Mike called. Let me run inside and tell Brother Josiah we'll be going straight to our hotel after the meeting. I wouldn't want him to wait for us unnecessarily."

"Certainly, Brother Dockerty. We'll wait right here."

Mike ran back into the sanctuary and grabbed one of the Delaware cops, and told him to call the station on the Maryland side to set up for the Delmar hotel. He told Josiah Covington to head home and they'd talk to him later and thanked him for his hospitality. He ran back to where Tomás waited with Fogg and Wardworth.

"Thank you for waiting, gentlemen. Josiah has gone to Miss Langsdale's home. I expect we'll see them both tomorrow."

"Ah, the lovely Miss Langsdale." Larry Wardsworth sounded a little bitter. Mike didn't know if it was the fact that Miss Langsdale was lovely or that she existed at all.

They went on to the small hotel. It had only two storeys. There was no elevator and only a single central staircase used by both staff and guests. It would be much easier when the time came to make their arrests. No chance of someone slipping down the back stairs, or of people running in four different directions. According to Josiah there were no suites in this hotel, and only two *en suite* rooms. The inhabitants of the other rooms had to share the bathroom at the end of the hall or use the thundermug under the bed.

Both Tomás and Michael wore shoulder holsters under their jackets, and each carried a second pistol elsewhere on their person. They were taking no chances. Katy had told Michael before he left that if anything happened to him on this mission she'd kill him. That, of course, had led to Katy sending him off in a manner he would remember with a broad smile for the next several days.

Barnaby Fogg knocked on the door to the room he shared with Gabrielle. "Sister Gabrielle? I have two gentlemen from Baltimore who want to meet you."

Chapter Nine

Tadhg spent Friday morning in Captain MacFarland's office. He'd been waiting for over an hour to see his commanding officer. Finally he was called in.

"What can I do for you Nagel?"

"I've gotten my orders for France, Sir."

"I know. You're supposed to leave in April."

"That was the original plan, sir. Mechanics can't get replacement parts damaged by sabotage in this country. The *Aéronautique Militaire* has decided I'm to complete my training in France. I'll be here until Christmas and ship out the day after."

"Damn, Nagel. We hate to lose you. What about your horse?"

"That's another thing I wanted to talk to you about, Sir. I'd like Johnny Allen to have him while I'm gone. That way he could do longer duty if you needed him."

"That's not the way we normally do things, Nagel. The way it works, another officer will move up to the mounted patrol and will take your mount, unless you have a place to stable him."

"Sir, he is my horse. That was what was agreed to when I brought him up from Aberdeen."

"He is, but..."

"Sir, Sergeant Allen is one of the few men who could handle him. Plus his own horse and mine get on well so they could be trailered together if necessary."

"There is a way around it. Sell your horse to Allen. I'd suggest a written agreement of some sort, so you could have him back when you return for the same price. Then Allen can use your horse and his own, or not as he sees fit. You sure you wouldn't rather send him to a farm somewhere?"

"No sir. The King wouldn't like that. And there's not many men he'll tolerate."

"So go see Sergeant Allen and set it up. So we have you until Christmas?"

"I'll need to have a week before to prepare to leave. I'm supposed to go up to Quebec and leave from there."

"I'll arrange it from this end. Now get out of here and get on duty."

Tadhg almost ran out to the street, and down to the stables to claim his horse. He had to go find Johnny Allen. He hadn't said anything to Allen yet about his plan for The King.. He only hoped Allen would agree.

Allen and Major were riding patrol around Hopkins Hospital, keeping taxi cabs from parking in the ambulance bay and moving loiterers from around doorways. Tadhg rode up to them, stopping along the way to exchange pleasantries with a couple of nurses standing outside on their break.

"Morning, Sarge. We've been looking for you."

"You found us. Had you been at turnout on time you would have seen me there."

"Sorry. I've been in the Captain's office. I got my orders. I'm shipping out right after Christmas."

"So you're really doing it? You're going to go fight the Bosch for France?"

"I am. But I need a favor."

Allen groaned. "What, you want me to keep an eye on your wife?"

"You keep your eyes and everything else off my wife. You've got your own girls." They both chuckled over that. "I don't want just anybody taking The King. I want you to buy him. For a dollar. When I get back I'll buy him back."

"You sure?"

"I don't have any place to send him. If he went to a farm somewhere it wouldn't end well. I'm afraid other coppers wouldn't know how to handle him. But he likes you and he likes Major. So what do you say?"

Allen rode his horse so Major and The King were side by side, and offered his hand. "We'll need something in writing to prove it to the department."

"Captain said the Kemp firm will draw us up a proper bill of sale at no charge. I'll call them this afternoon. At least we've got time. I can get it drawn up, and we'll just need to get together to sign it. Why don't you come to the bakery Saturday for lunch. We're both off."

"Have you looked at the schedule?"

"Not today. Why?"

"Because between now and Christmas, we're working Howard and Lex every Saturday." He named the primary shopping corner in Baltimore, where the major department stores were located.

It was Nagel's turn to groan. "Are we at least off Monday?"

"We are."

"Good. So come round Monday. Lunch is on me."

"Where is this bakery again?"

"Baltimore and Luzerne. Just follow Marshal Farnan. He's there a couple times a week."

Allen nudged his horse into motion and Tadhg turned the King to follow. Allen called back, "Since you didn't bother reading the schedule you may not know. We're expected at Mount Vernon after lunch today. The City Electrician is putting up lights on the Monument. They want us there to keep traffic moving. And probably to hold the ladder."

The pair patrolled the hospital for another hour and began to work their way over to Charles Street. It took a while. They had to stop at a conveniently placed trough and water the horses and to let them rest with their feed bags. The department did not insist their officers get lunch on a set schedule. However, their horses were fed, watered and rested regularly.

They reached the Washington Monument in the center of Mount Vernon with plenty of time to spare. An electrician in the City's employ was already there with a small child around five. Tadhg rode up first and dismounted, making sure The King was up in the grassy verge and out of traffic.

"You must be the City Electrician."

The man looked up from his work. He was a few years older than Tadhg and could have been a matinee idol. "Henry Schneider. My son Paul. He's 'helping' today."

The kid never looked up from his task of screwing red, green and yellow bulbs into the long string of lights laid out on the grass.

"We're supposed to direct traffic here. What else do you need us to do, Mr. Schneider?"

"Keep those foolish girls from bothering me. Every time I try to do any work I wind up with them vying to get my attention. I figured if I brought Paul along it might dissuade them. So far it's only encouraged them."

Sure enough, Tadhg spotted two young women he judged to be housemaids or nursery maids by their clothes. They were staring holes in both men in the park and giggling behind their hands.

Tadhg thought it best to greet them from a superior position. He grabbed a handful of The King's mane and swung up into the saddle, much to the delight of the two ladies. He watched as they hurried across the street to the park. Nagel nudged his horse forward to block their way.

"Excuse me, ladies. You'll need to go back to the sidewalk. We can't allow anyone to be injured." They both looked up. And up. And up. They apparently hadn't realized how big a six foot tall man on a draft horse actually was.

"Wowzer!" one girl said, while the other giggled behind her hand.

"Ladies, I'm going to have to ask you to move. You're in harm's way here." He moved The King another step into them.

The giggler gasped and almost fell backward.

He realized they were still in their teens. "Come along now. I'll see you get safely across. Which way do you need to go?"

Wowzer pointed to the far side of Charles Street.

"Come along then. We'll see you make it across safely." Tadhg kept The King at a walk, and escorted the girls to the corner of Monument and Charles. Once he had them to a place of safety, Officer Nagel leaned on the pommel and bent over so he was almost at eye level with the girls. He spoke to them firmly. "Now ladies, if you try to come across that park again while Mr. Schneider's trying to string those lights, you'll get arrested. Do you understand?"

"Will you be doing the arresting?" the giggler asked, with yet another giggle as she bit her thumb coyly.

"Oh I'll be doing the arresting. You see that ring on the lamp post there on the corner?"

She nodded.

"I use that to tie my horse at times. I also use it to handcuff prisoners." He lifted a pair of cuffs from the hook on his saddle to show her. "One bracelet on your pretty wrist, and one on the ring. Then I ride down the block to the call box and we wait until the Paddy wagon comes to haul your little bustle off to jail. Now go home and be good little girls. Maybe when you grow up you can find a nice policeman to take you to a dance."

The thumb biter had the nerve to flutter her eyelashes at him. "Will you take us, nice officer?"

"I don't think my wife would like it. And I don't fool around with little girls. You see that man on the big black horse?"

They both nodded.

"He's my sergeant. If you don't get out of here now he'll make me arrest both of you. Now go on. Git!"

The pair scurried down Monument Street and turned in at an alley.

Allen rode up. "How'd you do that?"

"What"

"Get them to go along quietly, and not scream and call you everything but a child of God."

"I told them you were my sergeant, and you were a real SOB, and would make me arrest you if they didn't leave. Then I showed them my handcuffs and the hitching ring on the lamp post. I said that's where they'd be secured until the Black Mariah arrived."

"I'll have to remember that. Blame it on somebody else. I like it. How'd you learn that?"

"From hanging around with detectives. Coppers have the right to lie to suspects so long as they tell the truth in court and on their reports. So lie your arse off, then confess it on Saturday."

"What if you're not Catholic?"

"Then how did you get on the force, boyo?"

They both had a good chuckle over that. For the next three hours they gently guided people away from the work being done and from the surrounding park. By the time the electrician was done it was time for the horses to return for the evening and for Allen and Nagel to start writing parking tickets. It was something new for the City. For some reason, it gave the men a sort of perverse pleasure to enforce the parking regulations.

*****

"Brother Dockerty, what is your position in the church?" Fogg asked.

Michael leaned back in his chair and crossed his legs, trying to look nonchalant. "I'm one of the deacons and treasurer of the congregation." He was painfully conscious that they were in a hotel bedroom with a small seating area.

Fogg turned his attention to Reverend Rivers. "How many in your congregation Brother Rivers?"

"We're a small church so far, but we're growing. Last Sunday we had around a hundred and twenty. We have about that many children in the school."

"What grades do you have?"

"Only first through sixth. We don't have sufficient instructors for any higher grades. Not yet."

"So you're looking for a revival for an infusion of cash?"

Rivers looked at his deacon. "Brother Dockerty? Would you explain our current situation?"

Mike leaned forward in his seat. "You see, Brother Fogg, our school is our primary ministry. But as our congregation is mostly from the lower social economic classes they can't afford much tuition."

"So why don't they send their children to public school? The Baltimore schools are considered some of the best. And the Catholic schools aren't expensive at all if the parents are parishioners."

"That's the problem Brother. Our people want no truck with papists and they disagree with some of the things taught in the public schools. Our school teaches the actual basics. Reading, but from Scriptures only. Arithmetic. Penmanship. We also stress American history, particularly the War of Northern Aggression." There. That should demonstrate they were a couple of ignorant bigots who could be fooled with an arithmetic dog and some phony Pentacostal babbling.

While the men talked Sister Gabrielle Lane Pennington and Velma Roland sat quietly as proper "Christian women" should. Brother Rivers finally addressed the evangelist. "Sister, how do you justify being a minister of the gospel when St. Paul said specifically that women shall not preach?"

Gabrielle shifted in her seat. She had been expecting this. "Brother, I do not make any claim to being a minister. I am an evangelist. I exhort. I invite. I beseech. I proclaim. But I neither preach nor teach."

"But you do teach, Sister." River's smile didn't reach his eyes. "Don't you teach women how to be proper wives? Don't you interpret the Word from your pulpit?"

"Brother, who better to show women how to be a wife than one who is a wife herself?"

"Yet I notice your name is Pennington and your husband's surname is Fogg. It all seems very peculiar."

Gabrielle waved her hand, the apparent signal for two men to leave the room. Fogg and Wardworth went into what was apparently the bathroom.

Velma Roland was looking at Brother Rivers, biting on her thumb in what she thought was a seductive manner. She started to rise as Gabrielle went to busy herself pouring coffee for their two guests.

Velma sat on the arm of Brother Rivers' chair, and ran her fingers through his mass of black curly hair. She whispered, "Is there something I can do to convince you to invite Sister Pennington to your church?"

"How old are you, Velma?"

She kissed the top of his ear. "I turned seventeen last week."

"Where are you from?"

Velma ran the tip of her tongue around the inside of the preacher's ear. "Ocean City."

"Un-huh." He stood up. "Sister Pennington, would you call the gentlemen back please?"

Gabrielle seemed to glide across the room as she went to the bathroom door, knocked twice then opened it. The two men came inside and resumed their seats. No one seemed to notice that Rivers had edged to the door that led to the hallway.

All four of their suspects were now in the same room. Michael stood and turned his back on the group, pulled out his badge and reached into his jacket for his service revolver. Tomás grabbed the knob and pulled the door open, admitting three Wicomico County Sheriff's deputies. Mike turned, showing his federal badge. "Gabrielle Lane Pennington, Barnaby Fogg, Velma Roland, Lawrence Wardworth, you're under arrest for multiple violations of the Mann Act, for kidnapping, attempted murder, assault on a police officer, assault and battery, absconding, and anything else we can think of." He turned to the deputies. "Gentlemen, if you would do the honors please."

The deputies had been briefed. They secured handcuffs to each of the four, cuffing them together. If one of them tried to make a break they wouldn't get far while dragging their accomplices.

The deputies marched the four downstairs. Michael and Tomás went about searching the room.

*****

The bakery was busier than usual Saturday morning. Of all days. Katy and Millie were going downtown with Rose and the kids to watch the Christmas parade, and to look at the displays in the department store windows.

Tadhg was no help at all this morning. He was downstairs putting a shine on his riding boots. He and Sergeant Allen were riding at the head of the mounted patrol in the parade up Howard Street. He had been late getting home last night because he had stayed behind to shine The King's tack.

Rose had pressed his dress uniform, and had polished up all the brass buttons on his coat. Tadhg had received two medals during his time on the force. Normally they laid in the collar button dish on his dresser. Today they had to be pinned on his coat.

An hostler at the stable was grooming The King right now. Tadhg wished he could have braided ribbons into the animal's mane and tail, but that sort of frippery was frowned upon by the department.

Dylan was going with his wife. He had finally made the executive decision that the bakery would close at ten o'clock. Whoever wanted to attend the parade could do so, and take care of some personal shopping at the same time while downtown.

Tadgh stopped behind the bakery counter on his way out. He had to get to the stables early to get his horse saddled and to make his way to the staging area near the harbor. His handgun, cuffs and nightstick were carried on his saddle, but now he carried them slung across his arm.He stopped to kiss Rose goodbye. "I'll see you downtown, darlin'."

Of course seeing a man kiss his wife in public drew hoots and hollers from the working men coming in for their breakfasts. Tadgh turned around to the bunch in front of the counter. "Eat your hearts out, boys." He bent, kissed her one more time, and pushed through the line to the door.

Millie was cheerfully filling bags with pastries as Rose tried to get control of the crowd. "Don't let them worry you, honey. They're just showing off." Millie noticed Rose was wiping tears. "What's wrong?"

"I'm only going to have him for four more weeks, Millie." She turned and ran from the counter into the kitchen, hoping to find a quiet corner.

Dylan was at the cash register. He looked at his wife, who merely shook her head. She knew the girl needed time. Dylan moved over and took Rose's place until Annie came from the kitchen a few minutes later.

Things finally slowed down enough for Dylan to leave the register. He went through the kitchen and back to his office. Rose was sitting on the stool behind his desk.

He braced a hip on the edge of his desk. "Rose darlin', tell me what's wrong?"

"Tadhg's going to be leaving in less than a month. We've had so little time together." She was still dashing tears from her cheeks. Dylan didn't know if it was because she was heartbroken or angry.

"Sweetie, you knew he was going to be doing this when you agreed to marry him."

"I know. But I thought we'd have six months. Instead we've had six weeks."

"Rose..." She was looking down at her lap. "Rose, look at me." She finally looked up. "What if Tadhg had decided to do the 'honorable' thing, and not marry you at all before he signed up? Because that's what a lot of men will be doing, on the off chance they leave a pregnant widow behind. How would you feel if he went to France, and you found out you were going to have a baby?"

"I'd be scared half to death. But I'd be so very happy."

"I thought so. Tadhg understands the risks he's taking by doing this, Rose. He's not a little kid. He has to do this, for himself, for the country of his birth. He sees what's happening in Ireland. He knows Germany is responsible. He feels honor bound to put an end to it."

"But why does Tadhg have to be the one to do it, Dylan? America isn't even in this war."

"A famous man whose name I don't remember said something like, 'the only thing necessary for evil to triumph, is for good men to do nothing.' Your husband is a good man. Oh, you could make him stay. But he'd hate himself for it for the rest of his life. And he'd eventually hate you for it. Didn't he explain to you how by doing this, he will be an officer? How he will be able to properly provide for you? You won't have to live on the three bucks a day a mounted officer earns. The French aircorps will offer him a skill, promotions, respect. He'll be an officer. In the American army, he'd be a grunt, cannon fodder."

"That's what Tadhg said. But I don't have to like it."

"No, darlin'. You don't have to like it. But you do need to accept it. Hate the war. Hate the army. But remember that your husband is a strong man who will do what he feels he must."

"I know. I'm afraid...afraid..." She dissolved into tears then. Dylan slid off the desk and pulled her into his arms, letting her sob it out against his shirt. When she finally seemed to slow down and the hiccoughs started, he held her at arm's length.

"It's getting late. Go get ready. We've got to get downtown if you want to see your husband and that dinosaur of a horse he rides lead the parade up Howard Street."

"Dylan?"

"Yes darlin'?"

"Thank you."

He hugged her one last time. "Now go get dressed. I've got to go get a dry shirt, and make sure the girls are dressed. You need any help? No, not me. Millie can come help you."

She giggled. "No. I'm a big girl. I think I can dress myself."

"Then go on with you. And make sure you have a scarf and gloves. It's bitter cold today."

Dylan hurried up the stairs to the third floor and checked on his daughters. They were wearing matching red dresses with white trim, making them look like little woolen candy canes.

He asked their nursemaid, "Hannah, are you coming with us?"

"Not today. I want to put my feet up, read a book and maybe have a long soak. Do you mind?"

"Not at all. You do what you need to do. I think we can manage these two on our own. But I will need you to help me get them downstairs. Do you mind?" Dylan still had some residual weakness in his left arm from the stabbing a few months ago.

"Of course not." Hannah finally got a good look at him. "Did you spill something on your shirt?"

He chuckled as he plucked at the damp fabric. "Rose needed to have a good cry. I was handy."

"Oh. I don't know how she'll do it."

"She'll do fine. But I'm glad she's got all of us here. Now, let me get a dry shirt and we can go downstairs. Make sure the girls are bundled up good."

"Yes, sir."

He was still changing his shirt when Millie came in. "Is Rose okay?"

"She is now. We talked, she had another good cry and went downstairs to get dressed. Everything's fine." He took a knitted jumper from the drawer and pulled it over his head, then shrugged into his jacket.

"No shoulder holster today?"

"Nope. But I'm not unarmed. Always be prepared." He turned his back to her, pulled up his sweater and showed the bulge in the small of his back under his trousers.

"I wish Michael and Tomás were here."

"I haven't heard from them at all."

They might be having trouble getting a telephone line through to the City with the holiday."

Millie sat on the edge of the bed and unbuttoned her bodice to change. Dylan sat down beside her and tried to help. She slapped his hand away. "If you help, I'll never get dressed."

"Oh, all right," he groused. "At least I can watch."

She finally managed to change her dress, layered on a jacket to wear under her coat, added a knitted scarf and gloves and she was ready. "Come on. Katy said she'd meet us by the back door."

They went to fetch their daughters, making sure they had both taken care of business before they left.

They went downstairs to meet their friends. Maria was waiting with little Benito bundled up in his fur-lined bunting.

Inga was the only employee who had decided to go downtown with them. She picked up little Declan when they reached the streetcar stop, and they all climbed on. Dylan paid their fares and the ladies managed to find seats.

The Number 13 took them right up to Cathedral street. They had to walk a few blocks down to Howard and Lexington where a crowd was already gathering, waiting for the parade. Dylan's superior size gave them an advantage when pushing through to the front of the crowd so they could all see.

He got some strange looks escorting five young women and five small children to the parade. Millie laughed when he mentioned it, and leaned back against him. "They think you're either a bad pimp or a Mormon."

"So either way they think I have a harem?"

"Probably. Because they have dirty little minds. And they're jealous."

"Let 'em be." He put his arm around her waist and pulled her a little closer. "I don't want you getting cold."

She leaned back, letting him support her. They could hear the sound of a snare drum down the street. Dylan pointed over the women's heads. "Look Mary Faith. Here comes the parade."

The sound of Christmas carols played in 4/4 marching time preceded the company of mounted police leading the parade. In the very front was Tadhg Nagel astride The King, and Johnny Allen riding Major proudly, followed by sixteen more mounted patrolmen riding four abreast. Behind the mounted officers came a marching band from City College.

Several display floats from the big department stores followed, each drawn by four horses. Another band, this one from Baltimore Polytechnic, played a different carol, also in marching time, making for an oddly pleasant discordancy. Several more floats, from McCormicks, Baltimore Gas & Electric, and other local companies made their way up Howard Street. Finally, the guest of honor, the Grand Marshal of the parade, Santa Klaus himself, his gold and silver sleigh heaped high with packages, and mounted on a horse drawn float. Beside the float walked half a dozen children dressed as elves.

The children and most of the adults clapped and cheered at the jolly old elf's appearance. Baby Benito began to cry. Maria looked around. Of all times for her son to demand to be fed and changed it had to be now, in the middle of Howard Street. The parade had passed by then. Millie gestured they should all go across the street to Read's, down in the soda fountain. They had tables and booths, and it would be easy for Maria to have enough privacy to nurse Benito.

Dylan managed to herd his flock across Howard Street, then down half a block to the big drug store. The first floor was typical of every drugstore in town, with patent medicines, tobacco and other necessities At the back was a druggist's counter, where a customer could get his prescriptions filled, or purchase enough poison to murder everybody in the city as long as he signed the poison book.

The group moved down the spiral stairs to the fountain. The place was busy, but Dylan managed to spot a couple of tables in the corner. He led them back and began shoving tables together, annoying the waitress. He apologized, gave her a fifty cent piece and asked her to come back in a few minutes to take their orders.

Maria loosened Benito's bunting, threw a blanket over her shoulder and settled in to feed her son. No one at their table thought anything of it. It was a natural thing to do, and no one could see anything. The restaurant manager pushed his way back to their group.

"Excuse me. I'm going to have to ask you to leave."

Dylan stood, towering over the prissy little weasel. "Excuse me?"

"We cannot permit females to expose themselves."

Dylan made a show of looking around. "I don't see anyone exposing themselves." He turned to Millie. "Millicent, do you see anyone exposing themselves?"

Millie stood beside her husband. "I see a man exposing himself for the pompous ass he is."

The pompous ass began to sputter.

"Sir, are you refusing to serve us?" Millie wanted to know.

"I'm merely asking the young lady to not expose herself."

Millie looked at Maria, who by now had buttoned her bodice, and was burping Benito. "Sir, I don't see anyone exposing herself. Although that blonde at the counter is showing far more bosom and ankle than proper." She lowered her voice, making him lean in to hear her. "Perhaps you should speak to her. Or are you her fancy man, allowing her to come in from of the cold for a few minutes?"

"I'll call the law!"

Dylan was grinning now. He reached into his pocket and pulled out his BoI badge. "I'm here. And I can tell you no laws have been broken. Other than you making a spectacle of yourself. My wife, our children and our friends were having a nice day out. Two of these ladies are married to City police officers, both of whom are working today. The young lady you accused of exposing herself is married to another Bureau of Investigation Special Agent. I don't believe any judge or any officer would be amenable to your complaint."

The little popinjay sputtered some more, gave up and walked away.

Their waitress reappeared, shaking her head. As Dylan sat back down, she put her hand on his shoulder and bent over so the manager wouldn't hear. "Don't pay any attention to Evil Eldridge. You see that girl at the counter?"

"You mean the one with the dumplings boiling over?" Millie asked.

"That's the one. Her man parked her there. Eldridge tried to throw her out and her man pulled a knife on him. She's on her third ice cream soda now, and Evil's been on the prod ever since."

"We'll try not to make any more trouble. Or let the kids make too much of a mess."

"Don't worry about it. Now what can I get you?"

"Do you have any soup today?" Even though it was called a "soda fountain", Read's offered a full lunch service.

"We've got some chili."

"What's chili?" Katy thought that sounded interesting.

"It's beans, tomatoes and meat with some spices. It's really thick and spicy."

"How spicy?"

"Not too hot. I can get you a taste of it first."

"Please." This sounded like something they could make.

The waitress disappeared, then returned directly with a coffee cup holding a half ladle of chili and a handful of spoons. She put the spoons on the table, so they could help themselves. Millie and Katy each took a taste, Millie fed her husband a small bite, then they passed the cup around the table. The only one who rejected it was Inga.

In the end, everyone but Inga ordered chili, with a small portion each for Declan and Donagh, Mary Faith and Chiara. Inga asked for a roast beef sandwich.

They were almost done when two uniformed officers came in. Dylan's first thought was that the popinjay really had called the police. Then he realized who they were.

Dylan waved his hand over his head. Tadgh Nagel spotted them and gestured to his partner. Tadhg went right to Rose. She touched his hand then recoiled. "You're cold."

He pulled up a chair beside her and sat down. "Millie, Dylan, you already met Sergeant Johnny Allen. Johnny, you know Rose. Let me introduce everybody else. Those two little girls are Dylan and Millie's. Mary Faith and Chiara. Then there's Katy Dougherty. Her husband's Detective Sergeant Michael Dougherty, and their sons Donagh and Declan. The lady with the baby is Maria Ribiero. She's married to BoI Special Agent Tomás Ribiero. Finally, this young lady sitting next to my Rose is Inga Rottmann. She's not married to anybody."

Allen greeted everyone, then pulled up a chair to sit beside Inga. The girl blushed prettily and looked at her lap. "So, you're not married to anybody?"

She shook her head.

"Are you seeing anybody?"

She shook her head again.

Rose volunteered, "She used to go with Alex when Tadhg took us to the local parish hall dances."

"Nagel, are there any dances tonight?"

"There is. The Knights of Columbus is having one tonight at St. Catherines."

"They let in non-members?"

"They'll let us in. Of course, we know Father Toolen and he works the door."

"Miss Inga, would you come with me to the dance tonight?"

Inga looked past him to Rose. "Are you and Tadhg going?"

Rose said, "I don't have to work tonight. And Tadhg doesn't have training tomorrow."

"It looks like we're going. Now, what are we eating?"

Chapter Ten

Michael Dougherty and Tomás Ribiero spent their Saturday sitting in the sheriff's office in Salisbury, Wicomico County, Maryland. Tomás had sent a wire to Dylan requesting his and one other detective's presence, for the transportation of four prisoners back to Baltimore. They were still awaiting answers.

Sheriff Bill Dryden, a typical rural sheriff with his broad brimmed Stetson, bushy beard and mustache, was plying the two visiting officers with bad coffee and good stories. The county had no full time deputies. The sheriff didn't have any sort of uniform other than a badge. Half the time he didn't carry a weapon.

According to the sheriff the last big crime they had had was some waterman had been caught stealing another man's crab pots and catch. Dryden said they had decided not to press charges against the man because the owner of the pots and the other watermen had beaten the bejesus out of the guy, breaking both his arms and all his fingers.

Mike and Tomás regaled him in turn with their own stories, including the bigotted woman they kept tossing out of the bakery.

It was getting close to supper time when the answer to their wire arrived. Dylan had sent a simple message. "Overnight train arriving first thing". Michael read it and handed the telegram back to Tomás. "He probably took the girls to watch Tadhg in the parade."

"I guess everybody went out. And I guess they closed up for the day."

"Meaning when I get home I'll have to figure out what the boys are telling me about seeing Santy Klaus in the parade."

Dylan Shay descended the day coach, accompanied by a detective in plain clothes the next day before lunch. Neither carried a bag as they were making a quick turn around. Shay spotted his superior on the platform and called to him. "Tomás!"

Ribiero pushed through a few clusters of people greeting other arrivals to get to Shay. "Dylan, I see you made it."

"We did. Special Agent in Charge Tomás Ribiero, This is newly minted Detective Manny Levy. Last time Mike and I saw him he was standing guard over a dead body."

"Levy," Tomás shook the younger man's hand. "I believe we've met before. You had guard detail at the safe house when we brought all those boys up from Aberdeen, didn't you?"

"I did, sir. I'm surprised you remembered."

"Well come on then. We've got four prisoners to transport back to Central District. The City gets to keep three of them. We may just persuade one of them to be a witness, but if she won't cooperate they can still hold her for prostitution."

Walking back to the sheriff's office, Dylan told Tomás, "Unless Maria wants to take this girl home with her I suggest you find someplace to stash her. We've got a full house as it is."

"I wasn't even going to suggest it."

Mike was sitting in the sheriff's office where Tomás had left him, his feet on a deputy's desk, half dozing. Dylan walked into the office first and saw his friend's compromising position. Once Levy and

Tomás were in the room, Dylan slammed the door shut and laughed when Mike almost knocked the chair over trying to get his feet on the floor.

"Detective Sergeant, I'm surprised at you. Here Tomás leaves you to mind the prisoners and you fall asleep."

Michael peered around Dylan's bulk. "Is that Officer Levy?"

Dylan answered, "It is."

Dougherty stood up and walked over to his friend. "Officer Levy, where's your uniform?"

"Hanging in the wardrobe at my mother's house. I'm Detective Levy now."

"As of when?"

"As of this past Monday. Chief of Detectives MacNally finally took pity on me and got me away from that ignorant sergeant in Southern District."

"Where are you stationed?"

"Central. Same as you. Except you don't come into the house much at all any more."

"Because I'm assigned to the BoI with these two."

The door opened behind them and Sheriff Dryden came in. "You can go get... Oh, I see you're here. It's going to take you until tomorrow to get home on the train. Why don't you go get you some lunch now, and get some box lunches for the trip. Tell Gert at the cafe I said to fix you up."

Michael introduced Shay and Levy to the sheriff, then the four men went across the street for some much needed sustenance. The lunch crowd was still thin at this hour. They found a table in the corner and sat down. The waitress was a tiny woman, with a face like a dried apple, and gray hair that frizzed in every direction no matter how tightly she tried to pin it in place. "What can I get you boys?

Dylan asked, "What's the special?"

"Hot turkey sandwiches with mashed potatoes and cranberries."

That was fine for all of them. Gert returned with the food, Dylan thanked her and continued. "Sheriff Dryden said you could fix us some box lunches. Any chance we can get eight lunches with turkey sandwiches with cranberries on the bread instead of butter. What else can you pack for us?"

"There's a sheet cake in the kitchen. I can wrap some of that for you."

"Is it frosted?"

"Of course. Chocolate cake with chocolate frosting."

"In which case put two pieces in each box. We'll pay for everything of course. You don't have to put it on account. Do you know if Sheriff Dryden has sent lunch over to the prisoners yet?"

"No. He said you'd take care of it."

"What did you send for breakfast?"

"Oatmeal. It came back mostly uneaten."

"In which case could you send a tray over to the jail with four specials please. And put a bowl of extra gravy on one of the trays."

"Yes sir."

Michael was already eating. "How come we never have hot turkey sandwiches at home?"

Dylan had to swallow before he could answer. "Because when they cook turkey, it's usually all gone and there's only enough left over for the soup pot."

They had almost finished their meal when Gert returned with a stack of white boxes, setting them on the table. "The kitchen boy took trays over to the jail. He said the two ladies dug right into it. Sammy didn't pay no attention to the men."

"Thank you Gert. Is there any more of that cake in the kitchen?"

"Enough for you each to have a slice."

"Good. Let's have it, and some coffee. Then we'll get out of your hair."

Mike stopped her. "Excuse me. Is your coffee any better than the stuff at the Sheriff's office?" He'd been drinking it for the past twelve hours.

"Well you can't use it to grease an axle like the stuff Bill makes, if that's what you mean."

"In which case, by all means bring us four coffees."

The cake wasn't as good as Katy's, but the coffee was considerably better than the sheriff's. Dylan paid for their food, gave Gert a whole dollar tip, which he had to remember to put on his expense account, and they headed back across the street to collect their prisoners.

*****

Sophia had spent the last hour trying to get her pyramid assembled before Gerhardt returned home. He had told her he had business in Washington and was taking the train over for the day. She was having a problem figuring out what went where because the directions were all in German. She finally put everything on the sideboard in a pile. She'd wanted to surprise him with it. He'd have to assemble his own surprise.

Instead, she went to the kitchen. Since she couldn't manage his pyramid, she could at least make the cookies. She'd found a special stamp at Thiebes, and had been given a recipe by *Frau* Thiebes.. Now she was determined to make *Spekulatius*.

The stamp she had looked to her like Santa Klaus. Mrs. Thiebes had told her he was *"Der Weihnachtsmann"*, Father Christmas. She had all the spices she'd need. Now it was a matter of mixing everything up and rolling them out. She pinched off a corner of the dough and tasted it. It was good raw so it would be even better baked.

She was taking the last pan out of the oven when she heard his key in the front door. Normally she would have hurried to meet him. The cookies wouldn't permit it. They had to be removed from the sheet while they were right out of the oven or they'd stick. She grabbed her spatula and began the delicate process. "I'm in the kitchen."

Gerhardt Weissmann, or Til Gerhardt, or Marcel Duprey, depending on his persona at the time, came in wearing his winter coat, blowing on his hands to warm them. "Something smells interesting."

"I got the recipe from Mrs. Thiebes." She handed him a cooled cookie. "Tell me if they taste right."

Before he bit, he examined his prize. "Father Christmas! I haven't had one of these in years." He bit the cookie in half, careful to catch the crumbs. "And you made these?"

"I did. Are they all right?"

"I'm not sure. I'll have to eat ten or twelve more to make sure."

She threw her arms around his neck. "I was so worried. I wanted everything to be perfect."

He returned her hug, then started to pull off his winter coat.

"Once you get your coat hung up I have something else for you. I wanted to surprise you and put it together but I can't." She took his hand and pulled him into the music room, then turned on the light.

He took in the pile of wood, the box of candles and the sheet of paper. "A *Weihnachtspyramide*! Another find at Thiebes?"

"Of course. I never heard of these before. It was so pretty and so cheap I felt guilty leaving it in the store."

"But you can't put it together?"

"I could if I could read the instructions. But I can't read German. Do you mind building it?"

"How long until supper?"

"Depends. Is pea soup all right for supper?"

"Of course."

"Then about an hour. Will that give you enough time?"

"This is..." He started separating parts of the carousel. "Four levels and the top?"

"It is."

"Then it should be just enough time." He took her in his arms again. "Thank you. I haven't had Christmas since I left home. My *Oma* always made sure we had a tree and presents, no matter how small. Since then, I haven't had anyone to share it with."

"I didn't know about a tree. My granny used to put magnolia branches up on the mantle, but we never had a tree. Even if I did know where to get one I couldn't have brought it home."

"Would you like a tree *liebchen?*"

She shook her head. "We don't have anything to decorate it with, and Thiebes' last day was yesterday. I don't know where else to buy things."

"This is more than enough."

"Now, let me go fix your supper or we'll be sitting down at midnight."

She pulled away after giving him one more quick kiss on the cheek, and hurried to the kitchen to throw the ingredients into a pot. She was thankful that split peas cooked so fast.

Just as she was putting food on the table Gerhart sauntered into the kitchen folding the instructions. He put the paper in a kitchen drawer, washed his hands and stood behind his chair.

"I suppose you're done."

"I am. Is supper ready?"

"It is. And if you sit down we can eat."

"Not yet. I want you to see." He took Sophia by the hand and pulled her into the music room. The electric lights had been turned off, the room illuminated by the five candles. The heat from the candles turned the blades on top, propelling the four levels, some clockwise, some counter-clockwise, depending on how the gears were set.

Sophia clapped her hands like a little girl. "Oh, Gerhardt! It's wonderful. How'd you make them go in different directions?"

"There's gears inside like clockworks. Depending on how it's put together, they can all turn the same way, or alternate. Now, can we go sit down and eat?"

"This was your idea," she giggled. "Come on. Before the soup gets cold."

*****

Dylan and Michael brought Manny Levy home with them when they returned on Tuesday. Lunch service was over, the front door was locked, and clean up was underway. Katy looked up from where she was cleaning the stove. She shoved three men aside to get to her husband.

"Took you long enough," Millie told Dylan from where she stood in the doorway to the bakery. "I thought it was an overnight trip."

"We forgot it was overnight each way."

Millie started across the kitchen, wiping her hands on her apron. "Some detectives you are. Send you to pick up some prisoners and you wind up getting lost on the way home."

Dylan had had about enough of her sass. He grabbed her then, not caring who else was in the kitchen.

Ribiero was watching the scene unfold. "Manny, get yourself some coffee. Annie, this is Manny Levy. You have any idea where my wife is?"

"Up in Millie's with Benito. She's been here since you left."

"Good. I'll be back."

He took the stairs two at the time until he reached the third floor. Tomás opened the door to the flat quietly, and walked down the hall to the guest room Maria used. He found her sitting in a rocking chair Dylan had apparently moved from the nursery. Benito had fallen asleep in her arms, and Maria had dozed off herself.

Tomás slipped into the room and put one arm under his son, and the other across the back of the chair. "*Querida*, I'm home."

Maria mumbled something that sounded like his name, and slid down further into the upholstered rocker.

Tomás tried to take Benito from her arms, but her hold tightened just enough. "Maria. Wake up. It's time to go home."

She mumbled something else and turned her face toward him. Tomás knew the moment when she realized he wasn't dreaming. "You're home," Maria said, sleepily.

"I am. And it's time for us to go home."

"Not yet. Wait until after supper."

"I wasn't thinking about food. I've been away for a week, *querida*."

"I know. They're going to be another hour cleaning up downstairs. The girls are down at Katy's."

"What are you saying?"

"I'm saying put your son in his basket and close the door. We've got plenty of time."

*****

The Christmas Recital performed by the students of the Marcel Duprey Conservatory went well. It had finally been decided they would perform on Christmas Eve.

Maestro Duprey had been in contact with some of the instructors at Peabody. Two faculty representatives had attended specifically to hear Barton Watterman's transcription of Cherubino's aria, which was the finale to the children's performance.

Both Barton and Isaac were offered scholarships to the prestigious Conservatory on Charles Street as soon as they finished high school. The violin master further agreed the school would fund additional classes in theory for Barton with his beloved *Maestro*.

All in all it was a good day, and had earned their little school two more students.

When everyone was gone and the tea cups and cake plates washed and put away, Gerhardt pulled Sophia into the music room and lit the pyramid. He had her sit in the chair he used to listen to his pupils and ran upstairs. The look on his face when he returned with a package wrapped in brown paper reminded Sophia of a little boy.

"Liebchen, I wanted you to have this tonight."

She felt tears in the corners of her eyes. She hadn't had a real present since she was a little girl. That was when an orange or a few pecans were a prize. "Open the door under the sideboard. There's something for you, too."

Gerhardt fetched her offering from the sideboard, likewise wrapped in brown paper. He sat on the end of the piano bench. "Shall we open them together?"

She nodded, and the two began ripping paper. "Gerhardt! This is beautiful." He had given her a beautiful Persian lamb coat with mouton collar and cuffs. Sophia rubbed the soft honey colored fur against her cheek.

He held up what had been his own gift. "Sealskin? With sable? *Liebchen*, this is far too much." He sat on the arm of the chair where she sat. "How did you ever find this?"

"From deGroot's back room. Remember, I picked this parcel up for you? I didn't know what it was, but I knew I wanted to get you something nice. Now, you know it's not polite to discuss the price of a gift."

"I know. But I know how much deGroot wanted for those furs."

"Then you should also know I never pay full price." She smiled sweetly at him. "I'd wager the old Dutchman charged you almost retail for my coat. Not that I'm complaining. I love it. But I've known him longer than you have. Try it on. If it doesn't fit, he has three more in the back room."

"You try yours on too."

They both stood and pulled on their coats. Gerhardt reached and fluffed her collar around her face. "Lovely. I'd like to have your photograph made in that coat."

She shook her head, the Christmas spell suddenly broken. "No. No photographs. Not now. Not ever."

Gerhardt reached for her, but she evaded his arms. "*Liebchen*, tell me what's wrong?"

"My husband, Rory. He took pictures. Photographs of me in my underclothes. Of other women, of men with women, of men with boys. He was selling them. It became an obsession with him. It's what got him caught and hanged."

"I'm sorry Sophia. I never knew." This time she went to his arms willingly. "I'll never bring up the subject again."

"But I do love my coat. And I must say, you look very suave and dignified in yours. Quite befitting the *maestro* of an up and coming conservatory of music."

*****

Rose sat on the edge of the bed, watching her husband pack his bag. She was determined she was not going to weep in his presence. Once he was gone, she fully intended to lie on their bed and cry until she was all cried out. But for now, she'd be brave.

"Tadhg, why don't they let you fly to France?"

"Because it's too far. No one has flown that great a distance yet, and none of the aeroplanes we have can do it. So we get on a boat in Quebec, dodge some German submarines, and eventually land in Normandy."

"German submarines? No one ever said anything about submarines." Maybe her promise to herself had been premature.

He sat beside her. "Don't you remember when they sank the *Lusitania*?"

She nodded.

"That was a submarine. They hunt in a wolf pack. We'll be traveling on a hospital ship, so we should be safe."

"How can you get from here to France on a hospital ship? We're not in the war yet."

"All right. We're taking a supply ship to Liverpool. Then we board a hospital ship and sail on that into Normandy."

"Tadhg, they sink hospital ships all the time and apologize after. I don't want to receive an apology from the French ministry of defense telling me you were blown up by mistake."

He put his arm around her, trying to jolly her out of her depression. "Would it be better if they told you it wasn't a mistake?"

The last thing she wanted to do was to fight with her husband today, when he was leaving in a few hours. "The only message I want to get is telling me when you'll be coming home."

"Would you object to getting a message that I'll be getting a medal?" He whispered it in her ear, trying to make the possibility sound seductive.

"So long as it's not being awarded posthumously."

He checked the time. "You know, I don't have to leave for another hour yet. And I'm done packing."

"Mm-hmm." She tilted her head back. "Did you have anything special in mind?

*****

Millie and Dylan drove Tadhg and Rose to catch the late train that would eventually get them to Montreal. The three flyers were already waiting at the depot for them. Genet had a small notebook filled with girls' names and addresses, including three who worked at *Zofia's Cakes and Tarts*. Tadhg and the three Lieutenants had had their photographs made by Robert Morrison, who had provided each of them with a collection of cabinet cards. Those would be handed out to all interested ladies at the drop of a hanky.

Millie handed out box lunches to the lieutenants. "Katy made these up. I hope you like fried chicken."

The box lunches earned Millie a kiss on the cheek from each of the three men. Dylan shook hands with the men. They grabbed up their duffles and moved to the front of the platform as the train was pulling in.

Tadhg kept Rose back as long as he could, holding each other. The B&O train ground to a stop, and the conductor began calling for passengers to board., Tadhg moved her slowly across the platform to where Millie and Dylan stood.

"You promise you'll come back?"

"You promise you'll be here when I come home?"

Dylan cleared his throat to get their attention. "We'll take care of her."

Aspirant Tadhg Nagel lifted his wife clear off her feet, kissing her one last time. He shook Dylan's hand, hugged Millie, getting his own kiss on the cheek from her, grabbed his duffle and climbed on the train.

Rose still didn't cry. Her handkerchief was in her hand, but she bravely managed to hold back the flow. Millie had made no such pledge, and let her tears flow freely. Dylan put his arm around his wife, but it didn't do any good.

Nagel and the three lieutenants were the only men in uniform on the train. They had seats by the window facing the platform, and waved wildly as the engine started forward with a jerk.

Rose waved with her handkerchief until their car was out of sight. That was when she let everything go and collapsed into Dylan's arms.

Her sobs slowed and asked if she wanted to go home. "Can we go somewhere else first?"

"Where, sweetie?"

"I don't know. I just don't want to go home."

Dylan checked his watch. "It's not quite nine. Would you like to go get a drink? Kelly's had a lady's entrance."

She shook her head. "I'm just being silly, I guess. Let's go home. But do you mind if I come up and stay in your spare room tonight?"

Millie nudged her. "Rhys is in there. You want to share with him?"

That made Rose giggle, then hiccough. "You think Katy would mind if I used her spare room?"

"No. Not at all. Or you can go down to your own flat and have the girls over. Tomorrow's Sunday. You can sit up and drink cocoa all night and cry and laugh and I can even sneak you down a bottle of Dylan's whiskey if you want."

She hiccoughed again. "I like that idea. Do you and Katy want to come down too?"

"Would you want us to?"

She nodded.

"Then we'll come down. Dylan, me darlin', take us home."

"Yes, dear."

Rose went right to the girls' quarters when they got home. She knocked on their door, and when Inga answered, told them they were all to come to hers to drink hot chocolate, eat Christmas candy, and talk. Only Inga accepted. The other girls claimed they were too tired. Rose thought they didn't want to be around the weeping grass widow tonight.

Inga wore her nightgown and robe and brought the box of fudge Millie had given her. Each girl had received a box of candy from Millie for Christmas: fudge, divinity, candied nuts. Katy had crocheted each girl a collar to wear with their work dress in the dining room. The employees had all pooled together and given their employers some new piano rolls.

They had just gotten settled on sitting in the middle of Rose's bed when Katy and Millie came in. Katy carried a quart of milk, sugar and cocoa, while Millie carried half a bottle of Dylan's good whiskey.

Katy lit the stove and put the milk on to heat while she mixed the cocoa and sugar with a little water. Millie got down four cups and poured a shot of liquor into each cup. As soon as the cocoa was ready Katy added it to the cups.

For the next two hours, Rose and Inga discussed keeping company with police officers. Johnny Allen had been paying attention to Inga since Thanksgiving, and the poor girl was in a dither about it. She'd walked out with Tadhg a few times when Thomas Mulalley or Alex Collins had taken Rose to a dance, but now Johnny was coming around every weekend. She didn't know what to make of it.

Millie and Katy tried to offer what advice they could, but it was limited, given their diversity of history and their lack of real courtships. Rose asked Millie, "When do you get used to them going off like this?"

"You mean like when Tadhg went to Aberdeen or Dylan went to Washington or Delaware?"

"I do. When do you get used to it?"

"I'll let you know when it happens. I hate it. But I put up with it."

"Why? It's so hard."

"I know, honey. It's damned near impossible." Millie reached over and took a piece of Inga's fudge. "I hate it. Every time he gets on that train or has to go anywhere but to the office I almost panic, particularly since he got hurt in West Virginia. But I don't say anything because it's his job, and because he loves it so."

Katy said, "Didn't you see how we acted when they were all in Delaware? Michael and Tomás were there for over a week and Dylan went with Officer Levy for three days. Maria came to stay and we all worked ourselves to death the whole time they were gone. Didn't you notice how many times I cleaned the stove?"

Rose shook her head. "I'm sorry. I didn't notice."

Inga told her, "Of course you didn't notice. You and Tadhg were too busy down here every night to see what was going on upstairs."

That made Rose blush and made the other three giggle. Katy got up to get some more cocoa and brought back the whiskey along with the pan. "So you've got an excuse. Let me ask you this: How did you deal with Tadhg going up in that aeroplane every Sundays?"

"I said a lot of rosaries."

"Exactly. That's all we can do. But why did you let him do it? You know, had you really objected, he wouldn't have gone."

"Because it was the most important thing in the world to him. And he would have eventually hated me if he couldn't go."

Millie took her hand. "And you love him too much to stop him, don't you?"

She nodded.

"When Dylan and I got married he was just a plain old detective. He made detective sergeant soon after. Same with Katy and Michael. Then Dylan got seconded to the Bureau. He got paid extra for that. It took a while, but last year the BoI decided to put on more agents. Dylan was able to get on. His salary almost doubled then. Not only does he love what he does, it makes him feel better seeing our bank balance go up every month."

"How come?" Inga hadn't been around long enough to understand the workings of their extended family unit.

"Dylan can explain it better than I can since he's keeping the books now. Breakfast pays for all the meat and supplies we need. Lunch pays for your salaries and taxes. The tea room and supper service are profit. Of course, that profit is what our families need to live on. But they bank their salaries every month for emergencies, or whatever. Does that make sense?"

"Millie, how come you pay us so much?" Rose had always wondered.

"You mean why do you earn twice what you'd

make working in a sweater sewing shirtwaists?"

She nodded.

"Because we both understand what it's like to not be able to earn enough money to live. I was fourteen and working in a sweater. I made a dollar a day. I could either eat or pay the rent. I couldn't do both. When a rat-faced little man offered me an ice cream, I went gladly. That's how I wound up working in a hot-mattress joint. Katy's story is pretty much the same. We both swore we'd never be responsible for another woman having to make that choice."

"But you let us live here." Inga still didn't understand everything. "You could charge us rent.

"It's to our benefit that you're here, Inga. If our employees are late it makes it almost impossible to run our business. Tommie and Annie still live in their rooming house. I wonder if Johnny would mind walking them to work in the morning?"

"He can't Miss Millie. He lives too far away."

"For now."

"What do you mean?"

"Oh, I wouldn't be surprised if Sergeant Johnny Allen decided he really needed to find a room over on this side of town."

"You think so?" That seemed to excite Inga.

"Maybe. But if you want to see him, you'll need to get somebody to walk out with Siofre or Marguerite to go with you. Unless you want your granny to chaperone."

That made Inga laugh. "Lord no. *Grossmutter* wouldn't approve at all. She'd say he was too Irish to be respectable." They all giggled, and Inga asked, "Can't Rhys walk out with Siofre or even Frances?"

"I don't think so, honey," Millie told her. "He's corresponding with Lucy Goodheart in Hagerstown. He has a bad case of teenage looooooooove."

"How does Miss Goodheart feel about him?"

"Well, I think she might like him better if he knew Morse code. She wants to be a telegrapher."

"Can ladies do that?"

"If they're trained. Her guardian has been teaching her for the past two years. By the time she's out of school she'll be as good as anybody at Western Union."

Chapter Eleven

January 31, 1916
Somewhere in France

My dearest Rose,

We arrived, reasonably safe and sound, although Genet spent most of the trip leaning over the rail. It didn't help that the other passengers aboard were primarily equine, and our quarters were attached to the hold where they were kept.

Someone hadn't checked the animals before they're loaded. We had an outbreak of glanders. I had to go with the mate and separate out the infected horses, help him shoot the animals and throw their carcasses overboard. I hope that's the worst job I ever have to perform.

So far the other difficult thing I've had to do is learn French. I thought Irish used a lot of letters we don't pronounce. At least there are rules about it. French puts the letters in a sack, shakes them up, and you say about a quarter of the ones that fall out.

I'm still training. I can't tell you much because we're not allowed to. But I have been flying some and helping deliver new aeroplanes to different bases.

Lieutenant Prince is hollering for me, so I'd best get this in the post before we have to go up again. Please write to me. My address is on the outside of this letter.

[The remaining three lines had been cut out with a razor]

Tadhg

"Millie look! I got my letter!" Rose ran into the kitchen, almost falling when her feet hit a wet spot on the linoleum.

Millie grabbed her before her butt hit the floor. "Careful. I sloshed soapy water there. Now sit down and read it if you can."

"What do you mean, if I can? I can read."

"I mean maybe there are some personal things you don't want us to hear?" She grinned at her friend.

"I don't know if there was or not. Somebody cut a big chunk out of the paper with a razor

"The army must censor the letters."

"I don't know why."

"Ask Tom when he comes over. He might know."

Rose spread the paper out on the table and waited until the other women in the store had gathered around. Thenshe read the letter aloud. She didn't know if she should be upset that there wasn't anything she couldn't share with them.

"Well, that's it other than this gaping hole at the bottom." She held the paper up so everyone could see.

None of the other young women had heard from

the three lieutenants. Only Hannah was upset. She'd spent several pleasant evenings with Lieutenant Prince, and had hoped he'd write to her. Now that Rose had Tadhg's address she knew they were still stationed together. Perhaps she could write to him first. She'd have to ask Rose.

Tomás came by to collect his wife and son. Rose caught him when he arrived and showed him her husband's letter. "Any idea why someone would do this?"

He made her sit at the table. "I'm pretty sure I know why. Tadhg wanted to tell you something personal, something he didn't want anyone else to read. He wrote it in...is it Gaellic or Irish?"

"Irish. Because Gaellic has about ten different flavors"

"He wrote it in the Irish language, so the censor cut it thinking it was some sort of code."

"At least I know he wrote it, even if I don't know what it said. I couldn't have read it anyway. Not all of it anyway. And I don't think I could ask Dylan or Mike to read it to me."

"I thought you'd be able to."

She shook her head. "I was born here. A lot of people from Ireland can't speak it either. The English did a pretty good job of wiping out the language in the last hundred years."

"So write to him. Send him some fudge or something. If you want to tell him anything really...personal, put it on the papers you wrap the candy pieces in."

"Tomás, isn't that espionage?" She was grinning when she said it.

"Probably. But since you were born here you can't be counted an enemy alien. Just make sure you write it in English. Remember, the Germans are sending arms into Ireland every day. If the censor doesn't read the language he could automatically cut out anything in a possible a suspect language."

Rose grabbed her letter and gave her friend a quick kiss on the cheek. "Thank you. Now I've got to find Katy's fudge recipe."

"Ask Maria if you can't find her. She makes it too."

*****

Royce Allardyce sat in his office at the Baltimore City Courthouse reviewing his file regarding Larry Wardworth.

The primary case was federal including multiple violations of the Mann Act. For some reason known only to God and the Attorney General of the United States Allardyce had been handed the initial trial of this Larry Wardworth.

The victim in this case was Inga Rottmann. Allardyce flipped through the reports. Good. He already had a deposition from Officer Tadhg Nagel. Sean Kelly was one of the arresting officers who would testify. Then there was this Rose O'Donovan. It looked like Rose lived at the same place as Officer Nagel. That could be questioned in court. He needed to talk to her first, and find out what the real story was.

He used the intercom to tell his secretary he was heading to Highlandtown.

An hour later Assistant State's Attorney Royce Allardyce pushed open the front door of *Zofia's Cakes and Tarts*. Lunch service was underway. Millie spotted him first.

"Mr. Allardyce! You're the last person I expected to see darken our door. Come in, please. Are you here to eat or on business?"

He looked at his folder. "I need to speak to Miss Rose O'Donovan. Is she around?"

"She is. Follow me." She told Renata she was going to the dining room, and led Allardyce through. She spotted Rose and gestured to her. "Rose, this is Mr. Allardyce. He's the Assistant State's Attorney. He needs to talk to you about a case he's handling."

Rose had been expecting this. "Do you need to see Inga too?"

"Miss Rottmann?"

"Yes sir. She's in the kitchen. I can get her."

"Let me talk to you first. Can we sit down somewhere we can talk?"

It was early yet, so the department dining room hadn't filled up. "Come through here. This is the police officers' dining room. It's early yet for them." She gestured for him to sit and she sat opposite.

He flipped his file open. "I know Officer Nagel is in France now, and we have his deposition. This was his address. But it's also your address. Were you two living... without benefit of clergy?"

Rose didn't know whose face was redder, hers or his. "No sir. Never. Mrs. Shay and Mrs. Dougherty set up dormitories downstairs. Two separate entrances, locks on the inside and everything. Ladies on one side, men on the other. I lived in the female dormitory with five other girls. Tadhg shared with three other men. There was never any mingling unless we were properly chaperoned.

"Tadhg and I were married before Thanksgiving. The Shays and the Doughertys converted the men's dormitory into a small flat for us."

"So where are the other men sleeping now?"

"Two of them went to Boston for work. The other one is Mr. Shay's brother Rhys. He's sleeping in their spare bedroom."

This was very interesting. He scribbled down some quick notes so he could bring this up on the stand. "So how did you and Officer Nagel happen to save Miss Rottmann?"

"Inga started working here after she got fired from Read's. Her grandmother called here looking for her when she didn't come home one night. She had been attending service at the Angelic Tabernacle on Fait Street. I was afraid she had decided to stay with them. Tadhg and I went over to the storefront. On the way he called Sean Kelly because he was sure they might need to make some arrests. We sat down in the church part, really the front of the house. I could see Inga sitting behind a curtain, staring into space. Tadhg said I should to pretend to be sick. He hustled me through to the kitchen and out to the outhouse. Mr. Kelly and his officers showed up and they raided the place. Inga had been drugged almost to death. We brought her back here and called the doctor. After she recovered she wouldn't go home because her granny wouldn't have let her out of the house. So she moved into the rooms downstairs."

"You know we're going to have to put you on the witness stand." It was a statement.

"Yes, sir. Tadhg already told me."

"I don't know who Mr. Wardworth retained as his attorney. But I expect he'll try to make you and Miss Rottmann sound like loose women. Do you think you can stand it?"

"Mr. Allardyce, my husband is in France right now, fighting for a country that isn't even his because it's the right thing to do. I know I've done nothing wrong. I know what those people did was not just wrong, but illegal. And they should be punished."

He was smiling, but he still had to ask. "Very good, Mrs. Nagel. But can you stand up to a man asking you how many men you've taken to your bed? How much you charge for your favors? How many other inmates are in this abbey?"

"I also know the history of my employers, Mr. Allardyce. Some of the girls here were...uh...in the oldest profession at one time. I can assure you, none of that goes on here. From the day Tadhg proposed to me, he and I were no longer allowed to live in close proximity. I was moved upstairs to the Shay's spare room. When Special Agent Ribiero and Maria became engaged, she slept in the Shay's flat, and he slept at the Dougherty's. The ladies are very careful of our reputations, simply for the reason they know how easily small-minded people can get the wrong idea."

"Very good, Mrs. Nagel. Now, if you can send Miss Rottmann out to me you may return to your duties."

"Would you mind if I stayed? Inga is very nervous around men since this happened."

He groaned inwardly. All he needed was a witness who was scared of men. "Surely. I'll wait while you get her."

Rose disappeared into the kitchen and returned with Inga, holding her by the hand. Both girls sat at the table but Inga couldn't quite meet his gaze. Rose made the introductions. "Inga, this is Mr. Royce Allardyce. He's the attorney who's going to put Larry Wardworth in jail. Mr. Allardyce, this is Inga Rottmann."

"Hello Inga."

She mumbled something. Rose told her, "Inga, you have to speak up. Nobody's going to eat you."

"Hello."

"Miss Rottmann, I don't know if anyone told you. When I take Mr. Wardworth into court I'll need you to testify about what happened to you in that phony church. Can you do it?"

She shook her head.

"Inga, if you don't testify, I can't send him to jail."

"Rose can tell."

Her friend squeezed the hand she still held. "Honey, I saw you sitting in the back of the church. I don't have any idea what happened to you or how long you sat back there."

"Mr. Allardyce, may I have someone in the courtroom with me?"

"So long as they're not a witness. See, witnesses aren't allowed in the courtroom until after they testify. Mrs. Nagel has to testify. Who did you have in mind?"

She whispered, "Sergeant Johnny Allen."

Allardyce looked at Rose. "He's a mounted officer. He worked with my husband. The two of them were sent to College Park for the airshow a few months ago."

The attorney scribbled down the name. "I'll speak with the captain and make sure he's there."

He went through what Inga had experienced. Finally he had one last question. "Miss Rottmann, I don't know what attorney will be retained. But I suspect he'll ask some questions intended to make you angry or to make you cry. I'd like to ask you these questions now so you'll know what's coming. Is that all right?"

She nodded.

"Miss Rottmann. What kind of name is that?"

"What do you mean, what kind of name?"

He smiled. She had her back up straight away. Anger was better than tears. "I mean is it German, Dutch, English, what?"

"Oh, it's German."

"So you're German."

"No sir. I'm American."

"You just said your name was German."

"My grandmother was from Germany. My father was born in this country. I was born in this country."

"What about your mother?"

"No sir. She was born in France."

"Do you speak German?"

She nodded. "Yes sir. Because I want to talk to my grandmother and she doesn't have much English."

"So you speak German. You're from a German family. But you profess to be American."

"I don't profess anything. I can show you my birth certificate. I was christened at St. Aloysius downtown.'

Allardyce was very happy with her answers. "Now at this point, I'll be jumping up and objecting, and the judge will tell you whether you have to answer any more questions of that sort. Now, I've already talked to Mrs. Nagel about this. Do you know about how your employers used to earn their living?"

"Yes sir."

"You know the lawyer could ask you if you have ever earned your living the same way. Do you think you can do that?"

"I've never done anything like that."

"I didn't say you had. But they will ask. They will imply you offered your services to Larry Wardworth."

"Is that why he gave me lemonade that tasted like old socks? Why he kept pouring it into me for more than a day, while I sat in a chair and soiled myself because I was too drugged to even know I had to go to the necessary?"

"Very good Miss Rottmann. So you were sitting in that kitchen for more than a day?"

"Yes sir. I think it was Thursday when I went to service. And it was Saturday when Rose and Tadhg found me. It took almost a week for me to recover."

"Why so long?"

"Dr. Marsh said it was because I was...what was the word she used...overdosed. He gave me so much laudanum that it could have killed me. I was lucky I survived, and I did only because I vomited after the third glass. It's almost a miracle I wasn't left a blithering idiot. You can get my record from Dr. Marsh. Her office is on St. Paul Street I think. Or maybe Cathedral. I've never been to her office."

"Do you know if anyone interfered with you while you were drugged?"

"I remember seeing people moving around me. I could see and hear everything that was said. I just couldn't respond. I think one of the men wanted to, but Sister Gabrielle wouldn't let him. She said I wouldn't be as valuable if I wasn't 'fresh'. I wanted to scream and beat them with bricks and run away. But I couldn't move."

"And you know it was Larry Wardworth who gave you that lemonade?"

"Yes sir. The three men there all dressed the same. But Wardworth, he was the one who played the piano. His teeth were broken in the front, and at least one was missing."

"I understand that when they were arrested the first time the men were dressed like tramps. Now they wear suits. Will that make a difference in your identification?"

"Not once he opens his mouth. His teeth will give him away."

"Who took care of you while you recovered?"

"My grandmother and Frances Murray. Sometimes Rose or Siofre Quinn. Everybody but my granny lives here."

"Very good. We're set to go to trial on the twenty-eighth of February. I expect it to take a week. Once you have testified you'll be excused, but you may return to watch any other day."

"Do I have to decide now?"

"No. I do need to get you a subpoena to make it official."

Inga told him, "I don't need one."

"I don't either," said Rose.

"You may not. But the rules say I have to. And if I don't play by the rules I lose the case. I won't lose this case. But I may just give them to Sergeant Allen to bring to you."

Inga smiled. "That's fine." She looked around. The dining room was beginning to fill up. "Mr. Allardyce, can I bring you some lunch?"

"Maybe I should move." Before either young woman could answer, Brendan MacCartland, Chief of Detectives, spotted him. "Royce! Are you dining with us today?"

"Apparently." He glanced at the two servers. "Won't you join me, Chief?"

MacCartland pulled out a chair and sat. "What are the specials, ladies?"

"Boxty with bacon and cabbage, cottage pie, gravy and biscuits. Poached eggs with any of it."

"Boxty with bacon, cabbage and a couple of eggs. And Brown Betty for dessert. What're you having, Royce?"

The State's Attorney was amazed at the selection. "What else is for dessert?"

"Apple cake or crumb cake." Inga was very happy to serve both men. "What can I get you, Mr. Allardyce?"

"Cottage pie and Brown Betty. With a lot of coffee."

"Yes sir. I'll have it right out."

Rose and Inga disappeared into the kitchen.

*****

"Good afternoon, Barton. Did you bring your music?" *Maestro* Duprey was always happy to see one of his two best pupils.

He pulled his manuscript sheets from his book bag. "Yes, sir. But Isaac's voice is changing. I don't know how much more I can write until he's done."

"Just keep writing. If he can't perform it, we'll find someone else. Meanwhile, start writing for the tenor range, and for baritone if you want to try."

"Are you sure, *Maestro?*"

"Yes, Barton. I'm sure. Now, you never told me. Do you have a piano in your house?"

"Yes, sir. My sister is trying to play but she's only had a few lessons at school."

"How old is your sister?"

"Nine."

"Is she any good?"

"She listens to music people play on their Gramophones, then she picks it out on the keys. But she can't read music."

"We'll fix that. Bring her with you Thursday. And you tell your mother her lessons will be added in with yours, and the Peabody will be paying for them."

"Really, *Maestro?*"

"Really Barton. Now, let's see what you've done." He took the music from the boy and studied it. "This is your own composition? Not just a transcription?"

The boy was grinning at his teacher. "Remember how we talked about the tocatto and fugues, and how Bach took a theme and inverted it? I took an old song, *Baggage Coach Ahead*, and broke it down into parts, inverted it, played it sideways, and twisted it all around. But if you listen, you can still hear the original song."

"Have you ever played piano?"

"Some, but not much."

"Sit down and play this for me." He handed Barton back his own music.

"I don't know if I can."

"Find me Middle C."

The boy hit the right key.

"Now put your right thumb there. Everything else falls into place. If you expect to write for the piano, you really should know how to play. We'll get on with your violin shortly. But play this for me."

Barton played a few experimental chords. "*Maestro,* our piano isn't nearly as fine as this."

"There's no difference in how it works. Just try it."

Barton played. For his first real composition, he did extremely well. Duprey stood behind the bench and watched as he played the notes on the paper.

"Barton, do you have the original song written out?"

"Yes sir." The boy ran to his bookbag and took out the sheet music.

"*Madame* Gareau! Come here please."

Sylviane hurried in from the kitchen. "Yes, *Maestro?*"

"Will you set this up for me on a stand please?"

She fetched a collapsible music stand from the corner and set it up, then put the music on it. It was the work of a minute. She could tell by the way he was studying the page it was a piece with which he was unfamiliar.

"Barton, would you start over please?"

As Barton played his invention, Marcel Duprey played the tune on his violin. He noticed Sylviane was mouthing the words as he played. He wouldn't ask her to sing in front of the boy . He knew she was sensitive about her voice and would never sing in his presence, although he knew her voice to be quite pleasant.

When they finished playing the piece through,

Duprey looked up at Sylviane again. He couldn't help but notice the lone tear that ran down her cheek. "Barton, excuse us for a minute please. Get out your violin, tune it, and play through the Cherubino transcription."

Duprey pulled Sylviane into the kitchen and took her in his arms. "What's wrong, *liebchen*?" he whispered in her ear.

"It's that song. *Baggage Coach Ahead.* Did you read the words? *While the train rolled onward, the husband sat in tears. Thinking of the happiness of just a few short years. But baby's face brings pictures of the cherished hope that's dead. For baby's cries can't waken her in the baggage coach ahead.*"

"I'm sorry. I never would have had you sit in."

She shook her head. "It's not your fault. I'm just a foolish woman, and sometimes songs make my eyes leak." Her watery smile made him hug her one more time.

"I have to get back to my pupil. But if you feel...leaky again, you tell me, all right?"

She nodded. "It doesn't happen often. Music excites me more than it makes me weepy."

"What music excites you, *liebchen?*"

"Oh, some of the arias from *Don Giovanni.*"

"Which ones?"

"*La ci darem la mano.* The Catalogue song. I know they're foolish. But I do love to hear a baritone or bass. And I know Giovanni was a rotter. But when he starts to sing, it just makes everything melt inside."

"I'll have to remember that." She started giggling when she realized he was humming the song Giovanni sang to seduce Zerlina.

*****

February 29, 1916

Zofia's Cakes and Tarts
Baltimore and Luzerne

Dearest Tadhg,

Inga and I testified for Mr. Allardyce today against that Larry Wardworth. You would have been so proud of Inga. I had to testify first. Mr. Allardyce was so nice. He had me tell the story. Then the other attorney had his turn. He was just so mean. But Mr. Allardyce objected, then Judge Stovall wouldn't let him be mean any more.

Inga went next, and I was able to sit in the courtroom with her. Johnny Allen sat in the front row and watched. Having him there gave Inga courage, I think. She told him everything that happened. Just like Mr. Allardyce said, the other attorney tried to make her out to be a little tart. She stood right up to him, and said he was a filthy minded little man. Judge Stovall told her she was out of order, but he still laughed. Then he told the lawyer that he wasn't allowed to ask a decent young woman those kinds of questions.

We got to hear some other girls testify, too. Inga wasn't the only girl he drugged. And that's just from Baltimore. Mr. Allardyce says he'll have to stand trial in Federal Court, too. I don't know what the difference is. Tom tried to explain it, but I still didn't understand.

Watch for a box of fudge in the post. I'll wrap the pieces individually so they don't get all squashed together.

Johnny says that The King is doing well, and loves having every other day off. Johnny did ride him in the parade for Washington's birthday. The King knew he was something special, dancing and prancing in front of all the other horses. Johnny said he'd like to teach him something called "dressing" or some such. I asked him what that was. He said it's when the horse dances and makes all sorts of fancy moves. I told him he'd best check with you first.

Inga and I are going back to court tomorrow. We really want to see what happens to Wardworth. So long as Millie and Katy can spare us, we want to go. Dylan and Tom said they'll take turns going with us. I wouldn't mind going with Inga alone, but she's still too scared.

Every letter you send has chunks cut out of them. I don't know what was so naughty. Tom thinks it might be because you said something really personal in the Irish. I'm afraid I'd have to have Dylan read it to me, so maybe that isn't a good idea.

Inga has moved into our flat for now. Somehow, sharing the bed with my best friend isn't the same as sleeping with my husband. And her feet are colder than mine.

Come home to me soon, my darling. We had so little time together.

Love,
Your Rose

Rose folded the letter and put it into the envelope. She'd already spent the extra money for postage stamps for France. Her original thought had been to enclose the letter in the box of fudge she was sending, but thought better of it. If the letter said she was sending fudge, maybe they wouldn't look. The candy was ready. Each piece was wrapped in a piece of the white paper Millie used in the bakery. On each small piece she wrote a personal note. Sometimes silly, sometimes a simple "I love you". She knew it was against the rules, but what was the worst that could happen? Someone else would get the candy?

Millie had given her a small bakery box. Rose put in the wrapped candy with a small PS, added on a card. *"Tell the three interchangeable Lieutenants they'd get their own boxes if they would write once in a while."* Hannah was dying to hear from one of them. She had been out with Genet, but at this point, Dylan was right. They were interchangeable.

The box got wrapped in brown paper, tied with string, and handed to the postman when he brought the morning mail. She knew Millie or Renata would see it went out. Rose made sure she left enough money to give him for the postage.

Inga was sitting in the small parlor in Rose's flat repairing the hem in her skirt.

"You know, Siofre gets paid to do that." Rose sat next to her on the settee.

"I know. But I'm the one who stepped on it and pulled it out. I figure I can fix it. Besides, I want to wear it again tomorrow. Have you seen the forecast in the paper?"

"According to the *News Post* it's going to be cold and sunny. According to the *Sun* it's going to snow."

"Fooey. And we have to go all the way downtown."

"You don't have to go, you know."

"I know."

"Tomás is going to drive us there in the Nash in the morning so we won't have to take the streetcar. And he'll bring us home after. We might have to sit in their office for a while, but that wouldn't be bad."

"Well, that's all right, then. What will we do about lunch? Johnny took us today. But what about tomorrow?"

"Either Tomás will take us somewhere to eat, or Dylan will carry lunch for everybody to eat at their office. Would you quit worrying about your stomach?"

"I'm just hungry all the time, and I don't know why."

"Didn't I see you upchuck this morning?"

"I don't know why. It's weird. Some mornings, I feel like I'm going to lose my breakfast, even before I have breakfast. Then the rest of the day, I can't stop eating."

Uh-oh. Rose wasn't going to say anything to Inga.

Not yet. But tomorrow she'd make sure she took Dylan aside and have a talk with him. And with Katy if she could catch her when she had a spare minute. She'd go now, but they were both already in their nightclothes and it was too dark to go upstairs this time of night.

Now Rose had to wonder who could possibly have gotten Inga in a family way. She knew it wasn't Wardworth. Inga's kidnapping was too long ago. The possibilities were Johnny Allen, one of the lieutenants or Rhys Shay. Unless there was somebody Rose didn't know about.

Just what they needed. An unwed mother in their little family. Dylan would make it right even if it involved a shotgun. What was bad was that Inga was so dumb she probably didn't know how she could have gotten that bun in the oven.

Rose went into the bedroom and looked at the alarm clock. It was only nine. She couldn't wait, and Millie and Dylan would still be up. "Inga, I have to run upstairs for a minute. Will you be all right?"

"Sure. Go ahead."

Rose pulled on her coat, headed outside and up the outside stairs to the third floor. She knocked on the kitchen door, hoping they could hear her without the necessity of waking up the entire neighborhood. Rhys answered it.

"Rose, what's wrong?"

"Is Dylan still up?"

"Sure. In the parlor. You need him out here?"

"Please?"

Rhys ran to fetch his brother. Dylan and Millie both hurried to the kitchen. Millie sat at the table. "What's wrong, Rose?"

Not waiting until she was invited, Rose pulled out a chair and sat opposite Millie. "I wanted to tell Dylan, but you need to know too. I'm pretty sure Inga's in a family way."

"Has she said anything?"

"No. But she's been nauseated in the morning, then eats like a horse the rest of the day. She came to stay with me when Tadhg left for France, but she hasn't gotten the curse once."

"You sure?"

Rose just gave her a look. "I'd know if the cloths in the bathroom were being used. I'm the only one who's used them."

"Any idea who could be responsible?"

"One of the three flyers, Johnny Allen or...Rhys."

Dylan groaned, then bellowed, "Rhys!" The boy came running. "Have you been playing slap and tickle with Inga?"

"Of course not. I mean, she's pretty enough. But I like smart girls. Inga's kinda...you know...dumb."

"Looks like I'll be talking to Sergeant Allen in the morning."

Millie put her hand on his arm. "Don't you think you should talk to Inga first?"

"No darlin'. I think you and Katy should talk to Inga. It's obvious her granny never did."

"I don't think either of you need to go to court tomorrow."

"Good. It's going to snow tomorrow anyway."

Chapter Twelve

The *Evening Sun* was right. When Inga and Rose went out the back door in the morning there was a thick coat of snow on the ground. It was getting close to time for the employees' breakfast in the first floor kitchen.

Inga had the dry heaves when she first got up. Rose had given her a cup of tea that seemed to settle her stomach. Now she seemed determined to eat her weight in groceries.

Millie and Katy were waiting for them. Katy grabbed the girls as soon as they came in. "Come upstairs for a few minutes. Tommie, you and Annie take over, please."

Up in Katy's kitchen, Dylan was sitting at the table nursing a cup of coffee.

"Are you taking us to court, Mr. Shay?" Inga asked.

"We're not going today. Didn't you see the snow? It's not good for you to be out in this weather."

"Okay." She seemed confused.

"Inga, I called Johnny Allen this morning before he reported to work."

"Yes, sir."

"Johnny said you two had been...intimate."

Inga looked around the table. "I don't know what you're talking about, Mr. Shay."

Millie held up her hand. "Inga, do you know where babies come from?"

"Of course, Missus Millie. Two people get married, then they have a baby. Is Rose having a baby?"

"No sweetie. Rose isn't having a baby. But we think you might be."

"How can I have a baby? I'm not married."

"Inga, it's not necessary to be married to have a baby. All that's required is that a man and a woman have relations."

She shook her head rapidly. Dylan was afraid she'd shake her brains loose. "No no no. *Grossmutter* says two people get married then they have a baby. That's all."

"I think maybe your granny was embarrassed. Trust me. I know."

Millie tried to help. "Inga, do you know how Dylan and I got Mary Faith?"

"You adopted her."

"That's right. Do you know who her parents are?"

She shook her head again.

"Her mother was a girl around twelve. Nobody knows for sure who her father was, just that he was one of her mother's customers. So trust me when I tell you. It is not necessary to be married to make a baby."

"But Missus Millie, we didn't sleep together."

The four other people seated around the table sighed in unison. Katy told her, "Inga honey, it's not sleeping together that makes the baby. It's what you do when you're awake. People just say 'sleep together' because it's more polite than some of the other words we could use."

Dylan asked her, "Now that we have that straight, we need to know, what do you want to do?"

"What do you mean?" She stared at him, her confusion obvious.

"Inga, you're going to have a baby. Have you been with anyone other than Johnny Allen?"

She stared at her lap and shook her head.

"Do you want to marry him? Because we can make it happen if that's what you want." He was thinking about how he and Michael may have to take Allen out in the alley to do the convincing, and found the idea oddly pleasant.

"What do you mean? If we don't get married won't the baby just go away?"

Jaysus. Could the child actually be that stupid? Dylan was beginning to wonder if the drugs she had been given had some sort of residual effect. "Honey, babies don't go away. Not unless something happens to harm the baby."

"Should I throw myself down the stairs?" She asked the question quite calmly, as if it was the most natural thing in the world.

Katy asked her, "Who do you know who threw herself down the stairs?"

"My mama. It was after my daddy died. She stood at the top of the stairs and stepped out, saying she wanted to take care of her problem."

"Did it?"

"She lost the baby. But she bled to death before the midwife came." Everything the girl said was matter-of-fact. There was definitely something wrong with her.

There was something else Dylan needed to know. "Where did you and Johnny get together? I know it couldn't have happened here."

"Oh no. He took me out to the stable one Sunday to see where Major and The King are. There was an empty stall."

"How many times did you go to the stable with him?"

"Let's see. That Sunday. Then the next three Sundays."

"Have you been with any other men like that?"

"You mean in the empty stall?"

"No, I mean doing the same thing you do with Johnny."

She shook her head again. "Just Johnny. I like Johnny."

"You never answered my question, Inga. What do you want to do? You can marry Johnny Allen, or you can stay here and have the baby. You can give the baby up for adoption if you like, or you can keep him. We won't make you give him away if you don't want to. But you need to decide."

"Dylan, before we let Inga decide anything, I think we need her to see Dr. Wollaston." Millie really didn't think the girl was competent enough to make any sort of decision.

Dylan Shay left the table to go make the telephone call. He returned a few minutes later. "Edmond said he'll be here in time for supper."

"We really need to deduct the cost of his food from his bill." Katy was only half joking. It seemed like every time he made a housecall, it was at mealtime.

"So feed him a lousy meal. Maybe that will cure him."

"But that means we'd have to eat a lousy meal."

Millie was laughing out loud now. "Then quit complaining." She realized Inga looked even more confused. "Don't worry. We'll see you're taken care of."

Dylan had to make sure she understood. "Inga honey, you have to make sure you don't tell anybody about the baby. You promise?"

She nodded. "Can I tell Johnny?"

"Not yet. You'll see the doctor first. Then Michael and I will talk to Johnny. When we're done, you can see him."

Edmond Wollaston was as good as his word, and arrived in time for supper. Katy kept Inga in her flat all day. She couldn't be trusted to keep her mouth shut or not do anything stupid.

Edmond Wollaston greeted Katy and Millie when he came through the kitchen door. He asked to see his patient first. He washed in the kitchen sink and carried his bag into the spare room where Rose was sitting, trying to keep Inga occupied.

Millie stopped him in the hall. "Doctor, we're afraid there's something wrong with Inga's mind. Around a year ago, some man fed her huge amounts of laudanum over several days. Dr. Marsh said it was only by the grace of God that she didn't die. She hasn't been quite right since then, and in the last few months she's gotten worse."

"Do you know how far along she is?"

"Rose estimates she's missed her cycle twice."

He nodded. "Do you have the ability to keep her if necessary? I can send her to an asylum, but I'm afraid that would be more harm than help."

"She's been staying with Rose since Tadhg went to France. I'm pretty sure between us we can manage. She could sit with Siofre in the sewing room during the day, then go downstairs at night."

"And you have the monetary means?"

"Edmond, we're not going to throw her out into the cold."

"Good. Now take me to my patient."

Rose and Inga were sitting on the bed, while they looked through a mail order catalogue. Wollaston noticed they weren't looking at baby things, which told him how detached the girl was.

"I'm Dr. Wollaston. Which one of you ladies is Inga?"

The chubby little blonde raised her hand.

"Hello, Inga." He was gentle with her, as if she was six, rather than eighteen. "May I call you Inga, or do you prefer Miss Rottmann?"

"Inga."

"Okay Miss Inga. I need to examine you. And I'd like at least one of these ladies to stay with us. Who would you like to stay?"

"Missus Millie?"

"I'll stay, sweetie."

Katy and Rose slipped from the room and went to the kitchen.

The two women started putting supper together. It wasn't what the good doctor had come to expect, but they'd been busy today doing everything but cooking. Rose went downstairs and collected some eggs from the case that would supply them for breakfast. On top of the two dozen eggs in her basket, she put the contents of two trays of par-baked biscuits. It took her a minute to see what else Katy could possibly need. She checked the icebox and found some mushrooms that were getting a little aged. Those would work.

She went up the inside stairs as the exterior stairs were beginning to ice over. Rose carried her basket through to the kitchen and set it on the table. Katy was already cutting up the leftover ham.

"Put the two big skillets on the stove and turn them on please. And turn on the oven." Rose did as she was asked.

"You want some butter in the skillet?"

"A little. What'd you bring me?"

"Eggs, biscuits, and a half a basket of mushrooms that are getting sort of disreputable."

"That's exactly what we need. Some disreputable mushrooms. Cut them up and toss 'em in the skillets."

"What are we having?"

"I thought about making omelets. But for seven people that's a lot of cooking. I figured I'd just cook everything up together and put it in a big bowl."

"You have any cheese?"

"In the cupboard. You want to grate some up?"

Rose found the muslin wrapped piece of cheese and the grater and got to work.

The biscuits were coming out of the oven and the eggs going in to melt the cheese when Dylan and Michael came in the kitchen door. Katy volunteered, "Millie's in with the doctor and Inga."

Rose asked, "Did you talk to Sergeant Allen?"

Dylan answered, "Not yet. We need to hear what Edmond has to say first. Then we'll have a discussion." He punched his open left hand with his fist.

Rose agreed with his sentiment, but said, "If she wants to marry him, don't mark him up too bad. You'll never hear the end of it."

Katy was getting dishes from the cupboard. "I don't know if she's capable of marrying anybody. She's not in her right mind, I'm afraid."

Edmond Wollaston came in and headed straight to the sink to wash. "She's getting dressed. And you're right, Katy. I doubt she has the capacity to contract a marriage."

Katy dropped into an empty chair. "God, Michael. What are we going to do?"

He massaged her tight shoulders. "Same thing we always do. We'll get by."

Rose asked, "Why is she like this?"

"You told me she was heavily drugged a year or so ago."

"That's right. Dr Marsh said she was okay."

"Physically, yes. And I'm afraid her pregnancy is exacerbating the situation. After she gives birth, her mind may well recover. But there's no guarantee."

"What can we do for her?" Katy wanted to know.

"First off, I don't want her working downstairs. She can work in the house. Sewing, dusting. But nothing with chemicals. And I want her to have lots of nourishing food, three or four meals a day. There's a chance that extra nutrients can alleviate some of her symptoms."

Katy thought back to her own pregnancy. "So fruits, vegetables, liver, eggs."

The doctor nodded. "And just in case, make plans for the baby. Because if she gets worse, I'm afraid she may wind up going to a home."

Rose had to dash tears from her eyes. "I'll need to talk to Tadhg…"

Katy reassured them all. "We won't let anything happen, Edmond. Now, take these plates and put them in the dining room. Supper's ready."

After supper, Dylan walked the doctor downstairs to let him out the kitchen door. "What do you suggest we do with the proud papa?"

"Make him leave town? Because I'm afraid she'll run right to him given half the chance, and I doubt he'll have the willpower to turn down what she offers."

"That's doable. Michael and I will have a talk with him and his captain in the morning."

Edmond said, "Just don't tell Inga. I also suggest none of the males in your house are alone with her. She's going around the bend, Dylan. She grabbed my wrist when I was examining her, as if she wanted to be gratified sexually. Ask your wife. And tell your brother to stay a mile away."

"Are you sure she's safe to have in the house?"

"I'm going to send you some Valerian tea. I want her to have a cup of it every night. It will help her sleep, keep her in her own bed, and isn't addictive the way opiates are. She's been sleeping downstairs with Rose?"

"She has."

"I'm honestly worried about that. I don't know if Rose is strong enough to mind her around the clock."

"We'll let her sleep down there tonight, then we'll discuss it with the other women in the house. They're involved too, and they need to have a say."

"I'll get hold of Miss Dombrowski. She can stay with Inga while you have your meeting."

*****

Michael and Dylan were waiting for Sergeant Johnny Allen after turnout the next morning. "Allen, we need to have a talk."

"Yes, Sergeant?" Allen considered Michael Dougherty his equal, although Mike was his superior.

"Let's go into the interview room. Don't worry. We've cleared it with Kelly." He named the desk sergeant.

The three men went into the interview room, and Dylan closed the door. Allen volunteered, "Listen, about Miss Rottmann..."

Dylan stopped him. "Yes, about Miss Rottmann. Didn't you think she wasn't quite right when you took advantage of her?"

He shrugged. "I just thought she was real friendly. I mean, why should a man refuse what's freely offered? Right?"

Mike was still standing opposite where Allen sat. "You refuse what's offered if it's obvious the one making the offer isn't right. Didn't you notice she started talking different, started behaving strange?"

"I thought she just really liked me."

Dylan slapped the table. "Christ, Allen. You're not stupid. You're a sergeant, supervising a dozen men in the field. Yet you allowed a poor, sick girl to get herself in a family way."

"You want I should arrange for a doctor? I know a guy."

"For what?"

Allen looked over Dylan's shoulder at a point in the corner of the ceiling. "You know, for the...abortion," he whispered.

Michael leaned across the table and backhanded the sergeant across the mouth. He turned and opened the door, then called out to Sergeant Kenneth Kelly. "Kelly, get the Captain down here."

Captain MacFarland took all of two minutes to come down from his second floor office to the interview room. "What's doing, Dougherty?"

"Captain, Allen here has been slipping around with a girl that works at our wives' bakery even though he was told we won't stand for that. The girl's not right in the head, but Allen still took advantage of her. He got her in a family way, and now he just offered to provide her with an abortion."

"Captain, I never..."

"Sit down, Sergeant Allen." The Captain fairly roared. He asked Michael, "Is that the little blonde girl?"

Mike nodded. "Inga Rottmann. She was snatched and heavily drugged by her kidnappers. She hasn't been quite right since, and since Allen here got hold of her she's gotten considerably worse. She may well wind up in an asylum! We'll have another homeless waif to look after."

"Allen, are you prepared to marry the girl?"

Dylan didn't give him a chance to answer. "Captain, the doctor told me last night she isn't sufficiently competent to make a marriage."

"Shay, what do you propose we do?"

"Personally, it would suit me fine if you closed the door on your way out and left me alone with him for about half an hour. But I know I'd get done for assault and he's not worth the trouble, or the paperwork."

The Captain agreed.

"I think it would be a good thing if Allen here went down to Virginia and signed up for the Navy. Or went to the harbor here and joined the Merchant Marines. He needs to get out of town now."

Allen started to object. Dougherty cut him off. "The Captain of the Homicide division in Baltimore County has a horse farm in Timonium. We'll relieve you of the responsibility for The King and take him up to Captain Bobbitt's farm."

"What about Major?"

"You want him to go, we can arrange that. Provided you're on the next boat out. And I want it in writing that you relinquish any interest in the horse. And you also sign a paper that you relinquish any right to the child. I'll pay to have the documents prepared." Michael turned to their superior and asked, "Is that all right with you, Captain?"

"I think you're being lenient on him. But it is an excellent idea. Allen, there's a ship in the harbor right now that's signing on crew. They're shipping horses and mules to France. They need men to handle them aboard ship. Go down now and sign on. Then come back here. Shay, how soon can you have the documents prepared?"

"As soon as Mr. Kemp's clerk can have them ready."

"Draft the papers Mr. Shay. I'll sign them.

*****

Gerhardt Weissmann came in the kitchen door of the house off Parkside and greeted Sophia. She kissed him quickly then backed away. "You're half frozen. Go hang up your coat and get some coffee. I'll have supper on in a little while."

"You'd think it would start to warm up in March." He rubbed his hands together over the heat rising from the oven.

"We'll have another ice or snow storm the end of the month. It happens almost every year."

"I wish I could have worn my new coat today but it wasn't possible. I had to fit in."

She handed him a coffee cup. "I know. How'd you do?"

"I completed my commission. Then I had time to stop by the music publishers and pick up some new sheet music for the students, and some manuscript pages. And I brought you a present." From the center of the pile of music pages he withdrew a ten inch wax disc. He handed it to her.

Sophia withdrew the disc from its paper sleeve reverently. "You remembered!"

"Of course I remembered. Go crank up the Victrola and see how it sounds."

She almost skipped into the music room and did as he asked. She set the record on the turntable, set the needle and released the catch.

Sophia sat on the end of the piano bench, her eyes closed, listening to the beautiful, seductive music. When it ended, she reached back to Gerhardt's hand. "I love it. I don't know what they're saying, but that is the most beautiful thing I've ever heard."

"You don't know what they're saying?"

She shook her head.

"Start it up again."

She did. Gerhardt straddled the bench and pulled her so she sat with her back to him. As Giovanni sang, he told her in her ear, *"Give me thy hand, oh fairest. Whisper a gentle yes. Come if for me thou carest, With joy my life to bless."*

She laid her head back on his shoulder. "My god. I've never really seen this on stage, only heard it from the cloak room. This must be really something to see."

"When this idiotic war is over, *liebchen,* I'll take you to la Scala or Salzburg to see it live, as it was meant to be performed. Or maybe we can go somewhere that doesn't have such stupid laws, where you and I can sit together in the theater to watch it performed."

"We'd probably have to go to Mexico or Canada."

"So, we'll go to Canada."

"I've got to get supper before it burns. Why don't you flip that record over and play what's on the other side."

He did as she asked. Sophia was putting dinner on the table as she listened to *Se Vuol Ballare.* Gerhardt went to the dining room.

"What's that from?"

"It's *Marriage of Figaro.* Figaro finds out his boss is lusting after his fiancee. He sings, *if you want to dance, little count, I'll play the tune."*

"That's from the same opera Isaac's song came from, isn't it?"

"It is."

"Is all of Mozart's music this much fun?"

"Fun? It can be fun to play. It can also be a hell of a lot of work. Mozart was a genius. He believed in the mathematics of music. Let me check with the Peabody. Their students may be putting on one of his operas or oratorios. We can go to that."

She finally had supper on the table and they sat to eat. "What did you have to do today?"

"Are you sure you want to know? If I tell you, you can't deny knowledge, and it could put you in harm's way if I get caught."

"Honey, in the past five years there's not much I've done that was exactly legal. I can get arrested just for the way we're living. So tell me what you had to do?"

"You know that ship in the harbor where they're loading all those horses and mules?"

"It was in the newspaper. The Glenmore, isn't it?"

"It is. They leave on the morning tide. Two days out, there will be an explosion that will blow a hole in the hull."

"And the ship will be lost with all hands?" She was smiling.

"We can but hope. Do you mind that I'm doing this?"

"Why should I? This country hasn't done much for me. I can't buy a house in most neighborhoods. I can't go into most of the stores downtown. If I got a job they're allowed to pay me half of what a white woman earns, and a quarter of what a white man would earn. You blow up whatever you want honey. Just remember to come home when you're done."

"I've got the telephone number for the director at the Peabody. I'm calling him right now. We need to take Barton and Isaac. You and I will be required to chaperone the boys." He jumped up from the table and went to make his call.

Sophia didn't know why her agreement that he could commit wholesale sabotage seemed to excite him. In fact, any time she agreed with him, or told him he did something well, he almost dragged her off to bed. Amazingly, even though he couldn't achieve gratification himself, he seemed to take pride in the pleasure he gave her. And pleasure her he did. She'd have to get him to translate the rest of that song for her.

He returned to the table. "The director is holding tickets for us for Sunday. Some of his students are having a voice recital, and they're performing Mozart."

"We definitely want the boys to hear that."

"I'll have to get the Runabout from deGroot's garage."

"I didn't know you still had it."

"It was too nice a car to lose. Adolf rented me space to store it. I'll pick it up tomorrow. Want to go with me?"

"Sure." She poured him a cup of coffee and put a piece of whiskey soaked fruit cake in front of him. "You never said. Are you getting paid sufficiently for this work you've been doing?"

"Of course, *liebchen*. Ten thousand for the ship. Well, two down and I get the rest when it sinks."

"Ten! And how do you make the bombs?"

"Benjy deGroot. The boy is an electronic genius. I pay him a thousand dollars, do my job and wait for the boom."

"Have you used his stuff before?"

"Of course. Remember that fire at the coal depot Curtis Bay?"

She nodded.

"And remember the day I came home covered in coal dust?"

She nodded again.

"I set the charge Benjy made. Two days later...*boom*. And the fire burned for a week."

"Does deGroot know his son is doing this?"

"I don't know. I don't intend to bring it up."

"So long as I know."

"Let's get the dishes done and I'll tell you what else Giovanni says to Zerlina. And you can tell me if it works."

*****

They left Johnny Allen sitting in the interview room when Dougherty and Shay went out to the station's lobby to discuss the state of affairs.

MacFarland was disgusted by the entire situation. "I'll write Allen a recommendation to go to the merchant service, then I'll have one of the men drive him down to the harbor. I want him gone as badly as you do."

"Thank you, sir." Dylan was amazed things had been settled without shedding more than a modicum of blood. Dougherty had backhanded Allen once and split his lip. "I need to go see the lawyers."

"Go on. And Dougherty, you go make arrangements for those animals. The city will house them until the end of the month, but they need to go someplace else. Otherwise they run the risk of being sent to France. You know what will happen then."

"Yes sir. May I use the station telephone, or should I go to our office?"

"Use the phone. Tell Kelly to get you a long distance line out."

MacFarland headed back upstairs to his office. Dylan asked Mike, "I thought Bobbitt's brother-in-law, the idiot, owned the horse farm. You think he's capable of taking in the horses?"

"I heard from Bobbitt while you were in Delaware. The idiot was kicked to death by his stud horse. So Bobbitt's sister Paisley has the place now. Chuck's moved his family out with her, and he says they're doing well."

"Good. That man was a menace to his wife. Go call him and tell him we can bring the horses on the train to Timonium."

"You want to take the kids up to see the horsies?"

"Mary Faith would love it. Chiara would think they smelled bad."

Mike went to make his call and Dylan walked out the front door to find the clerk at the Kemp law office.

When McFarland returned, Dougherty let him know that arrangements were made to take Major and The King to Timonium in a week. Bobbitt had even invited them to come to his house on Ash Wednesday and to bring their wives. His wife would be cooking codfish cakes and fruit compote., "You think they'll go on Ash Wednesday?"

Michael grinned. "I don't see why not? They know Chuck from way back. And you know Katy will want to find out about this fruit compote."

"So we'll leave the kids home. And we'll have to make arrangements for Inga."

"I think Rose will be able to do it. You know she wrote to Tadhg this morning. She wants to take the baby?"

"I know. And if he says no it will break her heart."

"I doubt he'll say no. But it is a hell of a way to find out you're having a baby."

"It's better than when I came home to tell Millie we were having a baby at the end of the week. At least Rose and Tadhg have time to prepare for it."

"And if Nagel does say no, Katy wants to take the baby."

"She may have to fight Millie. Maybe we should pray for twins."

*****

"Millie are you around?" Coming into the kitchen

door at close to nine 'o clock Dylan dropped his briefcase on the floor.

His wife came from the nursery. "I'm around." She went to the door to greet him properly. "You're cold. Hang up your coat and get some coffee."

He opened the cupboard over the sink. "Where's the whiskey?"

"Next door over. Top shelf. You're the only one tall enough to reach it."

He poured a dab in his cup and topped it off with coffee. "Sit down with me. We need to talk for a minute."

"Oh, gawd, Dylan. You sound like you're going to tell me you want a divorce."

He grabbed her hand and pulled her into his lap. "Never that. I'm sorry I sounded so serious. It's been a long day. I've got a couple of things to tell you."

"You're not leaving town on a job?"

"Not exactly. Johnny Allen leaves town tomorrow morning. Captain gave him his papers today. He signed up for a merchant cruise handling horses bound for France, Allen signed both horses over to me. On Ash Wednesday, we're taking them to Timonium. Mike and I have to ride in the stock car with them, but you and Katy will be in the day coach. We're going to the Bobbitt farm, and he really wants to see you."

She hugged his neck. "That's wonderful. And we don't mention it to Inga."

"How's she been today?"

"Wandering around the house humming and playing with a string. Katy says we need to teach her to crochet. Knitting needles could be dangerous. But it's hard to stab somebody with a crochet hook."

"Do we need to hire somebody to mind her? I don't mind."

"Let's wait and see."

"I've got one more thing to tell you." He hugged her just a little tighter. "Mike and Tomás and I are going to the Peabody on Sunday afternoon to hear a voice recital of Mozart's music. I thought you might like to go with us."

She kissed him one last time and put a soup plate in front of him. "I never thought my big, strapping Irishman would tell me he was voluntarily going to a Mozart concert. I must have created a monster."

"You'll probably have to translate a lot of it for me."

She filled his bowl with navy bean soup, and put a basket of hot rolls on the table. "And if they sing his *Missa Solemnis* you'll have to translate that for me."

They finished their meal and Dylan got up to help with the dishes. "Are the girls asleep already?"

"I was tucking them in when you got home. I said you'd spend time with them in the morning."

"I'll make sure we have breakfast together."

"I need to let Hannah know that Benito will be coming over on Sunday."

"Good. And arrange for Rose and Frances to mind Inga."

"I'll make sure Rose has the key to the piano. They can play some rolls and have a fun afternoon on their own."

As they finished their supper he asked, "Should I tell Inga about Larry Wardworth? Going to trial with him was about the last lucid moment she had."

"What about him?"

"He got seven years. He still has federal charges to face."

"Oh, no. Will Rose have to testify again?"

"I talked to Allardyce today and told him everything. He says they have the transcript of her testimony. He can possibly get it admitted with a motion if she's not available. He was concerned that testifying might have put her over the edge."

"I never thought of that. I'll mention it to Edmond when I see him again."

Sunday morning Maria and Tomás brought eight month old Benito to Millie and Dylan's flat. Tomás had brought Maria's clothes in a carpet bag. Maria carried Benito through to the nursery and sat down in the rocker to nurse him one last time before dressing.

Millie followed her and sat down on the extra chair. "How's he doing with eating solid food?"

"He loves the taste of chicken. I remember you telling me to give him a stripped chicken bone once he got his first tooth. He couldn't get enough of it. I made meatballs the other night and handed him one. The little stinker made short work of it."

"Good. I know you cook with more spices that I do. Has he eaten anything like that?

She grinned as she shifted the baby to her shoulder to burp him. "I think he'd teethe on a pepper if I handed him one. I was fussing with Tomás about feeding him *ropa vieja* last week. He stopped and Benito started yelling and grabbing for the spoon. So yes, he is definitely his father's son."

"You think he'll manage until we get home?"

"Of course. He's weaning himself. He's down to three or four times a day, and he's even sleeping through the night."

Millie groaned. "I wish mine did. Both of them were up at two in the morning every night for almost a year."

She called for the nanny. "Hannah, can you come get Benito? I think he's ready to play with the girls."

Millie laughed. "How much playing does he really do?"

"He loves being the center of attention. Mary Faith plays dress up with him like he's a living doll-baby. So long as Hannah's there to make sure they all behave everything will be fine."

"If you say so. Come on. Let's get dressed. We've got the Nash today so at least we'll be inside for the ride."

"I just wish there was heat inside the cars. It's as cold as riding the streetcar."

"At least in the Nash, we don't have to worry about needing to keep a hatpin handy to fend off mashers."

Chapter Thirteen

Maestro Duprey pulled the Stearns-Knight Toy Tonneau Runabout up in front of the house off Parkside. The two boys waiting on the porch began to clap and jump around at the sight the "boss machine", so named by Barton, and driven by their beloved teacher.

Madame Sylviane Gareau herded the two boys down to the car. Barton sat up front while she sat in the back with Isaac. The boys would switch places on the way back.

They found a convenient place to park just off Charles Street. Duprey led them directly to the box office where he asked for their tickets. The director had made sure they had the best seats where the acoustics were perfect. The Duprey Conservatory party was one of the first to arrive, so they had no problem finding their seats near the center of the auditorium.

The last time they had put their ten pupils between them. Today Duprey instructed the boys to sit on either side of their two chaperones, so he and Madame could sit together. He knew they might get some stares. He didn't care. He'd never see these people again.

As before, Sylviane wore her hair wrapped in a wide silk scarf. She doubted anyone would recognize her dressed as she was with two young teen boys in her care. She settled into her seat, and was surprised when Duprey pressed his knee against her's.

The auditorium filled up quickly. Dylan had managed to secure six tickets together in the last row, which suited him fine. They didn't have the benefit of a balcony today, but he was still quite happy sitting next to his lovely wife.

Maria sat next to Millie and spent her time looking around at the other patrons. She saw most of them were students of the conservatory. She was surprised to see two younger boys who couldn't possibly be students there, seated several rows in front of them.

Something about the woman looked familiar, but Maria couldn't put her finger on it. She kept watching but finally gave up and began looking through the program she'd received when they came in.

Maria showed the program to Millie. "Look, this is a vocal recital and they've got eight students performing. Do you recognize this?"

Millie looked. The names were in Italian or German or French. She pointed as she read down the list. "Marriage of Figaro, this one is *Cosi fan Tutti*, it means 'They're all the same'. Two stupid people don't recognize their fiances in costumes. Then *Abduction from the Seraglio*, from the harem. Don Giovanni you know, I'm sure. This one is from the *Missa Solemnis*." She turned to her husband. "Dylan, what's *Quoniam tu solus sanctus* mean?"

He looked up from his own program. "It means, 'You alone are holy'. The priest sings it at the high mass."

"Guess that's what I get for never going to high mass."

"Would you like to go?"

"Only if we go to Callum's mass. Father Toolen can't sing to save himself."

He put his arm around the back of her seat and gave her shoulder a squeeze, leaving his arm there.

A quartet came on stage and began to tune up, followed by a harpsichord player. They played incidental music as the remainder of their patrons assumed their seats.

Finally, the house lights went up, then dimmed, and the eight singers progressed across the stage from two different directions, taking their place in the center in front of the the musicians.

The music director, who was acting as conductor as well as announcer, turned at his rostrum and called out the name of each of the eight singers, and those of the five musicians on stage. A round of polite applause followed.

They opened their performance with the Octet of the second act of *Nozze di Figaro*. Millie closed her eyes as they sang, taking in the complexity of the vocal acrobatics and listening to the words. Then the tenor performed a piece from the same opera. Millie buried her face in her husband's shoulder to mute her laughter.

"What's wrong, darlin'?"

She shook her head, trying to catch her breath. "They almost always cut that song. He's saying he was saved from accidents in his youth by wearing a donkey skin."

Dylan looked down into her face. "Does that mean what I think it does?"

She nodded, and started laughing again, covering her mouth. Her husband did the same.

Maria noticed a blond man sitting with the woman and two boys was also sniggering. She'd have to ask her friend what that song meant.

The next piece was far more staid. Maria saw the blond man lean closer to the woman beside him so their shoulders touched. There was something familiar about him but she couldn't quite place him.

Intermission came. The man in front of them took the boys out to the lobby, probably to use the restrooms. The woman stayed where she was.

Maria was still watching her. The woman had turned so her profile was exposed as her companion stood. A flash of memory and she knew.

"Tomás, do you remember Sophia?"

"Sure. Why?"

"Because she's sitting about seven or eight rows in front of us. You see that woman wearing a yellow scarf, and the green dress with the yellow collar?"

"I do."

"That's her. She's with a blond haired man with a beard, and two boys who look around twelve or so."

"What about the man she's with? Do you recognize him?"

"He looks familiar, but I don't know who he is."

Tomás reached across his wife and tapped Dylan on the wrist. "Come with me." Then he turned to Michael and did the same. The three men stood and stepped into the aisle so they could get a better look at the woman in question.

The three strolled down the aisle a way, stopped and appeared to chat and made their way back to their seats. They were just sitting down when the man and the two boys returned and the house lights flashed, announcing the start of the second act.

Tomás leaned down and whispered to Maria. "You're right, *querida*. That's Sophia. The one we ate with that night, and who we tried to arrest at the Flower Show."

"What are you going to do?"

"We're going to try to take her as she leaves. I don't want to have to climb over a bunch of seats to get to her. We wait and see which way they come out then reach out and grab her."

"What about the man she's with?"

"You're right again. He looks familiar but I can't place him."

She patted his knee. "It will come to you. Maybe he'll come to post her bail." They observed for a long moment. "Tell Katy to trip her."

"Huh?"

"Katy's sitting on the end. Tell her when the woman comes past to stick out her foot and trip her. Then you and Mike grab her."

Tomás grabbed his wife and hugged her. "You're brilliant." He turned to Michael. "See that woman in the yellow scarf?"

Mike nodded.

"That's Sophia O'Fallon. We can take her when she's on her way out. Tell Katy to trip her as she comes past."

Mike whispered Tomás' message in his wife's ear. She nodded and whispered something in return. Michael told Tomás, "Katy says when the last piece is almost over, she and I will stand up and stand behind the seats as if we're waiting for someone, then you and Maria should move to our seats. Make sure you're on the end."

Tomás looked across Mike and Katy, grinned and nodded. He then turned and repeated the message to Millie to relay to Dylan. In turn, Dylan let him know he and Millie would go to the opposite end of their row, just in case their prey exited to the left rather than the right.

The remainder of the program seemed to drag. Millie found herself unable to even pay attention to her favorite piece from *Don Giovanni.* She did notice that the two people they were watching seemed to feel the same about the duet Millie usually did. They leaned together, and it appeared he might be holding her hand beneath the side of her skirt.

The woman had on a rather expensive Persian lamb coat, and the man wore a lovely sealskin coat with a fur collar. That told Millie at least he was doing well if he was providing for both of them.

The final composition began, the trio from the *Missa Solemnis.* Dylan reached across Millie and nudged Tomás. They all went to their appointed positions.

The applause at the culmination of the performance was much more enthusiastic than at the director's initial introductions. Six pair of eyes were on the woman in question.

Once the crowd had thinned out, the man in the sealskin coat said something to her, and took the two boys forward to see someone still on stage. The woman stood and moved a little gingerly, apparently getting the stiffness out of her limbs.

The man must have told her to wait for him in the car. She started up the aisle toward the rear of the theater, and would pass right in front of Tomás and Maria. When they spotted her headed their way, Katy stepped behind Tomás' seat and bent down as if she was speaking to him, effectively blocking part of the aisle. The woman in the scarf started to step around Katy, who stuck out her foot and caught the other woman's ankle.

Michael was right there, and caught her as she fell forward, saving her from hitting the floor. "Are you all right, miss?"

"Yes, thank you. I'm not usually so clumsy."

"I know you're not, Mrs. O'Fallon." Michael had a

firm grip on her left arm. Tomás moved in and grabbed her other arm. Mike continued. "Sophia O'Fallon, you're under arrest for receiving stolen property. Please come along quietly."

Sophia looked over her shoulder to see if Gerhardt had seen what happened. She saw he was watching, but could make no effort to protect her now. She was on her own.

She went along peacefully as Dylan went out to the street to find a uniformed officer.

*****

Tomás drove the ladies home, then returned to Central District where Michael had transported Sophia O'Fallon. He walked in and spotted Kenneth Kelly behind the desk. "Don't you ever go home, Kelly?"

"Not recently. Seems like half the men on the force are down with some sort of grippe. Everybody's doing double shifts.

"Glad I'm not on the force then. Can you tell me where Shay and Dougherty have taken their prisoner?"

"She's in the interview room with the matron. Our two lost lambs are upstairs in the Captain's office."

"You think they'd mind if I joined them?"

Kelly grinned, "I think they'd expect it."

Tomás returned his smile. "Top of the stairs?"

"First door on the right. Don't knock, just walk in and be prepared to duck."

Kelly could hear Tomás grumbling something in Spanish as he climbed the narrow stairs.

Contrary to Kelly's instruction, Tomás still knocked before he opened the door.

Captain MacFarland called, "Special Agent Ribiero. Come in. We've been waiting for you."

Okay. Maybe it wasn't going to be as bad as he

expected. Not that he had anything to worry about personally. Neither Ribiero nor Shay were under the purview of the Baltimore City Police.

"Sit down, the three of you."

They sat.

"This woman you brought in. What's her name again?"

Dougherty answered. "Sophia Davies O'Fallon."

"That's right. She married that Irishman just before we executed him, didn't she?"

"Yes sir."

"What have you got her on?"

"Possession and sale of stolen property."

"What sort of stolen property, Detective Sergeant?"

"She had some Australian black opals that were stolen from a house in Annapolis about a year and a half, two years ago."

"Set in gold?"

"In plate."

"That's what I thought. Cut her loose."

"What do you mean, cut her loose!" Dylan was on his feet. He knew better than to shout at his former commander as it could make things hard on Mike.

"Just what I said, Special Agent Shay. Cut her loose. You're too late. What she had doesn't rise to the level of a felony, and the statute of limitations on a misdemeanor has expired. Don't you have anything else on her?"

Dylan shook his head. "Nothing that will stick."

"Then release her. And give her cab fare home. You can't have a woman out on the streets after dark, even if she is a colored woman. I don't want to get blamed for something happening to her because she was mistakenly taken into custody."

"Yes sir." Dougherty sounded as if somebody had just shot his dog.

"Now get out of here and go have your Sunday dinners."

"Yes sir."

The three men filed down the narrow stairs. As Michael was the only City officer among the three it was up to him to release their prisoner. He shuffled across the lobby to the interview room. He opened the door and stepped inside, leaving the door open.

The matron was standing to one side, leaning against the wall. Beside her on a small shelf was a telephone prisoners used to make their one telephone call.

"Mrs. O'Fallon, we're releasing you. No charges have been filed against you. Sergeant Kelly is calling a taxi for you and we'll see to your fare."

The woman shrugged into her coat, collected her purse from the matron who had put it aside, and breezed out as if she were the Queen of Sheba.

The matron started to leave, but Tomás grabbed her arm. "Just a minute please, Matron. Did Mrs. O'Fallon make a telephone call?"

"Yes, sir."

"Do you know who she called?"

"I wrote the number down she gave the operator. She told whoever answered the telephone what had happened, and could he go up to her flat and let her cat out." She gave the paper to the Agent.

"Did you get her information?"

"Yes sir. Here it is." She handed him a folder containing a single page of statistics. Her name, address, employer.

"The address is a second floor alley flat off Baltimore Street. See if this sounds familiar." Tomás passed the folder to Michael.

"Son of a bitch. It's deGroot's."

Dylan asked, "What's it say for employer?"

Dougherty read from the form. "Assistant and housekeeper for Duprey Music Conservatory. That must have been Duprey at the concert today."

"You think she's gone straight?" Tomás asked.

Dylan thought for a minute. "Maybe. Maybe not."

"Should we keep track of her, boss?"

Tomás nodded once. "It won't hurt. Since she's not been charged the file won't be needed. Is that correct Matron?"

"Yes sir. Normally, I'd tear it up and throw it out."

"I'll save you the trouble." Tomás folded the form and put it inside his jacket pocket.

Dougherty didn't want to talk about Sophia O'Fallon anymore. "Captain gave me orders to go home and have Sunday supper. I suggest we do so, before Kelly finds something else for me to do."

They climbed into the Nash and headed back to Baltimore Street. They climbed the outside staircase stopping first at the second floor, then going up to the third to Millie and Dylan's flat.

Their wives were sitting at the table trying, rather unsuccessfully, to feed supper to their five collective children. Mary Faith had been doing well on her own until she spotted her beloved Da. She climbed down from her chair and ran to him, sticky face and all and jumped into his outstretched arms.

"Now you know better than to get up from the table without asking, dumpling. Sit down and finish your supper." He plopped her butt back in her chair and sat beside her. "What'd your Mam fix for your supper?"

"Meat and taters."

He grinned at his wife. "You mean shepherd's pie?"

Mary Faith crammed a spoonful of potatoes and lamb into her mouth. "What I said," she mumbled as she chewed.

Katy was having the hardest time of all, trying to feed both children at the same time as they sat with their mouths open like baby birds. Michael picked up a spoon and began to feed three year old Declan, while Katy fed Donagh. Both boys were capable of feeding themselves, but they still wanted to be fed their supper on occasion, particularly after their nursemaids had gone downstairs for their half day off.

A few months younger, Chiara was doing well on her own, only relying on her mother to catch globs of gravy before they could run down her chin.

Benito, on the other hand, didn't want any part of the delicious dinner. He clamped his little mouth shut and was turning his head away every time his mother tried to give him a spoonful of potatoes.

Tomás took his son from Maria and propped him up on his lap. He picked up a napkin and wiped his face before they went any further. "What's wrong, *hijo*?" He ignored the spoon, instead using his fingers to pick up a piece of the fork-tender lamb. He pinched a piece off and put it in Benito's mouth. The kid's eyes got huge, as if this was the greatest treat in the world. He took the spoon and tasted the gravy that surrounded the meat. "Millie, do you have a little cayenne?"

She went to the shelf above the stove to fetch the small metal tin, then watched as Tomás sprinkled a little on her shepherd's pie. He gave it a stir, then tasted it again, and gave a nod. This time when he put a spoonful into Benito's mouth the child smacked his lips and opened wide for more.

"Well! I think I should be insulted." Millie laughed when she said it. "Imagine, my food has been critiqued by an eight month old and found wanting."

Maria got up to wash her hands. "I wouldn't worry about it. I told you, the kid's all *cubano*. Any day now I expect he'll want *cafe* after supper, instead of nursing."

"At least my kids don't insist on eating boiled dinners every meal." Katy never let Michael forget that his mother boiled almost everything she cooked except for boxty, and those started out being boiled. They loved the old woman to death, but her dinners were less than appetizing. It was no wonder Mike had eaten so many meals at their bakery before they married.

Finally the kids were all fed, cleaned and tucked into bed in the Shay's nursery, and in their spare room. Now the adults could eat their own late supper, and the women could find out what was going on in the outside world.

Millie put the food on the plates, ready to take to the kitchen, where they would eat. Carrying them through, Millie said, "Dylan, get the paper out of the parlor. An extra came out right after we got home. I put it in there for you."

"An extra? Have we gone to war?" He headed into the parlor and found the two sheet *News Post Extra*.

"Well, what's going on?" Mike asked.

"Oh shit." Dylan dropped into the chair. "The *Glenmore* was sunk two days out of port."

"Torpedo?"

He kept reading before he answered. "According to this, the radio reports said a bomb exploded in the hold. The navy said there were no German submarines in the area."

"So sabotage."

"Exactly."

Millie sat next to her husband. "Oh no. That's the ship Johnny Allen was on, wasn't it?"

"Yeah." He covered his face with his hands.

She put her hand on his shoulder. "Dylan, you can't feel guilty about this."

"Why not? If Michael and I hadn't threatened him he never would have been on that damned ship."

Mike went to the cupboard and pulled out the whiskey and glasses and passed them around the table. "Dylan, we may have roughed him up a bit. He had it coming. But if you remember, it was the Captain who told him to sign onto that crew. You and I were perfectly willing to put him on a train south. If Johnny Allen hadn't been such an egotistical bastard he'd still be alive, and Inga wouldn't be up the duff."

Tomás poured himself a shot before passing the bottle down the table. "I talked to Edmond Wollaston yesterday. He said he suspects Inga's first experience with Allen may have been...forced, and that's what caused her final slip into madness. She compensated by thinking she was in love with Allen and succumbed to his desires every subsequent Sunday. Somehow I can't see a girl like Inga voluntarily losing her virginity in an empty stall in the City stables."

Millie put the shepherd's pie on the table, but it seemed they had all lost their appetites. She reached around.d grabbed the coffee pot and filled their cups, adding a dab of whiskey to her own. "Now, do we tell Inga?"

"I think we need to consult Edmond before we decide," Michael told her. "I'd hate to make her go even crazier than she is."

"Call him in the morning then. Call Chuck and tell him. He can decide what to do about Major I guess."

Dylan said, "I think we'll wait for Tadhg to get back. It's his decision really. We'll need to tell Rose so she can let him know about Allen."

Millie broke down in tears, burying her face against her husband's throat. He pulled her into his arms and rubbed her back. "It's not that bad, darlin'. This isn't anybody's fault, nobody but the person who set the bomb."

She sniffed, pulled his handkerchief from his jacket pocket and blew her nose, then stuffed it back in his pocket. That made him laugh. "I know. It's just so stupid. When did our lives become so complicated, Dylan? Millie and I only wanted a nice, quiet little bakery."

"I know, darlin'. Then those two big Mick detectives walked in. That's when things got complicated."

She giggled and sniffed again. "Maybe it is all your fault."

*****

"Gerhardt?" Sophia called as she came through the back door.

Weissmann hurried through the kitchen and pulled her into his arms. "Are you all right? How'd you get away? Do you have to go to court?"

She started giggling. "One question at a time." She allowed him to help her out of her coat. "Come on. I want to sit in the parlor. Do you have any wine open?"

"I will. Go sit and I'll bring it in."

A few minutes later, he handed her a glass of red wine and sat beside her. "Now, tell me everything."

"First off I'm fine." She took a long drink of the wine. "I didn't get away. They let me go."

"What do you mean, they let you go? You're out on bail?"

She shook her head. "No. I was sitting in an interview room, and three coppers came in and told me I was free to go. Apparently those opals were so cheap they didn't rise to the level of a felony. So the statute of limitations had expired."

"What exactly does all that mean?"

"To be a felony, the stuff stolen has to be over a certain amount of money. I think it's a hundred dollars. Under a hundred, and it's a misdemeanor. A statute of limitations says the coppers only have a certain amount of time to charge someone with a crime. There's no limit on a felony, but on misdemeanors it's only a year."

"And they only charged you with receiving?"

"That's it. They never said a word about Landry or Georgia or anything else."

"What address did you give?"

"The flat over deGroots. I used my one telephone call to get him and ask him to let the cat out. So he'll put some clothes upstairs and make it look lived in."

"How'd you get home?"

"The coppers put me in a taxi. And no, I didn't come straight home. I had him take me to the back door of deGroot's. I went inside and told him what happened, then he put me in another cab to bring me home. They asked where I worked. I said I was a housekeeper and assistant to the Duprey Music Conservatory. They never asked for an address."

"The cop who arrested you must have been in the auditorium with us."

"It was the same two guys who grabbed me at the Flower Show. When I was in the interview room with the matron, she mentioned how I escaped last year. I told her I was terrified, all those men grabbing me and marching me away from my stall. I was afraid for my virtue since most policemen seem to treat every colored woman as a prostitute. I was afraid of being stuffed into a Paddy wagon without a matron."

"And this time they had a matron?"

"They did." She drained her glass and handed it to him to refill. "How did you explain my absence to the boys?"

He handed her the newly charged glass. "I simply said you met some old friends, and you'd be back later." Marcel put his own glass aside and pulled her close to him. "I was so worried about you, but there was nothing I could do."

She leaned her head on his shoulder. "I know. I didn't expect you to. If they had done me for receiving, the most I would have gotten was a year and a day. Had you showed up trying to defend me, you'd wind up at the Cut facing a rope. No, sweetie, I don't want that. I lost my husband that way. I don't want to lose you, too."

That was the nicest thing anybody had ever said to him. "Are you hungry?"

"Starved. Come on to the kitchen. I'll heat up something."

"You can come to the kitchen. But I've got something in the oven."

She followed him out, and he opened the oven. Inside, he had been keeping warm food from *diNitti's* in Little Italy. "I wasn't sure when you'd be home. I asked Mama deNitti to wrap me up something I could keep warm. She gave me some polenta with pancetta and ribollita."

She took plates out of the cupboard and set them on the table. "Now would you like to tell me what that is?"

"Polenta is cooked cornmeal, with sweet bacon mixed in. She pours it into a pie pan and bakes, then slices it. Ribollita is bean and vegetable stew. She sent along that wine, bread and oil."

"Should I get bowls?"

"The stew is really thick. I don't think so."

Supper was more than she could have hoped for. After spending the evening at the Irish Clubhouse she had expected to come home to cold sandwiches. Instead, she found her man had secured her a wonderful hot meal.

That thought surprised her. "Her man". She'd had men before him. They had always used her. Gerhardt didn't. He treated her as an equal.

*****

"Inga, will you come sit down a minute, please?" Katy called her in from where the girl was sitting with Siofre.

She sauntered in, playing with the end of her braid, humming to herself. "Yes, Missus Katy?" Inga swung her body back and forth. She put Katy in mind of when Mary Faith was trying to be cute. "Oh, Dr. Wollaston. I didn't know you were here." Her body language suddenly changed, and she went from cute to almost seductive.

The doctor was sitting beside Katy, while Millie sat opposite them, leaving one chair open for Inga. Wollaston told her, "Sit down, Inga. We need to talk to you."

"Okay." She sat beside Millie. The girl sat and chewed the end of her braid, glancing at the doctor through half lowered lashes, trying to look cute.

Wollaston went on. "Did you see the Extra that came out yesterday afternoon?"

She shook her head. "I don't read much anymore."

He wondered if she even remembered how to read. "The Germans sank a transport ship the other day. Everybody on board was lost."

"Oh, that's too bad." She sounded as if someone told her it was going to rain tomorrow, rather than that fifty men had been killed.

He sighed and tried again. "Inga, when was the

last time you saw Johnny Allen?"

"Sunday."

"This past Sunday?"

"Uh-huh."

"And where did you see him?"

"He took me to the stable, like always."

"Excuse me a minute." He pulled Millie into the next room. "Has she left the house at all?"

"No, not at all. Since we found out, she hasn't been past the door, and someone in this house has supervised her every minute of every day. And there is a lock on the outside of her bedroom door. You want to ask Rose? I can call her." It took her a moment to realize. "Allen was on the ship when it left on Thursday."

" It's not necessary to call Rose. But I'm afraid she's slipping farther into insanity."

"Should we hire someone to mind her full time?"

"Let me talk to the people at Hopkins. We may have something available for her."

"Doctor, what about St. Joseph's? Would you mind checking with Sister John Anthony?"

"She helped you get your daughter, didn't she?"

Millie nodded. "Her mother was quite insane from repeated rapes. The last I heard, the girl is making progress there."

"That's an excellent idea. I'll call her first thing. Has any decision been made on what will happen with the baby?"

She shook her head. "Not yet. Rose is waiting to hear back from Tadhg. If he says no either the Shays or the Doughertys will adopt him. Or her." She grinned.

"Good. If you allow me to use your telephone, I'll call Sister now."

Millie returned to the kitchen and found Inga

sipping a glass of milk.

"Missus Katy says I have to drink milk for the baby. When will the baby get here? I want to play with him."

"It'll be a while, Inga. Just keep drinking your milk and eat all the good food so the baby will grow, and you can stay healthy."

"Okay, Missus Millie." She took another swallow. "Where's Doctor Wollaston?"

"He's making a telephone call. He'll be back in a minute."

The doctor did return, smiling. "Sister John Anthony said she'll be here for lunch. She asked if you could have creamed chip beef.

Chapter Fourteen

Easter Sunday

Dearest Tadgh,

I pray this letter finds you well. I have much to tell you, and so little space.

I told you that Inga is having a baby, but because of what happened with Sergeant Allen, her mind is gone. She has gone to stay at St. Joseph's.

According to Sister John Anthony, she is slipping further away and cannot keep the babe once he is born. Tadhg, my darling, I would love to take the baby as our own. You know how well Millie and Dylan did with Mary Faith, and this situation is much the same.

Naturally I will make no decision until I hear from you. I know you will ask why the father can't take some responsibility. Johnny Allen was aboard the Glenmore on her last voyage.

Michael and Tomás arrested that

Sophia O'Fallon, the one who escaped at the Flower Show. They had to let her go, because too much time had gone by. Dylan can explain it better than I.

I see the horrible news from Ireland. For once, I'm glad you are in France my darling.

Please come back to me safe.

All my love,

Rose

Rose walked down to the mailbox and posted her letter. Since she no longer had to contend with Inga, she had far more time to herself. She was surprised how quickly she had adjusted to living alone in their little flat.

She came in the door of the tea room in time to meet their postman. "Mrs. Nagel. I just left a letter for you in the kitchen."

"Thank you, Mr. Robinette." She almost kissed the man. Even though it was only half a dozen steps Rose ran to the kitchen and began sifting through the stack of envelopes. There, at the bottom, under the gas bill and an ad for a spring clearance at Stewart's, was a letter from Tadhg.

15 April, 1916
France

Rosie my love,

I hate what's happened to Inga. I never expected Johnny Allen to be such a cad. I read about the Glenmore, and the list. It's really a blessing.

I hope this part of my letter passes the censors. Our superiors have finally decided that, with so many Americans here, they would be best served by forming a single unit. We are now the Lafayette Escadrille.

When I flew yesterday, I had my first combat experience. I dare not say more. Let me simply say I came home, and Fritz did not.

I'd like you to think about something while I'm gone. We both know Inga won't be capable of taking care of a baby. Do you think you could find it in your heart to take him or her in once he's born? I've watched Dylan with Mary Faith, and have seen how easy it can be to love a baby.
You needn't decide now, love. Nothing will happen until October or so.

The claxton just sounded. Prince wants me in the air.

I miss you more each day.

Love,
Tadgh

Notes on the Book

The Bureau of Investigation was still without many of the powers they would obtain in later years, when they became the Federal Bureau of Investigation. They still lacked any power to arrest. Agents were permitted to carry a weapon for "personal protection" as private citizens. But they were not allowed to use their weapons for protection of the public as a police officer would. The FBI website has a lovely timeline that outlines their history. https://www.fbi.gov/history/timeline

Yes, in 1915, Baltimore City began illuminating the Washington Monument.

You can find he song to which Sophia is partial, *La Ci Darem a Mano,* here https://youtu.be/8aAHxjCo_64. I've loved Samuel Ramey since seeing him live back in 1972 at the Harford Opera Theater before he made his Met debut. I admit to fudging a bit on the recording. The first disc registered with the Library of Congress wasn't listed until 1920. But there may (and I stress *may)* have been others recorded in Europe at an earlier date.

The song that made Sophia tear up, *Baggage Coach Ahead,* is here. https://youtu.be/zWDQ_9LKums Keep tissues handy.

I really do try to make these stories as historically accurate as possible. The medical treatment used was taken from contemporaneous texts, the news from the

Sunpapers and other contemporary papers. For some unknown reason I have been totally unable to find any articles from the *News Post*, which was published up until 1986. If something isn't exactly accurate I might have made a mistake, or decided to "adjust" historical data to fit the story.

Thanks, Hon.

Books in the Series

Why Are You Weeping, Sister?
The House That Jack Built
That Was Before I Met You
Oh, Mr. Porter
Goodbye Muirsheen Durkin
Everybody Two Step
There's a Girl in the Heart of Maryland
After The Ball
Somewhere in France There's a Lily
Come to the Church in the Wildwood
When the Roll is Called Up Yonder
　Coming soon:
Johnny Has Gone for A Soldier